Ringer

They say it's the quiet ones you have to worry about, and she was quiet, very quiet – when she wasn't busy despising me with a burning passion.

Ringo 'Ringer' James has a no-strings-attached policy.
Love them, leave them, and remain the eternal bachelor.

After a summer in which every one of his mates has succumbed to settling down, or so it seemed, Ringer is on the lookout for a quick exit. Having had enough of the stomach-turning love fest witnessed over the past three months, Ringer jumps at the opportunity to help out his mate, Max, by heading to Max's dad's property for a working holiday.

It's just what he's looking for. A remote, dusty homestead in Ballan, with only hard work, a cold beer and a comfy bed to worry about – no women.

Until Miranda Henry.

The privately educated daughter of his boss has returned home from overseas and things are about to get very complicated, very fast. As summer draws to its end, Ringer is about to learn that sometimes attraction defies all logic, and that there really is such a thing as 'enemies with benefits'.

Ringer

Ringer

C.J. Duggan

Ringer

By C.J. Duggan

Copyright © 2014 by C.J Duggan

Ringer
A Summer Series Novella, Book 3.5
Published by C.J Duggan
Australia, NSW
www.cjdugganbooks.com

First edition, published April 2014
All rights reserved.

Edited by Marion Archer
Copyedited by Anita Saunders
Proofreading by Sascha Craig

Cover Art by Keary Taylor Indie Designs
Formatted by E.M. Tippetts Book Designs
Author Photograph © 2014 C.J Duggan
Contact the author at cand.duu@gmail.com

A Summer Series Novella: Book 3.5.
May be read as a stand alone or in the following order:

The Boys of Summer
An Endless Summer
That One Summer
Ringer
Forever Summer

Look out for

Kiss the Girls (A Kincaid Brothers Novel)

Someone Like You
All the Right Moves
The Anita Bowman Diaries

www.cjdugganbooks.com

Dedicated to all the misfits in the world.

"It's so easy to fall in love, but hard to find someone who will catch you."
- Anon

Chapter One
Ringer

I was suffocating.

I could feel it restricting my brain, exhausting me in ways I could barely describe.

"Do I look fat in this?"

I rubbed my eyes, sighing in disbelief that my best mate beside me was about to actually answer the question.

Seriously?

I rested my elbows on the clothes rack, in the only women's fashion outlet in Onslow. I raised my brows questioningly at Sean who stood on the opposite side of the rack. *Ha! Sean.* A six-foot-three grown man rubbing the back of his neck with guarded unease as he half laughed his answer.

"Of course not."

He only visibly relaxed when his girlfriend, Amy, beamed a winning smile at him.

Ding-ding-ding – that's the right answer!

Amy's adoring eyes glimmered with approval until they shifted towards me.

Her shoulders slumped. "What's wrong with you, Ringer?"

Without too much emotional investment, I lazily tore my eyes away from her accusing stare, casually running my hand down the sleeve of the silky shirt that hung in front of me.

"Who, me?" I asked, examining the overpriced tag before stepping aside with disgust. I returned my glance towards my awaiting audience.

Nope, nothing wrong with this scene. When a mate rings me up to say, "Do you want to catch up?", what better way to do it than waiting outside a women's changing room while his girlfriend tries on the latest fashion to hit Onslow?

I gave her my best sickly sweet smile. "I'm just fine and dandy, but, hey, thanks for asking," I offered sarcastically.

Amy shook her head. "You're an idiot," she said, before she stepped back into the alcove, parting the curtains with a diva-like flick.

My eye roll was short lived by an unexpected whack to the back of my head.

"Hey, what was that for?" I said, clasping the back of my skull, my outcry loud enough for the permed-hair shop lady to dip her head with a squint of disapproval through her bifocals.

I tore my eyes away, annoyed at the Judgy-McJudgment death stare; anyone would think we were in a fucking library.

Sean offered her his best dashing smile, as if nothing untoward was happening. His demeanour changed somewhat when he fixed his gaze on me and lowered his voice.

"Stop being such a snappy arsehole, Ringo."

Here we go.

It would never be the words snappy or arsehole that made my blood boil; I had become quite accustomed to those. It was the fact he called me by my actual name—something he knew only my parents used when I was in the shit. If I had learnt one thing about Sean Murphy in all our years of friendship, he enjoyed deliberately winding me up. He knew I would never actually tell him what was pissing me off unless he wound me up so bad, I would explode.

Yeah, well, fuck that for a joke. I was out of there.

I pushed off from the clothes rack, refusing to stray from Sean's challenging stare. It wasn't entirely a pissing competition; I could see a glimmer of something in his eyes, concern or whatever. Not interested.

"Have fun shopping, I hear Beauty Bliss do great bikini waxes if you're interested."

I flipped on my Oakleys from the top of my head and offered my best 'fuck-you grin'.

Sean shook his head, but a smile creased the corner of his mouth.

"You need to get laid, Ringer, you're turning into a grumpy old prick."

Before I could retaliate, a cough from behind Sean sounded. The bifocal-devil granny's lips were pursed in disgust. She obviously wasn't used to a couple of Onslow boys hanging out in the aisles of the women's department.

"Miss Henderson will take these." She motioned with an armful of clothing.

"Thanks Mrs C, just put them on my account," Sean said, before turning and pausing before me. "What?" He frowned.

I flicked my sunnies back on my head, propping my elbow back onto the rack.

"You have an account at Carters?" I asked, laughter threatening to rise in my chest.

Sean straightened. "Yeah, what of it?"

"No, nothing." I shook my head. I had had enough. I moved past him and Mrs C who was still holding the pile of clothes.

I paused, turning towards Sean, and said, "But you really must look into getting your vagina waxed before the day's out."

I didn't linger long, but it was long enough to hear the gasp from Mrs C, and almost ran into Amy as she came out of the changing room, still tucking her shirt in.

"Where are you going?" she called after me.

I waved without a backward glance. "To get a drink." Because, God knew, I needed one.

I twisted the top off my VB stubby and turfed it into the tray at the base of the bar.

"Do you ever feel like you're drowning in a sea of goddamn love?" I asked Max as I took a deep swig of my beer, a sip that still didn't manage to lift the scowl from my face.

"Hmm? What's that?" he asked half-heartedly, lifting his eyes from his Nokia screen as he read through a text. Max, the barman, and incidentally one of the last of the dying breeds amongst men—yep, he was single—was one of the rare few I could hang around comfortably. At least, so I thought.

Maybe he was texting some chick. Great.

You wouldn't usually see Max hovering over a phone, but it was the graveyard, Sunday shift. 'Hotel California' playing in the background, and I, his sole company. That, and whatever had him frowning at his screen.

I sighed. Surely not him, too? Against my better judgment, I put down my beer, and asked the million-dollar question I wasn't really interested in. Still, I reasoned, he was a mate.

"Trouble in paradise?" I pressed.

Max's eyes slowly broke away from the screen. "Hmm? Oh shit, sorry, mate," he said, shaking his head and pocketing his phone.

It was as if he were seeing me for the first time, instead of having agreed to every part of my insistent whining for the past half hour. Had he heard a single thing I had said? Probably just as well.

"What's up?" I asked.

Max ran his hand through his matted blond locks. "It's my dad."

"Everything all right?"

"Yeah, yeah, no, he's fine, it's just that …" His phone beeped. "Oh, for fuck's sake," he growled, delving into his pocket and pulling his phone out.

By then he had my full attention as I rested my elbows on the bar top, watching intently as he read through another message with a stony expression.

Max shook his head. "He is such a cranky old bastard sometimes."

I couldn't help but smile, lifting my beer to my lips.

Ha! Cranky old bastard, hey? Sounds like my people.

'He wants me to drop what I'm doing and go man the farm, while he and Mum go to the Wahroo Cattle Auction. As if I can just up and leave like that. Yeah, right, no worries."

My eyes drifted over the lean, gangly frame of the blond, baby-faced Max. He didn't strike me as a farm boy and it was certainly news to me that he was.

"Where's your family's farm?" I asked with genuine interest.

"Ballan; it's about five hours from here."

I nodded. "Yeah, I know the place." As in, you would blink and miss it. It had a pub, a corner shop-slash-post office-slash-petrol station, and a little school that probably had about twenty students from surrounding properties.

If Onslow was a one-horse town, Ballan was a no-horse town, and that was based on the horse who would probably die of starvation. If memory served me well, Ballan was not famous for its rolling grassy hills, either. It was as flat as a tack and drier than a biscuit. A stark contrast to the rolling green ranges and lake that surrounded Onslow.

Yeah, Onslow was beautiful; it was also bathed in romance. Sweet doe-eyed looks, hand holding, giggles, freakin' sunshine and rainbows. It was enough to make your beer go flat.

"So, I take it you're not tempted to obey Dad's orders?" I asked, motioning for another stubby.

Max scoffed. "No freakin' way."

Interesting.

I suppose I could understand; escaping the dusty plains of Ballan to Onslow would seem like a massive inland sea change. Hell, Onslow would seem like paradise. A great escape.

Escape.

It was only the dull thud of Max placing my stubby in front

of me that shook me from my thoughts.

Max laughed. "What's up with you, then? Woman troubles?" he asked, seriously misreading my troubled expression. I now had no doubt that he hadn't listened to a bloody word I had said before.

I broke into a grin. "Not bloody likely," I said, twisting the cap off my beer.

"Look out. I've seen that look before." Max shifted uneasily, as he noted the devious glint of mischief in my eyes.

"Max, my old mate," I said, toasting him with my beer in the air. "I think I have just thought of an offer you simply won't be able to refuse."

Chapter Two
Miranda

"I'm not going back, I don't care how desperate they are."

I folded my arms indignantly as I sat across from my aunty at her kitchen table.

"Oh, you're just jet lagged." Aunty Megan waved me off.

"I'm fine." I straightened. "I just don't need the guilt trip right now."

Not ever.

From the streets of Paris to the dusty plains of Ballan: no way, I thought, as I studied the gloss on my manicured fingertips.

"Well, you know your brother's not going home?"

My eyes flicked up. "What?"

"Max has a job and he can't go home."

A new panic surfaced inside of me.

But Max always goes home.

It was the unspoken agreement that he would do the dirty farm work, and I would travel around, because, well, that was just the way it was meant to be. I had wanted to escape Moira Station so badly, I had resorted to hitching rides into town, any which way I could, to get out of the most boring place on earth.

"Well, they will just have to make him."

Aunty Megan curved her brow at me, as if to say, "How can you make a Henry offspring do anything?"

Damn straight, I thought, because if there was one thing I was completely, totally, whole-heartedly defiant about, it was that I was not going back to bloody Ballan.

Four years.

That's how long it had been since I had been back home; I couldn't believe it had really been that long.

I had been kind of a nightmare—playing up, getting drunk at the only source of entertainment, the local pub. I had planned to gain some of my parents' attention in a way and, boy, had I ever. They decided that perhaps a private all-girls' school would be best. And I had completely agreed, aside from the all-girls' thing.

My school became a welcome reprieve from the dust and solitude. I excelled academically, probably because it had given me hope that I wouldn't end up a farmer's wife. Instead, I did so well that my parents allowed me to be a foreign exchange student in Paris for my final year of high school, and even supported my desire to stay on afterwards. Mum and Dad had been good to me— so good—but expecting me to come back home to do something so completely foreign to me was a bit of a joke, and an absolutely ridiculous ask. I had been in Australia for less than a week, and they wanted me to come home and play caretaker because my dad didn't want to hire someone in place of Max? And it's not like my little sister, Moira, could be anything other than a thing under foot; she was only thirteen. And, yes, she was named after Moira Station, so naturally she thought she owned the place, little brat.

It's not like I hadn't seen my family. They had holidayed overseas frequently to see me, the times when Max was around to take care of things. Max had even come over for a stint. I'd probably had better quality time with my family being an ocean away than I would have had at Moira, locked in my bedroom, hating the world.

The same claustrophobic feelings of my childhood bedroom

clawed at my soul: even after all these years I couldn't think of a worse place to escape to.

Escape to? Ha. More like escape from.

"I won't go," I said, pushing back my chair and heading for the kitchen door.

"Mm hmm," managed my aunty, as if she didn't believe a word I had said.

I paused at the doorway, piercing her with a poignant stare. "I. Am. Not. Going."

Famous last words.

Chapter Three
Ringer

I careened my '77 canary yellow Ford down the dirt track, admiring the trail of dust that rose from my rear-view mirror.

My suntanned arm rested on the wound-down window as I tapped my free hand cheerfully on the steering wheel to Air Supply's 'Lost in Love', a song I disturbingly knew all the words to. I paused from my singing, a smile creasing the corner of my mouth; if only the boys back home could see me now. I shrugged. It wasn't exactly my choice of driving music; still, my tape player was stuffed, so I had to put up with any outback radio station I could get reception for. The music crackled momentarily with white noise.

"Not now. This is the best part." I growled in frustration as I banged my fist on the dashboard.

Aside from the rather dubious romantic tunes of Air Supply, I was relishing the solitude. A true stroke of genius on my part that had me escaping the loved-up fools of Onslow. My offer to help out Max's dad by volunteering to work on the family farm in his place had been met with mixed emotions from Max. First uncertainty, and then fear. A fear to hope I was serious.

But I had been deadly serious, obviously, as I fishtailed along the desolate farm road towards…I squinted.

"You've got to be kidding me?" I groaned.

Slowing down to a full stop I tipped my sunnies down and shook my head. In front of me was another farm gate. The fifth one I had been faced with having to open. I didn't grab the details of how big the Henry's property was; I wasn't interested in the logistics. All I wanted to know was if there was a comfy bed and a cold beer waiting for me at the end of the day. Being assured of both, I was satisfied. But what I really should have asked was how many fucking gates the property had.

I opened my door and slid out of the leather driver's seat. I pushed my arms to the sky, groaning with the satisfaction of stretching my muscles as I slid my hand up my T-shirt sleeve to retrieve my packet of Peter Jacksons. I opened the packet, delving in and grabbing a smoke that I flipped into my mouth with expert ease. I reached for the zippo lighter from my back pocket, flicking it to life; I blocked the hot summer wind from the flame as I lit up and inhaled my addiction. I stood next to the opened car door, turning slightly, taking in the great nothing of my surroundings with each slow draw. Flat, desolate scrubland, with no pinnacle to focus on, no homestead in sight, no cattle or sheep to be seen. Only yet another divide of fencing and a weather-beaten farm gate.

I shielded my eyes from the penetrating rays of the February sun, before taking another drag and ducking into the console of my Ford to retrieve Max's mud map to 'Moira Station'.

Scribbled crudely on the back of a Carlton Draught beer coaster (my one and only token from Onslow), I studied the squiggly lines that proved to be a pretty easy route, now that I had turned onto Sheehan Road. All I had to do was just go straight, straight until the fork in the road. Left was Moira, right was the Sheehan's property.

Simple enough, I thought. When it came to Ballan, I had predicted that everyone and everything would be pretty simple, laid back to the point of slipping into a coma. Nope, complication was not on the agenda here. I may have been standing in the middle of nowhere, surrounded by salt, bush and dust. But the silence, the red earth and rusty gate I walked towards and started to unchain, all of these elements were beautiful to me, oh so beauti—

I paused. Cocking my head slightly to hear the distant thrums. *Was that a car?*

I stilled my hands on the gate, turning to see. Sure enough, a distant billow of dust burst into the sky as a little speck gunned along the track. I could have heard it from a mile away; the car was a shit box and in desperate need of a service. The sound sliced through the stillness of what was once a silent and heavenly existence. I shielded my eyes as I watched the white hatchback Mazda speed closer. Maybe this was my would-be boss? Max's dad, or maybe a Sheehan from the neighbouring property? It would be more than a surprise as most farmers drove flash four-wheel drives, not the screeching bomb like the one nearing.

Regardless, I threw down my cigarette and swivelled it out in the dirt, waving my arm in the air as a way of a friendly greeting while I slowly worked on opening the gate. I smiled, ready to meet my new acquaintance—the new acquaintance that wasn't slowing down. I worked on the chain faster—the new acquaintance, who was now beeping their horn like a raving lunatic. I clawed and tugged at the chain, glancing up from my hands only long enough to afford myself the view of the fast-approaching white rocket that barrelled down the track.

The horn sounded in a long, insistent beep-beep-beeeeeeeep. *Oh shit! OH SHIT!*

The psycho wasn't slowing. I had visions of the buzz box driving over my car like a monster truck, pinning me to the gate while it smashed its way through.

Beep-beep-beeeeeeeeeeeeeep.

I unlatched the last of the gate with enough time to latch onto it and catapult myself, attached to said gate, away in a wide swing. The beaten-up hatchback swerved violently around my car and sped through the barely opened gap.

The force of the gate slamming into the wire fence knocked

me from my hold; I fell backwards into the dusty shrubs with an *oomph*. I heard the car come to a skidding halt. I rolled onto my side, catching the breath that had been knocked out from me. I may have been in a momentary world of pain, and my life may have just flashed before my eyes, but it did little to stem the tide of anger that rose to claw its way out of me.

Clasping my ribs, I slowly got to my feet and glared at the rattling-arse end of the car before me.

"Hey! Hey, what the fuck?" I screamed, hobbling over to the car and slamming my palm on the back window before doubling over in pain. It was then I saw the driver's window was being wound down slowly, not because the driver was doing it deliberately slow, but because it looked like it was being shunted downwards by force; the window was clearly stuck and was taking considerable effort to open. I stood to the side, clear from the car, my brows narrowed, waiting for an apology, for a question of concern maybe? Instead what I got was a glimpse of a delicate feminine hand as it appeared from the gap in the tinted window, a turquoise beaded bracelet, and immaculately pearl polished, manicured nails. I was momentarily stunned by the unexpectedness of it, more so when the dainty little hand extended me the middle finger.

What the fuck?

My lips pressed into an incredulous smile as I quickly stepped towards the car wanting to get a look at who was behind the wheel, but as I skidded to the driver's door, grabbing onto the handle, the car spun its back wheels and gunned it down the track, leaving me in a shower of dirt and a Mazda door handle in my grasp.

What the fuck?

I coughed at the dust that was lodging in my throat, a cough that turned into hysterical cackling as I fixed my eyes onto the door handle. I wiped the tears from my eyes as I watched the Mazda thunder down the track until it was a speck in the distance, a speck that had me raising my brows with interest as it veered right. Taking the fork in the road that I couldn't quite make out, the car blazed its way towards the Sheehan property.

Interesting.

Chapter Four
Miranda

I wasn't ready to go home.

Not just yet; in fact, despite my erratic, maniacal driving (I had never been a good driver), I had wanted to avoid getting back to Moira Station at all costs. So my decision was clear; as soon as I had veered left off the main highway and saw the Sheehan Road sign, my first point of call would be to pay my dear old friends a visit. Right after I inadvertently almost kill a stranger. I grimaced, casting my eyes into the rear-view mirror, seeing nothing more than a hazy speck in the distance. I had felt bad, kind of. But how was I supposed to know he was so bloody slow at opening up a farm gate? It wasn't bloody rocket science, he would have had to have opened at least four before then, the idiot. Must be from the city? Although his car and attire hadn't screamed so. I bit my lip; what if he was visiting the Sheehans? Or worse – Moira? Either way, I was screwed; my hands became clammy on the wheel and I wasn't sure if it was down to the fear of running into the clearly crazy, swearing man, or the fact that my car had no air conditioning? At least with the window wound down I afforded myself some fresh air: fresh air for life now that it was firmly wedged open. You always took your life into your own hands each time you chose to operate anything in my car; still, it was mine and had been since I had driven away in it four years ago.

I neared the final gate that led towards the Sheehan's homestead; mercifully there was no canary-yellow Ford blocking the way, and no stunned stranger with fear in his eyes. A smile pressed the corner of my mouth, thinking back to the look on his face when I had flipped him off. Absolutely priceless. It had been so worth almost running him over for that look.

I stopped the car with less violent force this time as I readied myself to get out to open the gate. The screeching unoiled hinge of my car door was music to my ears; sure I copped a lot of flak about it, but she was my car and I loved her just as much as the day I got her.

I went to unhook the gate, but was stilled by distant screams and the sound of footsteps.

"Oh, my God. Oh, my God. Oh, my God. MIRANDA." Melanie Sheehan knocked the wind out of me, hugging me so severely she restricted my breathing, her arms circled around my neck like an anaconda crushing the very life out of me, pinning me, and my chest, into the gate between us.

"Dad said you were coming home, but I didn't believe it." She stood back, grasping my shoulders and studying my face as if what she was seeing before her was a mirage. "Why didn't you tell me?" she asked.

Dear, sweet Mel, my lifelong childhood friend and astonishingly dedicated pen pal. She was a few years younger than me, but she had been my only playmate as a child. How I had missed her clear blue-sky-like eyes, and the light dusting of freckles across her nose. She wore her hair in a constant ponytail; the lighter wisps of her brown hair bleached by the sun swept around her face. She looked just like her dad.

I smiled, an actual real smile that I hadn't done since I couldn't remember when. "I'm sorry, it's been insane since I got back, I haven't had much time to find my feet really. It's not like Mum and Dad gave me much choice," I said, trying to sound light about it.

The brightness in Mel's eyes dimmed and her mouth gaped in a question that was stilled when we heard a distant wolf whistle. Over Mel's shoulder stood a man I would never be able to forget, a man whose essence no photograph over the years had ever been able to capture. Mel's dad was tall, built, and had an electric presence of power and masculinity. Even though he was my dad's best mate and more of an adopted uncle, any female could appreciate his draw. Aside from that, to me he was just Bluey. Luke Sheehan, nicknamed 'Bluey', a namesake that drew much popular debate. Some say it's because he only owned Blue Heeler dogs, others put it down to his affection for blue dungaree pants and blue checked flannel shirts, but the one I believed true was because of the piercing blue of his eyes. Had to be.

He leant casually against a verandah post of his homestead, watching on at our reunion.

A crooked curve lifted his mouth as he shook his head. "There goes the neighbourhood," he said, straightening from his casual stance and making his way down the steps towards the gate.

I tilted my head. "Oh hardy-ha! I could probably teach you a thing or two, old man."

"Old man? Ouch," he said as he approached, towering next to Mel. He rested his elbows on the top of the gate. "Your old man will be glad to see you," he said, ruffling my hair up.

I pulled away, feigning annoyance as I brushed my hair back into place. "I bet he will, his own personal slave he can push around the farm."

"Slave? More like princess," Bluey scoffed.

"Ha! What kind of princess is asked to man the fort while her parents leave her to go to cattle auctions? I think not," I said, brushing a layer of dust off my jeans.

Bluey's eyes dimmed in the same manner Mel's had before; it was a look of genuine bewilderment, more so when Bluey shifted uneasily and caught the eye of his daughter.

"Man the fort?" he asked.

"Yeah, can you believe it? I haven't even been home for a

week and he wants me to babysit Moira Station, as if I have a clue what to do; it's preposterous."

"You wouldn't."

"Exactly. Thank you."

"That's why he's hired someone."

"What?"

Bluey shrugged. "He's hired someone Max recommended."

"But … but he said he needed me home."

"Needed or *wanted* you home?" Bluey emphasised the latter.

I blinked; thinking back to the conversations that had gone on, the only link in my mind, now having thought about it, was Max wasn't going to be there, so naturally I would be the one expected to … oh God! They had merely wanted me to come home, lured by my own stupidity.

Mel laughed. "You running Moira, now that I would like to see."

My eyes narrowed.

"You said so yourself it would be pretty preposterous." Bluey smirked.

Right!

I stormed back to the car, madder than hell: mad at my dad being shady on the details; mad at Max having a life; mad at the Sheehans for making me feel foolish.

"I'll see you later," I called, rage bubbling under the surface, because most of all, I was mad at myself.

I reached to grab the handle of my door.

"What the … ?"

My hand hovered over the bare alcove of my missing door handle, and a new dread swept over me.

He hired someone.

Someone Max recommended.

Oh shit!

Chapter Five
Ringer

"You're more than welcome to stay in the house."

Steve Henry walked in front of me down the long hallway that led into a pristine, cream-coloured kitchen with stainless steel modern appliances. He was tall and wiry like Max, except for one obvious difference: Max didn't have a beer gut … yet. Steve's sandy-blond hair and weathered face from working outdoors no doubt made him look older than he actually was. Still, he had a firm handshake which immediately put him in good stead—it's all any bloke could ask for in order to make a good impression; well, that and an offer of a cold beer that I gladly welcomed. After the long drive and near-death experience, I must have looked a sight. I arrived at Moira station covered in dust, my jeans torn on the side and a skinned elbow. Max's dad, Steve, had looked me over with guarded humour.

"Rough trip?" he asked.

Nothing like a bit of smart-arse humour to lighten the mood. I think I would like Steve Henry just fine.

"Like I said, there's plenty of spare rooms in the house if you want to claim one for yourself."

"Thanks, Mr Henry, but I've stayed in shearers' huts before, I'm happy to crash there."

"Ha. Maybe you better inspect them before committing, and if you call me Mr Henry one more time I'll force you to sleep in the shearing shed with the sheep."

I smirked, picking at the VB label of my stubby. "You're a subtle man, Steve."

"Ha. Just ask my wife: subtle as a sledgehammer, she says." He finished the last of his stubby before slamming it onto the kitchen sink, smacking his lips together as if he had satisfied an insatiable thirst, before belching like a champion. "Come on," Steve tilted his head towards the screen door that led out to the verandah, "you can check out the shearing huts, see what you think."

I followed his long strides out of the kitchen. The cream-coloured dial telephone mounted on the kitchen wall by the door sounded, causing us both to jump with the unexpectedness of it.

Steve paused in the open door frame, briefly closing his eyes and groaning as he looked up to the sky as if silently asking God to give him strength.

"Speak of the devil," he said before turning to me. "The Mrs."

I nodded my head with silent understanding as he let the wire screen door slam shut and reached for the phone.

"Hello … oh, hello, luv," he said cheerfully before giving me a smug wink. "Yeah, no I was just giving Max's young mate a tour of the place … yep, no seems like a good bloke … ah-ha, ah-ha, ah-ha …" Steve rolled his eyes at me, as he barely got a word in on the one-sided conversation. He placed his hand over the receiver.

"Ah, this might take a while, why don't you grab another beer and go relax in the lounge room, it's pretty cool in there," he whispered, before returning to his conversation. "Yeah, I am listening," he snapped.

I backed away from the display of wedded bliss, cringing at the thought of having to answer to anyone like that; to be accountable to anyone other than myself seemed … *exhausting*. I placed my empty stubby on the sink next to Steve's, going against the idea of grabbing another until he did. Instead, I made my way to the lounge room, delving my hands deep into my pockets as I casually took in the tidy room. The plush carpet had me wishing I had wiped my feet a little more vigorously before entering the home. I had wiped them pretty hard anyway, having seen the impressive, mansion-like homestead—the large, pristine weatherboard home with its sweeping verandahs that surrounded the whole building, acting as a shelter over the freshly oiled merbau decking. French doors led out onto the deck, no doubt designed to allow access to what cool airflow there was when the sun went down. The main entrance was grand with its ornate leadlight windows surrounding a heavy front door, detailed with Victorian scroll moulding. It screamed decadence. It opened into a long hallway; the gloss of the Murray pine floorboards shone as light filtered through the open door. My eyes had then been drawn forward to admire the decoratively corniced arch that divided the hall. A chandelier held grandly from the fifteen-foot pressed metal ceilings. It was the second thing that really struck me about the place: that and everything was cream. Cream curtains, cream couches, cream carpet. And if it wasn't cream it was white: white architraves, white mantel, white doilies lining the side tables with photo frames. It would have been a farmer's worst nightmare knocking off for the day and having to tentatively creep through the house, not daring to touch anything for fear of smudging an immaculately kept surface.

Cream was bullshit, and with that in mind, I chose to stand.

The white mantel was aligned with matching silver frames of alternative patterns and sizes; I lazily cast my eyes over them, staring from the left and walking to the other end, slowly taking in the mostly unknown faces.

I spotted a pimply-faced Max first, looking miserable and pubescent in his grammar school burgundy jacket and tie. I smirked to myself; of course they would have been privately educated. Next to Max's frame was that of a beaming girl with black hair and a smile full of metal; she looked about thirteen. She also wore some kind of hideous uniform. I shook my head.

Poor kids.

I glanced towards the kitchen where a weary-looking Steve was rubbing his eyes and nodding on the phone. For me, right then, he was the classic poster child for all the reasons why you would never dedicate yourself to one person. Get hitched, pump out a couple of kids and live mundanely ever after.

No thanks.

I sighed, thinking I would make my own way to the out buildings, check out the shearers' huts for myself. God only knew how long Steve's ear was going to be chewed off by his Mrs. Speaking of.

Hello.

My eyes rested on a wedding picture of a much-younger-looking Steve Henry. Decked out in a hideous-looking 70s-style suit, with criminally large lapels and flares that looked like he might have been whisked away like an unattached jumping castle should a gust of wind catch them. I grimaced.

The young Steve had his blond curls plastered down in a ridiculous side parting as he adoringly looked down at his not-too-ridiculous-looking wife. Sure, she looked like a giant meringue in that dress, but there was no denying it. Mrs Henry was a bit of a fox. Jet-black hair cut into a bob, she too looked adoringly up at her husband. I almost allowed myself to be lost in a romantic sense of nostalgia. Almost.

I shook my head, tearing my eyes away to move on to the next frame and paused.

This time is wasn't a picture of some miserable-looking private school kid, or some dated olden-day photo with questionable fashion. Instead it was a picture of a girl. It was different from the others; her smile was bright and authentic, her blonde hair captured in the moment as if blowing in a breeze. She looked carefree, happy, exotic. And it wasn't just the fact she was taking some kind of awkwardly angled selfie next to the unmistakable Eiffel tower, she was exotic in another way I couldn't wholly describe. Her eyes were shielded by sunglasses, and annoyance flashed in my mind of how it spoilt the image of the girl. I very much wanted to see what those eyes looked like; my eyes darted along the mantel, searching amongst the frames. Searching for a pair of eyes. And then I found them. But they weren't the light, smiling eyes I had expected; instead, they were sad, and humourless. A girl once again sitting in a stiff school uniform, her blue-green eyes haunted by something. I looked once more amongst the frames, but aside from the odd child or baby photo I couldn't see any other image with those eyes: eyes I had wanted to see in any other way but sad. They were far too pretty for that. Against my own understanding, I picked up the Paris frame and looked at it more closely; her smile was framed by brilliant white, perfect teeth, her cheeks flushed from excitement.

The corner of my mouth creased; well, well, well … who knew Max Henry had a hot sister. I shook my head, thinking to quickly place the frame back on the mantel before Steve Henry caught me perving on his daughter. Just in the nick of time I heard the phone slam down, followed by a deep sigh, before Steve appeared in the large arch between the kitchen and the lounge.

He shook his head. "Women."

I smiled with good humour.

My thoughts exactly.

"Everything all right?" I asked.

Steve crossed his arms and leant against the arch.

"Penny is in town with our youngest, Moira; some formal dress they're on the hunt for, for some ridiculous town hall disco. They actually asked me if they should go with silk or satin?" He laughed incredulously. "How the bloody hell should I know between silk or bloody satin? All I know is wool, and when I suggested how about Nana Henry knit Moira a formal dress, well, that went down like a bloody lead balloon, as you could imagine."

I couldn't help but laugh. "Shame, nothing says disco like a knitted evening gown."

"Yeah, well, my next line of thought was for her to accessorise it with a bloody chastity belt, but thought against getting myself into more trouble than a rat with a gold tooth."

22

Our laughter echoed through the room in our bonded moment of man talk. Steve caught his breath from laughing at his own joke; he cocked his head as if listening to something in the distance. My own laughs died and I fell silent. My humour faded; instead, I watched Steve intently for a long moment. It was like he was frozen in time. I was about to voice my concern when his serious face slowly broke into a brilliant smile.

"Here she is." He smiled.

My brows lowered, thinking that he had maybe completely lost the plot; I went to ask what he was talking about before pausing. That's when I heard it: the distant, yet familiar hums of a struggling motor, a sound that caused the hairs on the back of my neck to stand on end, and my pulse to quicken as a familiar rage bubbled in me.

No. Fucking. Way.

He gave a wide grin. "My little girl's home." He quickly stepped towards the wire door, before turning to me. "Come on, come meet my daughter, Miranda." He beamed.

A sense of dread filled me as I cast a fleeting glance back to the mantle and then moved to follow Steve. My expression grave as I neared the kitchen door, the unmistakable, and all too recognisable sound became louder. It was the equivalent of running your nails down a chalkboard. And sure enough, I had lost all interest in Steve's cheery demeanour as I stood next to him on the verandah. Instead, I stood in stark contrast to his animated waves and smiles as the daughter of the devil made a wide, semicircular sweep in the drive, in none other than a white hatchback Mazda.

Well … this is fucked.

I glared down from the verandah, maintaining my stoic stance as Steve descended the steps two at a time, eager to greet his charming little cherub. There was little doubt in my mind what the hell child from behind the wheel would look like, and sure enough, as the door swung open in a pained screech, a blonde head poked out and the Parisian goddess on the mantel slid out from her car.

Oh for fuck's sake.

Tall, slender, and dressed in a way that definitely screamed European, her black ankle boots and black skin-tight jeans accentuated the length of her long legs and the perfect curve of her slender, womanly figure. All would be distracting, but none more so than the sunglasses that framed her face, shielding those mysterious eyes like they did in that photo. I then reminded myself that I really couldn't give a shit what her eyes looked like. The black widow herself had almost killed me merely an hour before. The fact she was wearing a light gloss on her bow-shaped lips, or the shine of her hair as the sun hit it at the right angle, or the way she moved to open the back passenger door with grace in such a short distance … no, I wouldn't let any of that distract me, not for a second.

If she had seen me standing on the verandah she paid me no notice as she reached into the back seat and retrieved a bag.

"Hello, luv." Steve was by her side, all smiles and open arms; the father-and-daughter reunion was destined to be a real tear jerker until Daddy's little girl thrust her bag into Steve's chest with an oomph.

His brows rose. "Rough trip?" he asked, repeating the exact same words he had said to me; this time, he clamped down his humour as if not wanting to poke the bear. And he was right, because even with sunglasses on, no one would have to guess too hard that there was a glacial stare behind the dark shades.

Without a word she shouldered her other bag and slammed the door.

Yep! A real piece of work.

Cyclone Miranda was now headed in my direction; now, more than ever, I wanted her glasses to be gone so I could see the look in her eyes. I backed my way towards the screen door and waited. Her expensive European heels clicked up the steps, her blonde hair partially framed her face. She looked exhausted, as if she was carrying the weight of the world on her shoulders. Poor little rich girl had no porter to carry her designer bags for her. I smiled against my better judgement and, instead, had great pleasure in reaching and opening the door for her.

"Seems like I am always opening things for you, Miss Henry," I said, with a crooked tilt to my mouth. I expected her to blanch, to look at me with a double take and some ounce of recognition— something, anything. Instead, she strode a defiant, determined line and without missing a beat, she said, "Oh, fuck off," walking straight through the opened door and leaving her dad and me in stunned silence.

A real piece of work.

Chapter Six
Miranda

"I don't give a damn, young lady. You check that behaviour and leave that attitude at the door, do you hear me?"

My dad was pissed, clearly. Gone were the warm, welcome smiles and niceties from mere moments before. Instead, a raging bear had come bursting into my room, his face so red, a vein pulsing in his neck; I thought he was about to burst a blood vessel. I had sat on my old bed, taken my shades off and rubbed at my fatigued eyes, zoning in and out of his rant-like speech but listening enough to take in words like 'ashamed', 'disgusted' and 'embarrassed'. All the strong ones. I hadn't the energy to argue, to say sorry, because I wasn't sure that I really was. Well, maybe taking my anger out on 'gate boy' was not really fair, nor had been nearly running him over in the first place; still, the moment I drove into the drive and spotted his yellow Ford, I knew for certain that this was the person Dad had hired to take Max's place. I felt my stomach twist at the memory of his hand pounding on my back window as he yelled obscenities at me. I had stopped because I had seen him come off the gate hard, and momentarily winded. I had had every intention of asking if he was okay, but as soon as he started mouthing off at me, the monster caged inside me reared its ugly head and instead I flipped him off and left him behind in a trail of dust, relishing the thought that I had the last say, or action anyway. A brave move surely, until I had come to the realisation that I was about to be face to face with him. My heart had pounded as I rolled into the drive. Maybe I would just apologise and explain that I was just having a life crisis with coming back to Ballan to do my daughterly duty. At the end of the day, I really should be thanking him. After all, he was going to be looking after Moira, meaning I wouldn't have to. I could probably just visit for a little while and be free again, as long as my parents didn't want to investigate what I wanted to do for the rest of my life now that I was home from Paris. To be honest, I really had no idea myself, and, try as I might, I was not becoming a farmer's wife. No way.

So sure, I would extend a peace offering of sorts to yellow Ford driver, and I had completely intended to, until I came to a halt out the front of the homestead and saw him standing there on the verandah looking mad as hell next to Dad. His arms crossed across his chest, glaring down at me.

Fuck!

Okay, so I had clearly not thought any of it through. I hadn't meant to be so hostile towards Dad; if anything, I wished I could rewind the moment and just have hugged him and said it was good to be home like any good daughter would, instead of stomping my way and telling a stranger where to go. So I took the lecture—took it with every hollered shout from my dad—as it really was a sign of being home. The amount of times I had been lectured as I sat on my bed was too numerous to count, but unlike all those times, I responded in a way that really did silence my dad.

"I'm sorry," I whispered, looking down at my hands. I felt like a child, not like some woman of the world I thought I was. Maybe it was the bone-jarring fatigue that had stripped away all my bravado, or the fact that I had never seen my dad this angry before, not even when I was caught underage drinking at Tyler Mackie's. No, not even then.

He was silent now. I didn't look up to see if his demeanour had softened, or if his face was still scarlet with fury; instead, a long silence settled in the room and just as I hoped he would finally speak, he did.

"Not good enough," he said, before turning to make his way out of my room and slamming the door behind him.

Right then, I really wished he hadn't spoken at all.

The room I once dreaded returning to now had turned into my sanctuary. A safe haven from broody fathers and offended farmhands. It served me well for the first hour as I busied myself by unpacking my bags, then heading to my en suite for a shower, slipping into something more comfortable, and crashing onto my bed before falling into a deep, much-needed sleep.

Hours later, as the simmering summer sun dipped from the sky, it wasn't the much-welcomed dip in the temperature gauge that stirred me from my slumber; instead, it was the feeling of my head slamming into the bedhead as a heavy, bony-weight body slammed me out of my sleep.

"Wake up! Wake up! Wake up!" the voice screamed, as my mattress bounced to the beat of the sing-songed chants.

"Ugh, get off, Moira," I said, feeling my palm on a face and pushing; it did little to stop her bony knees in my rib cage.

"Sacre-bleu," she exclaimed. Always with the French words.

I blindly fumbled with the side table, awkwardly feeling for the lamp switch. I squinted at the offending beam, blinking as my eyes adjusted; it didn't help that Moira lay a mere inches away from me, her head resting on her hand, smiling her metal-mouthed smile, her eyes sparkling with glee. My icy façade thawed seeing my little sister, seeing that look of happiness on her face, expecting her to voice how much she had missed her big sis'.

"Oh my gosh, Miranda. Have you seen the hottie Dad hired? Hubba-hubba," she said, wiggling her brows.

The smile slipped from my face—my adorable boy-crazy little sister: some things never changed.

I pulled the blanket up to my chin. "He's not that hot," I scoffed.

Moira sat bolt upright. "Are you serious? You don't think Ringer is smoking hot?"

My head snapped around to frown at Moira. "Ringer?"

"Yeah, that's his name, how cool is that?" she said with intense enthusiasm.

"What a ridiculous name."

Moira sighed, hugging one of my pillows. "I think it's awesome." Her eyes had glassed over with gooey affection; it was the same moony expression each time Bluey brought the shearers out to Moira in shearing season. She was so embarrassing; the day they had shipped her off to an all-girls' boarding school couldn't have happened soon enough.

Moira snapped out of her daydreaming and shifted herself into a cross-legged position. "So, what did you bring me back from Paris?"

"Nothing." I yawned.

"Yeah, right," she said, playfully nudging my shoulder.

"It's true; what could I possibly get a girl who has it all?" I mocked seriousness, causing Moira to pummel me some more; the only protection was the doona I laughed and hid under. The squeals and squeaks of the bed mattress soon came to an abrupt halt at the sound of a cough from the doorway.

I slowly peeled the cover over my head, wiping the wisps of hair from my face; I instinctively knew who that sound belonged to.

My mother.

And, unlike my dad, she was less than thrilled to see me.

Chapter Seven
Ringer

Dusk settled into night and I found myself languishing in the peace and coolness of the evening.

Rocking on the back legs of the chair in front of the shearers' huts, I had wasted little time relocating myself to the out building. No matter how big the house was, it was never going to be big enough for Miranda Henry and me. The wench should have come with a warning label.

I blew on my cup of tea before shaking my head and taking a sip.

Tea.

I had to laugh: hours from home in a simple shearers' quarters drinking tea, alone, on a Saturday night.

What the fuck was I doing with my life?

The sleeping quarters were pretty good, actually: a long line of individual rooms that led onto their individual decked verandah. It wasn't far from the main house, the view offering the comings and goings of the Henry household. Including what I assumed was the mother and youngest daughter. Moira, was it? Returning home in their flash Land Cruiser after a day in the big smoke. I had hoped that the shadows might have concealed me, but Moira leapt from the passenger seat, fixing her eyes straight on me. I offered a casual wave that caused her to smile as she turned and skipped into the house with a heap of bags swinging from her arms.

"Miranda's home! Miranda's home," she sing-songed up the steps joyously as she struggled to open the door with her cargo and raced inside.

Pfft, at least someone was happy about it.

I slurped on my tepid cup of tea as I watched Mrs Henry shut the passenger door. As predicted, she wore cream-coloured capri pants with a navy linen shirt pressed to perfection. Her sunglasses propped on her immaculate jet-black bob, as she gathered some shopping and some wrapped flowers before locking the car and moving towards the house without a backwards glance.

Ha! Don't worry, luv, I won't steal anything.

It had made my stance to not stay in the house a good one. Steve had said to come and grab whatever I needed from the kitchen, but I didn't wholly feel comfortable with that arrangement. The house was spacious, grand, but I never felt anything more than claustrophobic in it, now more so that the older devil child had returned. I was out of there, I couldn't have cared less about her eyes, they no doubt shot laser beams from them anyway. No, I was best here in my simple room, with my single cot bed: clean, comfortable, no TV, a rickety ceiling. That was all that mattered. I knew I wouldn't exactly find a mini fridge and a mint on my pillow but that was okay. It was the change of scenery I had wanted. This was now my man cave.

Orientation would begin early on Monday, which gave me the weekend to settle in, of sorts, get my bearings, become accustomed to the lay of the land, all the while avoiding Miranda Henry. Should be easy enough; she didn't much strike me as the outdoorsy type.

Cuppa tea downed and now butting out my last cigarette, I let the two front legs of the chair fall to the deck as I stretched and groaned, ready to turn in for the night. It was only eight o'clock, but with little else to do, I stood to make my way inside, pausing at the sound of clinking cutlery and footsteps crunching into the dirt. I squinted into the darkness, seeing the silhouette closing in from the house.

"Hello," chirped a friendly voice.

"Hi," I said, guarded until the form was visible. The glinting metal smile of Moira, carrying a chinking tray of food.

"Mum thought you might be hungry." She grinned, stepping up to the verandah and setting the tray on the rickety side table next to the chair.

"You bloody ripper," I said. Sitting back down on the chair, feasting into a tray of biscuits, cheese and fruit. It wasn't exactly two meat and veg. Still, I was grateful nevertheless, not realising how hungry I actually was until I saw the tray of food.

"Thurnks," I managed through a mouthful of food, as Moira poured me a drink from a clinking ice-cubed jug.

"You're very welcome," she said, her beaming eyes staring at me.

Oh-O. I swallowed my food roughly. "Well … um … tell your mum thanks for me."

"There's cake under here." Moira lifted a lid off a small plate like she was a magician. "I made it myself," she said with pride.

"Wow, thanks." I nodded in good humour; I'm not sure how much more I could say. Guessing that would be it, I thought she would simply skip back to the house. Instead, Moira propped herself up on the beam of the verandah and wrapped her arm around the post, making herself quite at home.

"Is your name really Ringer?" she asked, cocking her head with interest.

Here we go.

I inwardly sighed, shaking my head no as I munched on some grapes.

"Really?" She straightened, her eyes alight with interest. "What is it?"

I slurped on my cold … cordial? Wow, tea to cordial. Things were starting to get wild.

I cleared my throat. "If I tell you, you have to promise not to tell anyone, okay?"

"Oh, I won't, cross my heart and hope to die," she said, physically crossing her heart. I was just about to reveal my actual namesake when I was beaten by the distant calls of Moira's mum.

"Moira? Come leave Ringer alone and have some dessert."

Penny Henry stood with her arms wrapped around herself as if warding off a chill that didn't exist on the tepid February night.

Moira grimaced. "Muum."

"Now, Moira." Penny's voice went down a few warning octaves; it was enough to have Moira jumping off the beam and rolling her eyes.

"I better go, she is in the worst mood since Miranda's come home."

Really?

I lifted my brows with interest, which only encouraged her to continue.

"Mum and Miranda always fight, you should hear them go at it," she said conspiratorially.

"I hope I never have to find out." I smirked.

"Ha. You'll be lucky." She laughed.

"Moira Henry!"

"Oh, I'm coming!" she yelled, before turning to me with a double eye blink. "Night, Ringer."

"Night, Moira." I stood as she skipped off towards her fuming mother. I lifted my hand to give a polite smile and wave, which elicited a head nod in acknowledgment. It was any guess why she would fight with her daughter, probably because they were so much alike … no doubt.

I dreamt of dust, and exhaust fumes, the whoosh of air as I had sailed through it, right before my life had flashed before my eyes. The images of my dealings with death played out in my subconscious like a horror movie on a continuous loop except each time it came to flipping me off, it wasn't Miranda doing it, it had been one of my mates. Sean, Toby, Stan … a different mate on each loop, always flipping me the finger, before tearing away, and leaving me behind in a cloud of dust. The sound of the car seemed so real, so loud, so …

I stirred. Lifting my face from my pillow I struggled to decipher my new surroundings. I gingerly rolled onto my back wincing at my rib cage where a bruise was slowly surfacing and providing me a constant reminder of my fall. I rubbed the sleep from my eyes, sighing in part relief that I had woken from my nightmare, a nightmare that seemed so real, so loud, so very … current. I froze, listening to the very sound that had plagued my dreams; I sat up, cocking my head to listen intently. It was the sound of the Mazda; the beat-up devil car (if you could call it a car) certainly sounded like it was manufactured in hell: wheezy, rackety and, in this case, failing to start.

Good.

It was about time it was put out of its misery, I thought, as I lay back down, linking my hands behind my head. I smirked in the dark, listening to its continued struggle as it refused to kick over and come to life. I waited for it to die so I could relish the fact of not having to listen to the sound again … *ever.* I yawned lazily, reaching for my Nokia on my side table to check the time.

I frowned at the illuminated screen. What the hell was the Mazda doing being started at one in the morning?

Before I could think too deeply about the reasoning, I found myself moving towards my door, clasping the handle and cringing as I twisted it slowly, hoping the sound of the creak of the hinge wouldn't alert me to anyone, not that they would be able to hear it over the sound of the ghastly, spluttering motor. Unable to see much through the crack of my door, I moved slowly to poke my head out and sneak a look down the verandah towards the Henry homestead, where the Mazda had last came to a stop. I slid along the wall of the huts, skimming myself along in the protection of the shadows as I neared closer, squinting to focus in the dark.

What is she doing?

The interior light of the car was illuminated with the driver's door left ajar. There she was, Miranda Henry, her face crinkled up in fierce determination with each attempt to start up her shit heap.

Come on, give it a rest.

Stubborn as a mule, she kept going and going to the point of me yawning and shaking my head.

You're not going anywhere, sweetheart.

And then the thought occurred to me. Why would she be going anywhere? She just got here. My attention snapped to a new sound. The sound of silence.

I edged my way closer, but still pressed far away from the rays of moonlight. Miranda's head was pressed against the steering wheel; she stayed that way unmoving for the longest of times. I half wondered if she was okay? Had some fumes filtered back through the car? No, she should be all right, the door was open a bit. Still unmoving, an uneasy feeling stirred inside of me, and my brow furrowed at the strange sensation, the feeling I could have sworn felt like … concern.

What a joke.

Now the noise had stopped I should have just turned around and headed back to my room, gone back to bed and enjoyed the fact that I would be safe from future nightmares about the ex-working Mazda hatchback. Instead, as I watched the unmoving blonde head bent over in despair, I sighed, straightened and stepped forward out of the shadows; my foot barely landed on the deck lit by a strip of moonbeam when I paused.

Miranda was on the move.

I jumped back, cursing at how ridiculous this all was, hiding like a child in the shadows, scared of the boogieman, or in this case, woman.

I watched on as Miranda flung her door open and slid out before slamming her door shut so violently, the sound echoed through the still summer night. How could I have been the only one woken by all the noise she was making, especially now that she had followed the door slamming with a kick from her expensive

European boot?

"Shit," she cried, latching onto her foot. Her boots were obviously not meant for kicking car doors.

A bemused smirk pulled at the corner of my mouth, watching her limp to the back passenger door as she flung it open with barely contained rage and grabbed for her bags. Much like she had when she arrived, Miranda Henry slung her belongings over her shoulder and slammed the passenger door. Shifting the awkward weight of her load, I waited for her to storm the exact same line towards the steps, onto the verandah and through the door. The only difference was I wouldn't be there to open it for her, or to be told to 'fuck off'.

I fought the urge to laugh at the memory, but then something happened that wiped all trace of humour from me.

She was headed my way.

Chapter Eight
Miranda

There was a good chance that I would get over my car.

Aside from the throbbing pain of my big toe, the ludicrously early hour of the morning, and the fact I was now stranded in the very last place on earth I wanted to be, I knew I would get over it. My fury had already started to dissipate.

Until I saw him.

Lurking in the shadows like a snake. I mean, did he honestly think I wouldn't be able to see him? The giant human-shaped shadow peering from the verandah?

Idiot.

When it came to lessons on sneaking around Moira Station I was fully qualified on the matter; I had enough connections in order to sneakily weave my way into town undetected every chance I had, so utterly desperate to escape, just like I wanted to now.

I didn't care how much noise I was making, I knew my parents would never hear me, their bedroom was right at the back of the house in their little parents' wing. Moira might have heard something if she wasn't snoring her head off and listening to music through her headphones.

All probably just as well. I had had enough of my parents' preaching and I had only been home for eight hours. I had hoped maybe they would have adopted the same kind of laid-back, carefree attitude when they would come and see me in Paris. In fact, I had really enjoyed 'holiday' Mum and Dad, it was almost like they were different people. But when I came home they were 'farmer' Mum and Dad: stressed, overworked, overtired, and full of questions and opinions. It had taken me two-point-five seconds to begin arguing with my mum when she came into my room. Instead of being glad to see me, it appeared Dad, the traitor, had relayed my dramatic homecoming, and my offensive behaviour. Yeah, of course I knew it was out of line; could I have stopped myself? Pfft. No! And furthermore, I really didn't want to have to be reminded of it every day of my time spent here, time I had hoped would be up as I threw all my belongings into the beast and drove off into the night.

Yeah, well, that wasn't going to happen. So my intention was, of course, to get as far away from my parents as possible. Seeing as it wasn't to be by blazing a dusty trail out the gate, it would just have to be in the shearers' huts. There was a less likely chance of my parents looming in my doorway with disapproving stares if I was out of sight, out of mind.

Aside from being pissed off about his spying, there was no doubt that Ringer (my dad's new pet) would have grabbed the best of the rooms, so much to my increasing burning hatred, I would have to settle for the room next to it. It still had a decent enough and less primitive set-up than the rest.

Before he had a chance to skulk away, as I approached the verandah steps, I called him out.

"Why don't you take a picture, it will last longer," I said, inwardly cringing as the words tumbled out of my mouth.

What, was I in a high school?

What had been scurried steps moving back along towards his room suddenly stilled. And by the time I had stepped up onto the verandah, he was standing in the open doorway to his room, looking at me with an incredulous dark stare.

"Nice night for spying," I said.

Ringer's mouth gaped, his brows knitted together.

"Spying?" he repeated, his anger barely contained. "Me?" he said, pointing to his chest.

I stopped before him, cocking my head and readjusting my bag on my shoulder.

"Do you see any other weirdo lurking in the shadows?"

"Weirdo?" he scoffed. "More like being woken up by that hideous sound your shit box of a car was making; I thought you were going to crash it through my fucking wall."

"It's not a shit box," I snapped.

"No, of course not, she purrs like a kitten," he said smugly, crossing his arms over his chest and leaning in the open doorway to his room. Right at that moment I really wanted to punch him in the face, but I think Mum and Dad might have me committed for acts of violence, or worse. Home detention.

"Hey, Ringer?"

His brows rose in surprise, as if the sound of me referring to him by name was not expected.

"Just do me a favour and stay out of my way," I said, weary with fatigue as I gathered my belongings and made my way to the room next door.

"Well, Mir-an-da," he said, deliberately emphasising my name. "It might be a little tricky, you know, now that we're neighbours and all."

"Just keep the noise down," I said, juggling to open my door as I twisted the handle and kicked it open. Making sure to give him a parting poignant 'I'm-not-joking death stare.' Unfortunately I was met with a devious grin as he watched on from his doorway.

"Don't worry, sweetheart, I won't rev my engine for you."

I dumped my bags inside the door and coolly and casually walked back towards Ringer, who watched my every move with guarded uncertainty, but that smart-arse glimmer was still in his eyes. I came to a stop right before him, close enough to be momentarily distracted by his breath that blew down on me.

I squared my shoulders, not thinking about that sensation. "If you call me sweetheart again, I will put sugar in your fuel tank; do I make myself clear?"

Ringer's jaw clenched, any trace of humour drained away with my threatening words. I had finally found his Achilles heel: his beloved Ford.

"My mistake." He nodded in a gentlemanly manner.

It was almost like my ego had been stroked as I took it as a small victory. I nodded in return before spinning on my heel and heading back to my door.

"Of course, in order to call you that, you would firstly have to have a heart."

I stilled, turning towards him, dumbfounded that he was still talking. My eyes locked with his.

"And as for the former," he said, pushing off from his doorframe, "there is nothing sweet about you."

Before I could even take in his sledge, he had walked into his room and slammed the door behind him.

Chapter Nine
Ringer

I thought at first I was hearing things, then as I pressed my ear to the wall the very reality hit me like a ton of bricks.

No-no-no-no-no. Fuck!

Miranda was crying.

A soft sob that made my shoulders sag in defeat; never before had I felt like such a giant arsehole. I hadn't even gotten a great amount of satisfaction in baiting her like I should. She was obviously planning to leave for a reason; something had obviously gone down bad enough for her to want to be away from her family, so bad that she resorted to sleeping next to me.

Definitely rock bottom.

I should have just walked straight up to the bloody car, asked if she was okay. Instead of getting my back up every time she was around me. Sure, she didn't exactly bring out the best in me but that gave me no right to accuse her of having no heart, because listening to the whimpers next door, regardless of her icy façade, she had feelings. I made a mental note to just be a bit more … *thoughtful* in the light of day.

Ah, Christ, I felt like shit.

I ran my hand through my hair, pulling away from the wall; I started pacing hoping that the distance from it would leave me unable to hear it. No such luck.

Even standing over the opposite side of the room, I could clearly hear her crying, as she became more distraught and consumed by emotion. It was clear; I was getting no sleep tonight. The guilt wouldn't let me. At first she tried to contain her sound, but now it seemed like it was the breath hitching, sobbing kind of tears, and they were the worst. Harder to control, impossible to ignore.

Please, please, anything but tears. Be a bitch, treat me like dirt, and make my life a nightmare. Just. Don't. Cry.

I sat on the edge of my bed, my head buried in my hands as a war raged inside of me. I blew out a long breath and lifted my head, staring at the thin wall that divided us.

Fuck!

Before reason or logic could come flooding into my mind, I stood and made my way to my door. I made no effort to creep around or worry about being heard, I let the full force of my footsteps be heard on the decked floor. And as I came to stand directly in front of her door, I inhaled deeply, praying that she would insist she was fine and tell me to go away.

I knocked lightly on the door.

"Miranda?"

I knocked a second time, this time harder, met by silence. I knocked for a third time, harder still.

"Miranda, are you okay?"

"Go away," she croaked.

"Listen, I just want to say … I'm sorry. I'm sorry for what I said."

"Yeah, right."

"I am, I didn't mean it … I just, wasn't thinking." Every word came out of my mouth stagnated and wooden; it was as if apologising was such a foreign thing to me, but thinking about it, it wasn't something I did, well … *ever.*

"Sure, easy to say sorry to a door," she scoffed.

I closed my eyes, praying for the strength; here I was debating my authenticity at some ungodly hour through a door, trying to comfort some princess. I counted to three, reminding myself to be more 'thoughtful'.

"Fine, I'm coming in," I called out.

If it was the last thing I would do, I would look her in the eye, apologise, take a hit to my pride and get the hell out of there. Surely with no car noise and no more crying I could sleep long and peacefully.

Without waiting for permission, I pushed the door open so quickly, there was little time to register the sensation of ice-cold water that came swooshing down on me, thoroughly drenching me, followed by the bucket landing perfectly on top of my head. I was frozen; the only thing snapping me out of my state of shock was the maniacal laughter, no, more like cackle sound muffled from beyond the bucket that sat skew-whiff on my head.

Son of a bitch.

I slowly pulled it off, whipping the water from my face and shaking my hair. I scowled above me, the bucket in my hand tied with a string that looped above the door, my dumbfounded stare then locked onto Miranda.

And she was far from crying; in fact, she looked positively radiant, not one tear shed, well, maybe from laughter as she stood on the bed, bouncing on the balls of her feet in hysterics. Her laughter finally caught in her throat as she noticed my murderous stare.

I thought she might have looked a tad bit worried, or held some form of regret; instead, she playfully bit her knuckle and winced, trying not to laugh.

"Oops," she said.

It was all I needed. I threw the bucket to the side and strode across the room. Miranda squealed, jumped off the bed and to the side as I tried to lunge towards her. I caught the edge of her black cardigan that she spun her way out of until all I held in my hand was the cardi itself.

Shit!

She dove for the door and darted outside. I dropped the clothing and took off after her into the darkness, our feet making loud pudding booms as we bolted along the decking away from the homestead, away from the shearing quarters. I was in hot pursuit, and she was fast, Christ, she was fast. I felt like a greyhound chasing a wild rabbit. I could see her blonde hair flailing in the wind, the warm summer night drying my clothes as I tore up the dirt and made up ground after her. She disappeared into one of the out buildings and I knew I was in trouble; she knew this place better than me and I knew if I lost sight of her that would be it. Luckily, inside was a massive open space, our movements tripping a sensor light and flooding the space with light. Save for an old bomb work ute that she sought refuge behind. Her breathing was laboured, and without the cardi on, she only had a skimpy, spaghetti-strap, sheer top underneath, low cut, her cleavage covered in a slight sheen of sweat. Her hair was wild and her cheeks were flushed. I tried to control my own breath as I leant my hands on the car; I also tried to control my wandering eyes. I'm sure she noticed them dip down to her chest.

Now was not the time for a raging hard on, Ringer.

We would be here all night; I had to make her move to the right, that way I stood a better chance of closing in the space with little escape. So I did what I knew would work; I glanced to my right, faking out as if my thought was to go that way, all the while my body went the opposite, as did she. She all but bolted into my arms and I latched onto her with my iron grip, her eyes wide with shock, her breathing shallow. After wondering what the mysterious eyes behind the glasses looked like, I was now in a position where I was staring into their arresting bluey-green depths, so close, I could make out speckled colours of lighter hues around the edges.

We were both breathing hard, her breasts pressed against my chest, the heat of her skin burning through my wet clothes. Miranda bit her lip as her cat-like eyes broke from mine and flicked to my mouth for the briefest moment. I couldn't help but smile; her eyes darted away so fast I could imagine she would be cursing herself for that moment of weakness. However brief it had been, it was still there, and the man in me soared to the surface. Could the wild-eyed beauty be tamed, I wondered? I became momentarily distracted by Miranda pressing together her perfect rosy lips, causing my own eyes to stray. I took it for an unspoken invitation. And just when I was about to loosen my grip a little, I saw something spark in her eyes, right before I felt the searing pain stab into my foot as she stomped the heel of her boot into me. I winced, instantly letting go, and she bolted once more.

"Fuuuuck," I said through gritted teeth. Her boots were obviously not made for kicking cars, but perfect for stomping on men.

I limped out of the out building, wet and injured. I spotted her running back up the verandah and diving back into her room, slamming her door. I glowered after her, dragging my foot in the dirt as I stomped my way up the deck. Stopping by her door, I felt like laughing—thinking only moments before, I was here pleading for forgiveness.

What a joke.

This time I was here for a whole other reason, as I twisted the handle and pushed.

Locked. Cute.

If she honestly thought that would keep me out she was sorely mistaken.

I stood back a little, aiming to kick with my non-broken foot; it took all but two swift kicks to have the rickety shearer's door burst open.

Miranda squealed, her back pressed up against the bedhead, fear wild in her eyes.

This time she had nowhere to go, she had backed herself into a corner. I smiled, because she knew it and I knew it. I felt it in her defeated slump as I reached out and snaked my hand around her wrist and dragged her from the bed with a yelp.

Without a word I pulled her to her feet and yanked her out the door, her steps working quickly to keep up with my long, determined strides along the decked verandah.

"Let me go," she cried, trying to twist out of my grasp.

"Umm … no," I said, flashing her a grin.

"I swear to God, Ringer, if you don't let me go I'll …"

Her words fell away as her attention turned to what lay ahead of her, her eyes wide and filled with fury as her head snapped up to meet my eyes.

"Don't. You. Dare."

Chapter Ten
Miranda

Fighting against him was useless.

No matter how I had resisted, or how much I tried to dig my heels in, Ringer yanked me forward like a ragdoll.

What had been an annoying accident of kicking the bucket that sat in my room near the door soon reminded me of a memory from long ago. I had picked up the silver tin bucket that had a frayed working of thin rope attached. A smile spread thin and devious.

I couldn't, could I?

Of course it wasn't exactly an original idea; it was an old classic prank that Bluey had masterminded back in the day. I didn't know if it was boredom that plagued the shearers or living away from home months at a time. But it usually had them scheming and setting up pranks on one another that would result in a chorus of riotous laughter thundering from the huts. Bluey had rigged up the bucket above the door for the unsuspecting target. If there wasn't a yabby in your drink bottle, your beds would be short sheeted. And seeing as I didn't have a spare yabby on me, and there would be no chance I would be going anywhere near Ringer's bed, I looked over the bucket and up to the door, grinning like the Cheshire cat. Of course, it may not have worked at all, and boy did I have to put on some Academy Award-winning skills. There had been a point when I thought he wouldn't come or call out. Maybe he was taking great joy in me being upset?

Bastard.

But sensing movement in the room next door gave me hope and I amped up my performance. Before I knew it, I heard his footsteps and the tap on the door. My heart had leapt into my throat.

Oh shit!

My eyes darted up to the precarious bucket over the door. I bit my lip, feeling a moment of regret until he started speaking. It sounded forced, uncomfortable, as if he just wanted me to shut up already. My brows lowered; I would give him something to shut up about, I thought, and as I got myself ready to stand on my bed with great satisfaction as he announced he was coming in, I waited for my moment of glory.

And, oh, don't get me wrong: it had been glorious, for about ten seconds. The one lesson I never thought to learn from the shearers' practical jokes was, were the ten seconds of joy really worth the torture of what may come?

And I knew what was coming; I could as good as read Ringer's mind as he pulled me towards the large water trough that caught the overflow of the shearers' quarters. Cold, murky and usually had some animal slurping out of it: my mind froze with horror thinking of my four-hundred-dollar Italian leather boots.

"Ringer, don't. I mean it," I pleaded quickly.

He spun me around, catching me by my wrists and leaning me precariously back as my butt rested on the trough.

I put on my best sad, pleading eyes of mercy. "Please, don't," I said.

Of course, I was talking to the one person I had almost ran over, flipped off, told to fuck off, woken up, accused of being a pervert, all before drenching him with water, and stomping my heel into his foot. Yeah, I'm sure batting my eyelashes would get me out of this one.

Ringer just smiled, slow and wicked, as he shook his head—as good as saying not a chance. He went to loosen his grip, but I hooked my legs around his thighs.

"Hang on, hang on, wait a minute, will you just wait a minute?" I blurted out, his brow cocking with interest.

My breathing was shallow; I felt like I was on borrowed time as I nervously glanced backwards. He probably wouldn't listen but I still had to plead my case.

"Look, you can turf me in as many times as you want, but my boots are really expensive, and …"

"Your boots?" He laughed.

"Yes."

"The ones that have their heel imprinted on my foot?"

I grimaced. "Yes."

Ringer looked down at me for a long, broody moment, before a smile pinched the corner of his mouth.

"Chicks and their shoes," he said, shaking his head. "All right then, it's more notice than you gave me, but you can keep your bloody boots dry."

My body visibly sagged. Until he moved my hands to his shoulders.

"Hold on," he said.

Seeing as the grip on his shoulders was the only thing that was preventing me from tumbling backwards, I did so without argument. I dug my fingers in, finding purchase in the corded muscular sinew.

A dimple creased on his right cheek when he smirked, and I wondered how I had never seen it before. He lifted my leg up and without breaking from my eyes once, he unwrapped my laces, roughly yanking at them one by one; it seemed oddly sexual, the way his eyes burned into mine, how each tug and unravel of his fingers felt like he was undressing me. I blinked, probably for the first time when my boot fell to the floor; he then worked on the other. I swallowed, trying not to think about the strength in his broad shoulders, the way they felt under my fingers that were white from the intensity of their hold. My other boot thudded to the floor and I blinked out of my daze, met once again with his hazel eyes. Okay, the boots would live to see another day, and my eyes dipped to my black sheer top; that had not been cheap either, I remembered, biting my lip as I took in the silken fabric.

Ringer reached out and bunched the fabric in his hand at my rib cage; my head snapped up in alarm.

"Do you want this off too?" he said, with a wicked glimmer in his eyes.

"NO," I said quickly.

Ringer sighed, letting go of my top. "Shame," he said, before, without even a moment's warning, grabbing my legs and flipping me backwards. I plunged into the gritty depths, clawing at the water that was turning into white foam as I coughed and spluttered, trying to find purchase on the bottom with my now bare feet.

I wanted to yell obscenities at him, to call him every name under the sun, but as I wiped the water from my eyes and locked onto him, I thought better of it as he stood by holding my boots.

I couldn't control myself not to glower at him.

Ringer laughed. "Might want to dry off before you put these back on." He placed them neatly on the deck, grinning up at me; the bastard was enjoying every minute of this.

"Night, Miranda." He saluted his brow and made his way back towards his room, pausing near my door. I looked on with annoyed interest as I fumbled my way out of the trough.

Ringer bent down and picked up the black cardi he had pulled off me earlier.

"Hey, put that back," I yelled, stumbling onto the decking. My bare feet padded a long determined line towards him, reaching out for my cardi that he lifted above my head out of reach.

Such a fucking child.

I took a calming breath, and held my hand out.

"Give me back my cardi."

"Actually," he said, thumbing the fabric and looking over it, as if it was a rare diamond. "I thought I might keep it as a trophy."

My hand dropped to my side in frustration. "Goddamn it, Ringer, give me it back."

Every time I lost my shit, it only served to entertain him to no end; his slow, wicked smile was not lost on me even as he turned and leant by his opened door. He made sure he was looking at me as he lazily turfed my cardi into his room, landing in a pile on his unmade bed. "You want it?" He tilted his head. "Go and get it."

My mouth gaped. He had thrown it expecting me to fetch it like a dog; furthermore, I would never step inside Ringer's room, not in a million years.

"We're even now," I bit out, my hands balled into fists as my eyes burned into his.

Ringer let out a blast of laughter, causing me to flinch at the unexpectedness of it. He shook his head at me. "Oh, sweetheart, we're not even anywhere near close to even." And with that, he turned and closed his door behind him, leaving me on the verandah barefoot, and in a puddle of water.

Yep! Ten seconds' bliss was *not* worth this amount of torture.

As the sun crept its way up to tinge the sky with colour, I tiptoed my way past Ringer's closed door, not without resisting the urge to mumble insults under my breath. I headed towards the main house past the Mazda, God rest her soul; I couldn't bring myself to even look at her. It was solely because of her I was heading to the kitchen at this ungodly hour on a Sunday morning. I decided to partake in the usual Henry tradition of a cooked breakfast, plus I had some major sucking up to do with my parents if I wanted to get this car fixed. It took every ounce of my being to clamp down the rage I had for my mother from last night as I pushed the wire door wide open.

"Good morning!" I beamed.

My mum stood frozen, hovering a spoonful of eggs between the plate and pan; she looked like she had seen a ghost, and even

Dad paused from his newspaper, a line pinching between his brow as he wearily looked at me as if seeing a stranger.

"You feeling all right, luv?" My dad folded his paper, pushing it aside as he watched me with guarded interest.

My smile dipped slightly. "Of course, why wouldn't I be?" I half laughed as I pulled a stool next to him at the island bench.

"Moira still snoozing?" I asked innocently, plucking a grape from the fruit bowl. Mum double blinked, unfreezing from her stance as she quickly started dishing out the eggs before they went cold.

"Ha! You won't see sleeping beauty before noon," said Dad.

"Sounds about right." I scoffed.

"From memory, you're not exactly a morning person either," said Mum, looking at me sceptically.

And she was right, I wasn't a morning person at all; still I hadn't exactly fancied running into Ringer this morning and I had planned to butter up my parents while I had the chance to have them to myself.

Mum sat a plate of bacon and eggs down in front of Dad. "Miranda, can you go knock on Ringer's door and see if he would like some breakfast?"

My grape caught in my throat causing a coughing fit; my eyes watering, I grabbed at Dad's orange juice to wash it down.

"What?" I croaked.

"I'll go," said Dad getting up from his stool, only to be quickly swatted back down with Mum's tea towel.

"No, Steve, your breakfast will get cold. Miranda, please duck out, I am putting more eggs on now," she said to me in a no-nonsense tone that always got my back up.

"All right, all right. I have to get some clean clothes anyway," I said, sliding off my stool.

"Where are your clothes?" Dad frowned as he cut into his buttered bread.

I paused. "Um, I camped in the shearers' huts last night."

Both my parents looked at me now, their eyes alarmed with

speculation.

"In the second room," I shouted. "On my own."

Unbelievable.

Dad squirmed in his seat. "Well just so long as …"

"Oh yeah, Dad, as if I am going to bunk in with Ringer," I said, turning only to slam straight into the chest of the devil himself, the devil and his taut, muscled chest, and damn him if he didn't smell amazing. Whatever cologne he was wearing was fresh and sharp, simple, yet very masculine. I double blinked, snapping myself away from the effect it had over me, as I clutched my shoulder, rubbing at the dull ache from having run into him at full force.

"Whoa, look out!" He laughed, stepping back.

I didn't have much time to show my annoyance as my eyes flicked down to his hands.

Oh dear God!

Ringer followed my eye line. "Oh yeah, you must have left these …"

"Thank you!" I cut him off, snatching them from his grasp.

I laughed nervously. "I must have left them on the verandah." I tried not to meet the judgmental stares of my parents, because I had known from the moment the words left my mouth, they wouldn't buy it for a second. Miranda Henry would never leave her shoes outside … Period!

Chapter Eleven
Ringer

I admit it.

When it came to Miranda Henry, I had this sick pleasure in pushing her buttons. Watching the cogs turn in her pretty little head, seeing the rage that burned in her eyes, the incredulous gapes of her mouth, and the thunderous steps she took as anger swirled inside of her.

Yeah, it was kinda hot.

I turned to meet the glacial stares of Miranda's parents in the kitchen; shit. It appeared I was also a dead man, and inwardly cursed myself for watching Miranda storm across the driveway towards the shearers' huts with an air of amusement; I also realised that I had probably watched her for far too long than was acceptable, especially with her parents watching on. I may have got the last laugh, but she had left me in the lion's den, so to speak. Lucky I was a charming bastard when I wanted to be.

I smiled. "Something smells good in here," I said, as I casually approached the kitchen bench, taking a seat.

I could feel Steve Henry's eyes boring into my profile as he spoke to me. "Make sure you eat up, son, because you and I are going to go for a little drive."

Fuck! Ringer meet lion's den.

I had thought that I may have been driven out to a remote part of his property where Steve Henry had a shallow grave waiting for me, the sentence had bore enough weight behind it for it to feel like I was about to be murdered by an over-protective father. But in typical Steve Henry style, he was upbeat and animated while we really did go for a drive. And it wasn't to an abandoned field; it was to his best mate, Bluey Sheehan's house, on the neighbouring property.

"If you need anything while we're gone, Bluey is your man," Steve said.

We spent the afternoon in Bluey's man cave, a refrigerated, air-conditioned shed with mismatched seventies-style lounges, a pool table, a dart board and a fridge full of cold beer.

He chucked a VB can towards me that I caught close to my chest.

"It's gotta be five o'clock somewhere in the world, right?" he said with a devious wink.

Steve sighed. "Penny will kill me," he said, looking longingly down at the cold beer.

"Penny can't expect you to have a business meeting without a beer," Bluey exclaimed, as he sat back down on the couch turning the volume of the cricket down a bit.

"Every meeting I have with you, Blue, is a business meeting." Steve smiled wryly.

Bluey shrugged. "I am a business man."

There were no two ways about it. I liked Bluey and when I grew up, I wanted to be exactly like him. My own man, doing my own thing, answering to no man. Or in Steve's case, woman.

Steve walked over to the fridge and placed it back inside. "Nah, better not, it's not worth the hassle."

Bluey shook his head. "Mate, you're under the thumb," he said as took a sip from his beer.

"Oh, piss off," said Steve.

"You have a big enough thumbprint on the back of your head it would be like driving over a corrugated road."

"Get stuffed, I'm going to use your loo," Steve said, walking out of the shed. The loo being the lemon tree out back.

"So, you reckon you can handle taking care of the place for a bit?" Blue asked me in all sincerity, his steel-blue eyes unwavering from me as he took a long draw from his can.

"Yeah, no worries, I did some jackaroo work on my uncle's property in Druin."

Bluey shook his head in recognition. "But did your uncle's property have a Miranda Henry to deal with?"

My eyes snapped up to meet his. What did she have to do with this? With anything?

"No," I said, wearily.

Bluey shifted, leaning his elbows on his knees, staring me down with such an intent look it could probably strip paint.

"Just let it be known that if you touch her or hurt her in any way, I will staple gun your genitals to the wall, do you understand me?"

Holy shit!

Striking the memory from the kitchen, now I really was IN the lion's den.

I swallowed thickly, not tearing my eyes away for a moment. I nodded firmly, causing him to mirror my image as he sat back. "Good," he said, melting back into the couch.

"Is this where Steve takes all the young men around town? To have a none-too-subtle word from you?"

A smile creased the corner of Bluey's mouth. "Not entirely, just looking out for a mate. Miranda doesn't exactly come without … issues."

My look would have said it all, a look of intrigue, because Bluey merely laughed. "And no, I won't tell you."

Steve Henry walked back into Bluey's shed and surveyed the scene before him. "What's going on? It's colder than a mother-in-law's kiss in here."

"I was, ah, just given some advice about how to best take care of things at Moira," I said quickly.

"I just told him to keep his eyes on the job at hand." Bluey winked at Steve.

It took a moment for Steve to catch on before reading the sullen look on my face. Before bursting into laughter.

"You mean Miranda?" he asked.

I squirmed in my seat, looking down into my beer before taking a sip. "It was not the most subtle advice," I said.

Steve continued to laugh. "Oh leave him alone, Bluey, this one's all right. I can't see him being any threat to Miranda's affections."

I did a double take, not entirely knowing if I should be honoured by his faith in me or offended with the fact Miranda would not give me a second thought. I had desperately wanted to call him out on it, but luckily Bluey did it for me.

"What makes you so sure, Steve-O?" Bluey asked sceptically.

"Because there is no way in hell Miranda would have any interest in a country boy."

A country boy? I was hardly a Ballan breed; I was an Onslowian through and through. And although it was hardly the cobblestone streets of Paris, we did have some substance. More alarmingly, though, why should I give a shit? So Miranda had a taste for European, Vespa-driving blokes that looked like they belonged in a Gucci catalogue. It seemed totally fitting to the stick-up-her-arse attitude. Good! Fine, who cares? I sure didn't.

I crushed my empty can in my hand and turfed it into the wool bale that was being used as a recycling bin.

"Don't think you need to worry, lads, as soon as that car is fixed I am pretty certain Miranda will be leaving Moira station in a trail of dust and burning rubber," I said matter-of-factly.

My words fell upon a silence, a silence I had created with my words.

Fuck! What have I done now?

Thinking I had majorly put my foot in it, I thought I might be met with some pissed-off expressions. Instead, to my surprise, Steve glanced sheepishly towards Bluey and then back to me.

"What?" I frowned.

Steve sighed, running his hands through his hair.

Bluey got up, wiping the barely contained smile from his face, chucking his crushed can in the wool bale. "Want a drink, Steve-O?" He ambled towards the fridge to get his long-time friend a well-needed beer.

Steve just nodded, his face a mixture of troubled emotions that wrestled under the surface. He rubbed the back of his neck in deep thought, before meeting my eyes. "Can you keep a secret?"

Some things you just didn't want to know.

I didn't necessarily need to hear all about Miranda's troubled past in Ballan, and about the low-life French boyfriend that had broken her heart a year ago. I didn't need to know that she had a temper and was generally untrusting and difficult to deal with. That her mum and dad constantly worried about her and feared she was destined to be a lost soul. And I certainly didn't need to hear that her dad had deliberately tampered with her car so it wouldn't start.

I'm sure, based on my reaction, that Steve regretted telling me the things that he had, but as the knowledge had slowly seeped in, and I swore that his secret was safe with me, he seemed to visibly relax, which must have been nice for him, because as it stood after his confession, I felt like I had a massive fucking weight on my chest.

Still, it did make one thing clear. Miranda had demons, raw ones, and I thought it best to leave well enough alone. No more smart-arse innuendoes, no more chasing in the dark. Aside from not wanting to get my testicles staple gunned to Bluey's wall, I had, after all, come here to escape everything complicated, and she was mega complicated.

They say it's the quiet ones you have to worry about, and she was quiet, very quiet—when she wasn't busy despising me with a burning passion.

Chapter Twelve
Miranda

I had debated whether to move back into the house or not.
The thought of dragging my belongings back inside, past my mum, past my sister, would be one thing I didn't want to have to explain. Besides the idiot next door, I had to admit I liked the seclusion, for as long as it lasted. My sister lay on my bed in the shearers' huts thumbing through a copy of *French Vogue*, going "Ooh La-La" at every beautiful dress that she set her eyes on. After fifty Ooh La- Las, it was enough to drive a person to drink, which gave me a bit of an idea of how I wanted to spend my evening.

"What's that look for?" my sister asked, peering up at me.

"What look?" I said, turning to hang one of my tops on a hanger.

"The look that says you're pretty pleased with yourself."

"Well, I am! I have finally unpacked my stuff."

"Tell me again, why are you staying in here?"

"I told you, I need my space. Besides, do you really want me and Mum fighting all day, every day?" I reasoned.

"No, that does kind of suck."

"Exactly! At least here I don't have to argue with anyone."

Well, aside from my arsehole of a neighbour.

"Why can't you two just get along?" Moira sighed, returning her attention back to the magazine.

"Because he's an absolute dickhead," I said, my glare still fixated on the wall.

"Huh? Who's a dickhead?"

Shit, we had been talking about Mum.

"Hmm? Oh no one, don't worry about it." I waved it off.

But it was too late; Moira missed nothing and she followed my angry stare to the wall I had held only a moment before.

She pushed herself into a cross-legged position on the bed, her eyes lit with excitement. "Oh. My. God. You saw him!"

"Oh, of course I saw him," I snapped. Annoyed that I was about to have this conversation.

"Isn't he gorgeous?" Moira all but squealed.

I deadpanned at her, refusing to answer the question. I guess he was all right looking, tall and toned in all the right places—his shoulders had felt like it anyway. When his white T-shirt had been soaked last night, I will admit that my eye did wander over the see-through fabric that clung to his chiselled stomach, but it wasn't exactly like I had gawked any more than he had at my boobs. I saw him; I wasn't stupid.

"He has wicked hair, and dreamy eyes; what are they, like a greeny-brown?"

"Hazel," I said, instantly regretting my answer.

My little sister grinned from ear to ear, blinding me with her braces. "Oh yeah, you have seen him all right."

I had seen him, more than I cared to want to or was going to. As soon as my car was fixed, and Mum, Dad and Moira were set to head for the Wahroo Cattle Station next weekend, I was out of there. When I returned to the kitchen that morning, I was annoyed to discover Dad had left for the day. Mum had said he was going to take Ringer to Bluey's and talk 'business'. Of course we both knew what that meant; they were going to have a beer and watch the cricket.

Typical.

So leaving no one else to talk to about the possibility of getting my car looked at, it had left me no choice but to hang out with Moira for the day. Where I went she went, chatting animatedly about boys mostly, and by the sound of it, she was Ringer's number one fan. It did make it less than ideal as I had planned to sneak into his room and get my cardigan back, but the last thing I needed was to get Moira to keep a secret about what my cardi was doing in Ringer's room. Because when it came to keeping secrets, well, Moira just couldn't. Fact!

I shoved my empty bag under the bed, slapping my hands together with a sense of achievement.

"How about we go for a swim?" It was part ploy to change the subject from Ringer, and partly to get Moira away from the huts long enough so I could sneak into Ringer's room and grab my cardi. The day was heating up and it was the only source of entertainment, aside from my plans tonight when I would make my way into town for a quiet drink, just like the old days. I didn't know how I would get there but I would find a way.

Moira's eyes lit up as I knew they would.

"You're on," she said, rolling off the bed and sprinting out the door. "Wait for me, I'm just gonna get changed," she yelled, all the while running backwards, almost falling over when she spun around to gun it across the dirt drive. She was so unco. I smiled, shaking my head as I watched Moira almost fling the wire door off its hinges as she ripped it open.

My smile soon fell away into a sneer as I turned towards Ringer's door. I would have to hurry; Moira on a mission meant I had only minutes to go in, find the cardigan and get out. The last thing I needed was to be busted by Moira or, worse, Ringer. I bit my lip, as I reached for the handle.

No, it would be okay. I could hear a car approaching from a mile away; hell I would hear Moira approaching from a mile away she was so bloody loud. I twisted the knob expecting the door to no doubt be locked, but as I slowly twisted, and pushed the door inward my breath hitched.

Eureka!

That's as stealthy as I got, as I quickly opened the door and dived inside, closing the door but leaving it slightly ajar.

Right. Should be simple enough. There wasn't much to the shearing huts: a bed, a wash basin, a rack mounted on the wall with some scraggly coat hangers, most of them housed some of Ringer's belongings, the rest of his things were slung over his unmade bed.

Pfft, such a boy.

I started rummaging through the pile; he had so much crap everywhere, it was like he had packed like a girl and yet they all seemed to be the same sort of clothing. Jeans, white T, Jeans, black T, Jeans, navy T. Well, at least he was always guaranteed to be clean. I bit my lip at the pile of clothes I had tossed onto the floor, *oops*. I quickly gathered them up and put them back onto the bed, organising them in such a way that seemed as if he had chucked them there himself.

Damn, no cardi.

I was running out of time. I stood with my hands on my hips. I blew a wayward strand of hair out of my line of vision as I turned in the room, examining every square inch.

Where the hell had he put it?

I pulled back the bedspread and dragged the pillows away, thinking he might have creepily stashed it behind his pillow.

Nothing.

I sat on the bed, a crease pinching my brow in frustration before I bent over and checked under the bed, spying only bare floorboards and a thick layer of dust.

I slapped my thighs in frustration as I moved towards the hanging clothes, checking behind them, seeing if he had it hidden it there. I was momentarily distracted when I came to a navy dress shirt. My fingers lazily ran down the sleeve. Soft to the touch, this would look nice on him, I thought, as my thumb grazed the pearl-coloured buttons. I brought the material of the sleeve up to my nose to smell the crisp scent of laundry detergent.

"What are you doing?"

I screamed, leaping away from the clothes at the unexpectedness of the voice from the door. My heart thumped fiercely against the wall of my chest, my eyes wild and wide as I spotted my sister, standing in the doorway with a confused scowl across her face, as if what she was seeing before her was truly disturbing … me in Ringer's room, smelling his shirt; well, that even disturbed me.

"Nothing," I said a bit too loud. "I was just, putting on the ceiling fan, it's going to be a scorcher today." Luckily the wall control for the overhead fan was next to the clothes rack, it made my casual move to turn it on seem more believable, even if I could tell by the sceptical curve of Moria's brow that she wasn't buying it. Not for one second.

How could I have not heard her? Not sensed her pushing the door open? Guess I had been lost in a trance of picturing Ringer in the blue dress shirt. I had to get out of there; being surrounded by all of Ringer's clothes was doing strange things to my mind. I quickly shook it off as I lifted my chin and walked a long, determined line towards the door, not meeting my sister's eyes as I brushed past her.

"Come on, let's go," I said, without a backwards glance.

Chapter Thirteen
Ringer

Well, well, well …

It appeared a rat had been in my room: a giant, blonde-haired rat with a smart mouth and a bad attitude.

To her credit, she had tried to make it seem like nothing had been touched, but I had guessed it the minute I had stepped into my room. An incredulous smile curved my lips as the shadows of the blades from the overhead fan flickered across my bed.

Instinctively, I moved and lifted up the mattress. My smile broadened as I reached and pulled out the soft black fabric of Miranda's cardigan. I thumbed the fabric, actually amazed she hadn't found it; it really hadn't been the most imaginative hiding place.

My first choice was shoving it inside my pillowcase the night before, but then all I could smell was her, and trying to sleep when all the blood was rushing to your groin was not easy. I ended up dumping the infuriating, sweet-smelling expensive scrap of material out from the case and shoving it under the mattress. Having no real intention of giving it back any time soon, I left it there instead. That was my plan anyway, but after having spent the day at Bluey's with Steve and being told way more than I cared to know, I had decided to lay off Miranda, even avoid her if possible. It seemed she was pretty messed up, so I was going to leave well enough alone and just put my head down and work hard like I intended to do in the first place. Of course, that's what I was thinking until I entered my room and noticed it had been tampered with.

Maybe just one last little push, I thought, holding the cardi up in the air and smiling like a Cheshire cat.

"I think the girls have gone for a swim," said Steve, as he busied himself watering the herb basket by the kitchen. "It's bloody hot enough."

Beyond a green, grassy strip of lawn and established garden that surrounded the homestead lay nothing but dry, dusty red earth and a blistering hot sun. It would be a full-time job keeping anything alive out here, and something that Steve was obviously pedantic about as he moved to untangle the hose to attach to the sprinkler. I made a note to self: don't kill anything while he was away; I guess that included Miranda. I smirked to myself.

"Why don't you go for a dip, cool off before I take you into town later?" Steve said, as he wrestled with the anaconda-like garden hose that was hooked around his foot.

Again I glanced beyond his little oasis. Apart from the water tanks, animal troughs and shearers' shower block, could there be any other drop of water?

"You have a pool?" I asked, thinking it possible that there might even be a tennis court stashed away as well, seeing as the Henrys seemed to like the finer things in life. I mean, I had a fucking cheese platter for dinner the other night, for Christ sake's; it was a far cry from a pot and parmi at the Onslow.

"Ha! Don't worry. I have been plagued endlessly from the kids to get one, and, sure, it would be great, but do you know who would be the poor bugger that would have to keep it clean?"

Steve finally untangled the hose, only to find there was a kink in it right down the other end. He swore under his breath and stormed a path to fix it, sweat lining his brow.

"So I take it that's a no then?" I mused, moving to help pull the hose out straight.

"I told the girls you have two choices. Run under the sprinkler, or duck dive in the dam. And seeing as they're not here—" Steve triumphantly clicked the attachment onto the tap, "—my guess is they're …"

"At the dam," I said, finishing his sentence. "Well, beggars can't be choosers, and seeing as I haven't run under a sprinkler since I was five years old, I think I might choose the dam, too."

Steve nodded in good humour. "It's that-a-way." He pointed towards the shearing shed, which I was guessing meant beyond.

"Right, thanks," I said, squinting up at the sun. "Well, might go for a dip then."

"Just come up to the kitchen when you want to head into town," Steve said.

"Will do." I saluted, before leaving the green, shady homestead behind me, making my way to get changed.

I didn't need the visual of Miranda Henry, arched back on a sun lounge, sunning in the blistering rays of an Australian summer. The image of her running under a sprinkler was enough to make me swallow hard; I didn't need this, too.

The dam was a fair enough walk from the homestead even from the shearing shed. It sat in the middle of nowhere, a big muddy hole in the earth that was a far cry from any chic, fancy-tiled in-ground swimming pool. It surprised me that Miranda Henry would be caught dead in it, of course, not that she was in it. She was reclined back on the rickety jetty that led out onto the dam. Her long legs were elegantly stretched out, her arms were resting on the armchair, her dark sunnies aligned her face, and her rib cage was clearly visible in her red bikini as she inhaled a contented sigh.

For fuck's sake, think ugly thoughts.

I thought about my task at hand and smiled to myself.

"Oooh, feel the burn," I quipped, as I crossed from the dust to the decking.

I heard the giggles from beyond and I lifted my shades, frowning at where it was coming from, until I spied Moira. She was in the water, her elbows hooked over a pool noodle, wearing goggles and a white swimming cap, which she quickly pulled off and fixed her hair in my presence. She pulled her goggles off, wincing as they got caught in her hair.

"Miranda, look!" Moira laughed.

Miranda sighed; this time it had nothing to with contentment, but everything to do with annoyance.

"I thought a black cloud had descended over me." She yawned, still bidding me no notice.

I stood above her, my silhouette cast over her, clearly spoiling her tanning session. The satisfaction made me want to stand there all day, but I had bigger, more infuriating plans.

"I'm sorry, am I blocking your death rays?" I asked innocently.

"If you mean sun, yes, yes you are," she replied, as if bored.

"Well, I best get out of your way then," I said, moving towards the edge of the decking. It only caused Moira to lose it in a fit of more giggles.

"Miranda." She laughed.

"What?" Miranda snapped.

I held my finger up to my lips, winking at Moira. Her smile spread broadly across her face as she stared up at me in a trance.

"What do you think, Moira? Do you think I should jump in?"

Moira's eyes widened as she shook her head vigorously – *No*.

"Really? I don't know; what do you think, Miranda, do you think I should jump in?" I turned, looking back towards Miranda who hadn't moved an inch.

"You can go jump for all I care."

"Hmm, I don't know." I sighed, crossing my arms and cupping my chin in deep thought as I looked back to the water. "Moira, I'm thinking I should; honestly, do you think I should?"

Before Moira had a chance to giggle a reply, Miranda slammed her palms on the armchair.

"Look," she bit out, pushing herself to sit up, lifting her glasses to the top of her head. "Why don't you just …" She froze, her eyes narrowing in a death-like stare.

Bingo!

Chapter Fourteen
Miranda

"Take. It. Off."

Ringer stood before me in nothing more than a black pair of footy shorts, thongs and my black cardigan that was ridiculously stretched tightly over his muscles.

His brows rose as if he didn't have a clue what I was talking about. "Are you trying to get me out of my clothes? Miranda, don't embarrass me, your sister's here."

Moira snorted, causing me to cut her an acidic stare.

Traitor.

I could feel my blood boiling under the surface of my skin, or it could have been the baby oil frying in the sun. No. Wait. It was definitely anger as Ringer stretched his arms lazily to the sky, the base of my overly stretched, expensive cardigan coming only to the top of his rib cage.

I pulled myself, rather ineloquently, to stand before him, fuming.

"Take it off, you're stretching it." I moved to grab him but he stepped away, his eyes confused until they fell to my cardi.

"Oh, you mean this old thing?" he said, pulling at the hem

of it.

My glower deepened, the urge to knee him in the nuts at the forefront of my mind eyeing his boyish grin.

He looked down at me, enjoying every minute. He stepped forward. "Do you want it?" he said lowly, suggestively.

I cocked my head; I wasn't telling him I wanted it, knowing how that would sound, knowing that's what he wanted to hear.

Such a smart arse.

I let my silence and murderous stare do the talking.

Ringer's smile fell away, but the devilish glint in his eyes remained.

"If you want it," he said, raising his arms up, "take it."

I weighed it up in my mind. Ten seconds of pleasure for a lifetime of torture, or even in this case, at best a week or so of torture depending on how long it was until I got my car fixed. I squinted at his smug face, his head tilted back, eyes closed, arms stretched, as if to say, 'I'm yours for the taking'. Oh, how right he was, I thought, a wicked smile spreading across my face, as I stepped forward, counting my losses one more time. A ruined top and further revenge, would it be worth it? Before I could think it through, Ringer did the worst possible thing he could have done: he peeked at me with one eye, his grin spreading even wider, if that were possible. It was all I needed, as I reached out and with all my strength pushed into his chest, sending him sailing backwards off the jetty and into the dam; it was a large, violent splash that caused rivulets of water to spray over me.

I dusted off my hands and watched with immense satisfaction as Ringer resurfaced, clawing at the water, coughing and spluttering.

"Seeing as you're into cross dressing, here's a handy hint. That cardi is not tumble-dry friendly."

Ringer eventually found his feet, still breathless from the shock of the water. "Thanks, I'll take that into consideration," he said, as he slapped at the side of his tilted head as if trying to dislodge water from his ear.

My instinct was to run like I had the night before, wary of a counter attack of sorts. Instead, I didn't feel like there was going to be one. Ringer was cool, calm, even slightly humorous as a wry smile creased his lips as he peeled off my wet cardigan.

"You did that, not me," he said, holding it up and chucking it onto the deck with a sodden splat.

He moved slowly, eloquently for his tall stature and even though there was nothing particularly threatening about his movements, it still caused me to take a step back. I was ever watchful as he planted his palms on the jetty and hitched himself up with ease. Now he wasn't wearing anything bar footy shorts, the weight of my eyes set on the muscled, taut curves of his slender frame. He was tall, lean, but toned to perfection, his shoulders square and broad. I felt myself swallow and then snapped out of my thoughts by a giggle from my little sister who was watching me with interest.

"Are you going to be in there all day?" I snapped. "You're going to end up looking like a prune."

"Hmph, never you mind about me, go back and bake yourself stupid," she said, kicking herself away defiantly with her chin in the air.

I rolled my eyes, turning to come up short and almost running into a wet torso, and flinching back.

"Don't stress, I'm not going to throw you in, it's too predictable."

"So you're just going to tell me to watch my back, sleep with one eye open while you plot some act of revenge on me?"

Ringer ran his hand through his saturated hair, flicking the excess water away. "This may come as a surprise to you, Miranda Henry," he said, looking directly down at me, "but not everything is about you."

My mouth gaped. "I … I never said it was," I defended.

"You don't have to, everyone knows it's the Miranda Henry show," he said with a shrug, sliding past me and pushing on his thongs that went flying off when he fell into the water.

I spun around to follow him. "What would you know? You've

been here, what, five minutes?"

"Well, let's ask someone who would know then, shall we? Hey, Moira, who's the golden-haired child in your family?"

"Shut up," I warned.

Moira swished around on her flotation device. "Ha! You're standing right next to her."

"Shut up, Moira," I snapped, grabbing for my towel and flicking it so violently over my shoulder Ringer had to veer away to save losing an eye.

I was out of there. If they wanted to assassinate my character they could do it without me, I thought. I stormed up the jetty and made my way towards the shower block opposite the shearers' quarters. A nice cool shower to wash away the baby oil, and cool off from my heated mood, was just what I needed.

I shampooed my hair with vigorous, violent aggression. "Golden-haired child," I mumbled under my breath. "The Miranda Show" I mimicked in a bitchy, whiny voice.

I was so sick of it: every corner I turned he was there, glorifying in making me feel paranoid, like that at any moment he could drag me and turf me into a water trough with ease, or making some kind of psychological assessment.

Well, fuck him.

I rinsed the last of the soapy bubbles down my torso, watching them fall and circle into the drain; I tried to use the symbolism of those bubbles with the aid of the cool water on my shoulder blades as a way of trying to relax. Let the cool, soothing sprays of the water let the tension melt and drain away with the bubbles; I titled my head back and let the water flow back over my hair.

Bliss.

It was working. With a deep, contented sigh, I could feel myself letting go of all the rage, all the tension, and it felt oh so go…

The shower in the next cubicle twisted on. The clank of the pipes and the unmistakable whoosh of water caused me to snap my eyes open and freeze in fear, as I suddenly heard the unnerving whistles of … oh God.

Whistling turned into joyous singing that echoed through the cubicles.

Lost in love and I don't know much was I thinking aloud and fell out of touch, but I'm back on my feet and eager to be what she wanted …

I winced at the shower wall.

Was he singing Air Supply?

"You just give a yell when you need your back washed," he called out.

Even though we were protected by the individual cavity of the shower cell, I still found myself covering my breasts as my scowl deepened.

"What are you doing in here?" I snapped.

"What am I doing in here? What are you doing in here? This is the boys' shower block."

"Pfft, no, it's not."

"Oh, it's communal then, is it?"

"No."

Fuck.

"Everything is an argument, isn't it?"

My knee-jerk reaction was to reply NO. But then I stopped myself from engaging.

Nice try.

Instead, I slammed my shower taps off and squeezed the excess water from my hair. This shower block was definitely not big enough for the two of us.

"Just stay where you are," I called.

"Why, are you coming to scrub my back?" he said.

"Ha! Not even with a thousand rubber gloves on."

"Well, that's extreme." He laughed.

I opened my shower door just enough to slide my hand out to reach for the towel hooked on the door, the towel that wasn't there.

Oh no-no-no-no.

I peeked through the gap of the door and spied my towel

sitting on the sink. I remembered now how I had stormed into here, leaving my towel, shedding off my bikini and dumping it all on the sink. The sink that was on the opposite side of the shower block.

Fuck-fuck-fuck.

"You need to leave," I shouted.

"Don't tell me your old man is a tight arse with water usage, is he?"

"No." I glowered, wrapping my arms around my torso, gooseflesh forming even in the humid shower cavity.

"Well, I can't leave now until my deep cleansing hair conditioning treatment has been in for five minutes," he called back.

Oh my God, I hope he was joking.

I was just about to call him out on it when the shower taps were twisted off. It was then I really felt the full weight of the situation. I was standing in a small confined space with only a wall dividing us: the two very naked us. Ringer started whistling his Air Supply tune again, as I heard him open up his shower door. I closed my eyes praying that he would just leave and didn't have some kind of cleansing, toning, moisturising ritual he had to carry out after his shower.

"Hello, what do we have here?" His bright upbeat voice echoed against the tiles.

Oh God. I had visions of him leaving with my things, of leaving me stranded naked in the cubicle for all eternity. Would anyone hear my screams? All of a sudden I felt hot and claustrophobic, as I took deep breaths and fanned myself.

"Just … don't … touch anything."

Deep breaths.

"What, like this?"

My beach towel was flicked over the top of the door, it was the most beautiful sight I had ever seen, and just as I was about to reach for it, it was pulled away with a deep-bellied chuckle.

"RINGER!" I screamed.

Oh crap! Would I ever learn? The ten-second joy was *never* worth it, not ever.

The towel appeared again, and just as I reached for it, the same thing happened, this time the laughter was louder and more out of control than before.

Fucking arsehole.

"Okay, seriously, I'm just kidding, I won't pull it away this time. Honest," Ringer said through barely controlled laughs; it didn't inspire much confidence.

And sure enough, for the third time it was flung over and torn away from my grasp. I sighed with boredom. I didn't have the energy to care or to feed him into baiting me. Instead, I thought of a new approach. It would probably open myself up to a whole new world of regret, but, hey, I had lived in Europe long enough to have adopted some form of worldly confidence. I just had to channel that liberated part of me that was buried deep, deep inside.

Oh my God, what was I doing?

It was the only thing I could think of in that very moment to do, and it wasn't ideal, but if I were quick enough, it would most certainly get my towel back. Before I had too much time to think it through, I took a deep breath, lifted my head with pride, and pushed open the shower door.

Chapter Fifteen
Ringer

Three times was the limit, even I could admit that.

I was about to fling the towel over the door for the last time, leaving it for her to snatch away from me, with a long line of insults no doubt, so when, instead, the shower door flung open and I was met with Miranda Henry in all her angry, naked glory, I almost slipped over in my shocked effort to spin around so fast.

"MIRANDA!" I all but yelped as I clung to the sink, turning my back to her, closing my eyes. "What the fuck?"

"I thought that might make you drop the towel," she said.

My eyes were squeezed shut, my hands holding the sink with a white-knuckle intensity. I could feel my heart pounding against my chest, and I felt like a fourteen-year-old boy spying a *Playboy* magazine for the first time. I went to say something, but I couldn't think of any smart comeback; my mind was mush, absolute mush. I had not expected that. I was clearly in shock.

I dare not peek an eye open at the risk of catching more flesh in the reflection of the sink mirror. As it were, I had the vision of Miranda Henry's breasts fused behind my eyelids. As far as flashbacks were concerned it was a bloody awesome one, but I could feel myself going red.

Fuck! Blushing like a fucking girl.

Having only a towel wrapped around my own nakedness, I seriously had to stop thinking about those visions if I didn't want to disgrace myself any further by pitching a tent. Christ, I had to maintain some form of dignity.

"Are you a virgin, Ringer?"

"WHAT?!" I said a bit too high, my eyes snapping open to see Miranda in the reflection, wrapped firmly in a towel, running her fingers through her wet tendrils. Her brows raised in question, a little smirk lining her mouth.

I turned to face her.

"You've got to be kidding me?" I scoffed.

She shrugged, moving to stand beside me at the sink, running a finger along her bottom lip as if applying some kind of balm before fussing over her hair some more.

"It just seemed like you have never seen a girl naked before," she said.

"Oh, I have seen plenty …" I paused; okay, that didn't sound real good saying it like that. My brows narrowed.

"That's none of your business." I glowered, moving away from her, making a line towards my shorts hanging on the back of the shower cubicle.

God, I was pathetic, storming around like a diva.

In one fell swoop Miranda Henry had managed to unravel me, gaining the upper hand in the war by turning me into a stuttering, blabbering fool. And what had I done? Played snatchy-snatchy with her towel.

Brilliant!

"So you are, then," she baited me. "Hmm, how about that?"

Against my better judgment I laughed, shaking my head. I wouldn't take the bait; instead, I peeled off my towel and flung it at her. It landed near her feet but she didn't move, didn't budge her eye line from firmly forward as I pulled my footy shorts on, zipping them up. Watching her with guarded amusement, I could see the stiffness of her shoulders even when she was trying her best to seem casual.

I walked slowly over to her, bending to pick up my towel from the floor, deliberately standing closely behind her as I locked eyes with her in the mirror. I pinned her there with my gaze. She had stopped fussing over herself and instead stood frozen; the only sign of movement was the shallow rise and fall of her chest. I stood so close I could feel the heat of her skin; I knew it was unnerving her, I could see it in the way she latched onto the sink like a lifeline. My lips curved into a knowing smile as I slowly but surely turned the tables around by simply eye-fucking her in the mirror.

I half expected her to throw an elbow into my rib cage, but she took it, she took every part of my gaze that licked every part of her like a hot brand. It was like I was seeing her all over again, her luminous silken skin. It wasn't more than a glimpse at best, but it was enough, enough to be burned into my memory for the rest of my days.

I leant into her, close enough for my lips to graze her lobe when I whispered,

"Lock the door."

"WHAT?" she croaked, her eyes all wide and panicked as she spun around, looking up at me, swallowing deeply as her breaths quickened.

A brilliant smile formed across my face, revelling in her bewilderment. She had turned around but I made no movement to allow her space, I let her mind race a million miles an hour before I spoke.

"Next time," I said, flicking my towel over my shoulder, "lock the shower block door, it will save you from deviants like me."

Miranda's eyes darkened as she took in the full weight of my words.

I mirrored her frown. "Why? What did you think I meant?" I teased.

Miranda straightened her spine, scoffing. "Who can ever

know, you talk so much shit."

She turned around back to the sink, attempting with the cold shoulder, but I could see enough pink in her cheeks to know exactly what she thought I meant.

My chuckle was the only thing that gained her attention with a murderous snap of her greeny-blue eyes.

I made sure I held her gaze as a crooked line tilted my mouth.

"Don't worry, Miranda, if I was going to fuck you, it wouldn't be up against a bathroom sink."

Her mouth gaped, my words causing her to visibly flinch.

Miranda Henry speechless and furious was a definite win for me, and I would wholeheartedly take it. Without giving her the chance to gain any kind of composure, I gave her a parting wink and made my way out of the shower block whistling, of all things, fucking Air Supply.

Chapter Sixteen
Miranda

Drunk!

I was going to get so, so drunk. And I didn't mean drinking alone in my room like a sad sack; no, I wanted to get as far away from Moira Station as I could manage, far away from *him*.

I had worked it all out.

"You have to cover for me." I made sure I caught Moira's eyes in the reflection of the mirror as I hooked in the last of my earrings. "Do you hear me?"

Moira looked confused. "Miranda, you're twenty-four years old, why are you sneaking around like a teenager? Just tell Mum and Dad you're going to the Commercial."

I knew it was ridiculous keeping secrets from my parents at my age, but the last time I was at the Commercial, well, it hadn't ended so well. Even though I was sure after all these years I had proven I had turned over a new leaf, as far as my first impressions were concerned, being back, well, I hadn't exactly done myself any favours. The last thing I needed was to hear any lectures from them, especially now that I was in the foulest mood possible.

"Please, Moira, just do what I ask. Remember, I have gone to

Mel's for the night. If they ask how I got there say you don't know, okay?" I turned from the mirror, smoothing over the fabric of my black skirt. "How do I look?"

Moira sneered in her usual fashion. "Overdressed."

"Shut up. I am not; this is smart casual." I nodded defiantly, turning to the mirror again.

"Exactly, and you're headed to the Commercial Hotel in Ballan," she added.

I bit my lip, studying my reflection. I hated to have to take fashion advice off my thirteen-year-old sister. Still, I met her gaze in the mirror. "Jeans, then?"

She smiled, jumping up from the bed and grabbing them for me. "You're not in Paris anymore, Toto."

She could say that again.

Okay, so I had to admit the jeans were a better idea, even more so now that I found myself straddled over one of Max's dirt bikes, my getaway rig for the evening. I gunned it across the paddock like Steve McQueen in *The Great Escape*, dust and the ear-piercing, high-pitched whines as I fishtailed it across the dirt, my adrenalin pumping as I put distance between me and Moira Station, but more importantly, from Ringer. The sound of the floorboards squeaking underneath his feet in the room next door was enough to make my blood boil, and then the memory would always inevitably flash back to what I had done.

Oh God! He had seen me naked.

I revved the accelerator some more and sped along the paddock hoping that the speed would wipe away my shame. Although the absolute look of shock on his face and embarrassment had been worth it, and I did get my towel back, it was almost like I had given him a small part of myself. Now every time he looked at me, I could feel the weight of his stare. I had empowered him, and I hated myself for that. It had taken every fibre of my being not to sneak a peek when he flung his towel towards me; at least I might have felt better about it. Seeing him equally exposed would have made us even. But then the real horror occurred to me; it wasn't the fact he had seen me naked that really bothered me. It was the fact that for the smallest of moments, as he looked at me, as he stood so close to me, I could feel the dampness of his freshly washed skin next to mine. It was the absolute horror that the way he looked at me excited me and the worst part of it was he fucking well knew it.

Having left just on dusk I had everything worked out, so I wasn't entirely lying. I was actually going to see Mel … kind of, in-as-much as we would rendezvous at the T-intersection where she would be waiting with my getaway vehicle. She would take the bike back to her place and I would take her work ute. It wasn't a grand entrance, but it sure beat heading down the main street of Ballan on a dirt bike. As it were, I could always park the ute up the street a bit. The one downfall that was clear was the high possibility of helmet hair. Still, these were my ridiculously limited options.

Sure enough, like a well-formed mission that had been planned down to every meticulous detail, Mel was waiting for me. I came to a skidding halt, kicking the stand out so I could climb off, making sure to remove my helmet before it did too much damage. Mel leant up against her Land Cruiser, smiling and jingling the keys.

"Just like old times, huh?" She laughed.

"Well, not entirely, I hope," I said, passing the helmet to her and grabbing the keys, swiping at the dust on my clothes and trying to tame my hair.

"You sure you can't come?" I asked.

"No chance, we're headed for Wahroo in the morning, got to be up by four." Mel winced.

"So you sure Bluey won't miss this?" I opened the car door to the Land Cruiser.

"Nah, it's mine anyway, and I usually keep it out back, so he won't even notice."

I climbed in and slammed the door shut. Mel rested her elbows on the open window.

"You're not going to get smashed and drive home, are you?" Her big blue eyes shrouded in concern.

My eyes rested on hers, but more vividly on the half-moon scar just below her left eye. It served as a permanent reminder of the last time I had been to the Commercial, of the trip back where we didn't make it home.

I swallowed the memory down and started up the car; I shouldn't have asked her to do this, to be an accessory to my dodgy ways, years later … and it was still the same shit, different story.

"I'll get a lift back, I won't drive," I said in all seriousness.

"Well, maybe just have a few, I'm sure that would be okay?" she said quickly, as if she had regretted saying anything.

"No, it's okay, I am sure someone can drop me home." I smiled.

"Well, if you walk up to the post office before eleven you can grab the last courtesy bus. They run one now from town on weekends," she said with a newfound hope in her eyes.

Eleven? Pfft.

"I'll work it out. Thanks, Mel, I owe you one," I said, starting up the Land Cruiser and flicking the lights on. "Have fun in Wahroo."

"At a cattle auction? I seriously doubt it."

"Well, you'll have Mum, Dad and Moira to keep you company next weekend."

Mel blinked in confusion. "Next weekend?" she repeated. "I thought they were heading Monday night?"

My head spun around so fast, I almost committed a neck injury. "Monday night? As in tomorrow night?"

Mel winced as if she regretted saying anything. "That's what I heard."

"But they weren't meant to go until the weekend; Dad was going to show Ringer the ropes and by then Bluey would be back in case he needed anything," I blurted out in a panic.

"I guess Ringer is going to get a one-day handover; your dad must think …"

C.J. Duggan

"Well, clearly he isn't thinking. The idea is ludicrous," I all but shouted, my hands clenched on the steering wheel with rage.

My mind raced; there would be no time to fix my car, and they would be away for two weeks. Did they honestly think I would just hang until they got back? Alone. Alone with RINGER?

I eyed the dirt bike, wondering if I could make my way back to the city on it?

"Oh God! What are you thinking?" Mel groaned.

I was thinking I was in deep shit is what I was thinking, and regardless of how I got home tonight, my objective was clear. I was going to get absolutely shitfaced.

Chapter Seventeen
Ringer

"Well, that's strange."

Steve glanced in the rear-view mirror of his four-wheel drive. I followed his line of vision.

"What's that?" I asked, turning to look back down the street.

"I could have sworn I saw Bluey's old Land Cruiser parked back there. What's he doing in town on a Sunday night?"

"Well, I'm guessing there's no late night shopping." I cast my eye around the desolate main street of Ballan, if you could call it a street, more like a strip.

"Yeah, not exactly. The only thing you will find open on a Sunday night is right here." Steve did a U-turn, swinging around to park directly in front of a double-storey brick building. The brick work was painted a deep burgundy that made the neatly penned white lettering 'The Commercial' stand out all the more. "He's probably inside having a quiet one before he heads tomorrow." Steve spoke mainly to himself.

I paused from opening the door. "Why don't you come in and say g'day?"

"Nah-nah, better not, the Mrs already has the shits from

me having a few beers yesterday." Steve looked longingly at the floodlights that lit the front of the hotel.

"Fair enough," I said, hopping out of the car and shutting the door, thanking the heavens above I was my own man. "Thanks for the lift."

"Hey, Ringer." Steve leant over the passenger seat. "Don't have a big one, hey? I know this will be your last bout for a while, but we have a full-on day tomorrow."

"No worries, watch is synced. Courtesy bus departs at eleven." I winked.

Steve nodded, pleased. "Good on ya, mate, have one for me, and tell that no-good drunk, Bluey, to get home."

"Will do!" I said, tapping the bonnet of the car before Steve backed out and sounded a cheerful blast of the horn as he veered off back down the street.

The muffled sound of Cold Chisel's 'Cheap Wine' filtered from the hotel. I leant casually on the verandah post, as I took the singular cigarette from behind my ear and flicked it into my mouth, before lighting it up and puffing it to life.

So this was Ballan's ground control, I thought, looking up at the pub: the place where Farmer John would meet up, and the local young blokes would converge on a Friday night to chase a bit of skirt. Seeing as it was Ballan, the male population no doubt outweighed the female, as any female within their right mind would surely flee this place at the first given opportunity. Just like Miranda had done.

My brows pinched together at the thought of her name; it had a way of weaving its way into my skull at any given moment, and I wasn't entirely happy about it. I had played with fire today. The line I had drawn in the sand had become blurry, even more so when I found myself thinking about Miranda Henry and her perfectly … perky body.

Ah Christ!

I took a deep drag of my cigarette and flicked it to the bitumen, twisting it into oblivion. Getting out for a bit was just what I had needed. A chance to clear my head by clouding it into a murky shambles of alcohol-fuelled good times. Steve was right; I did have a big day tomorrow, but that was only the beginning of my hell. He thought that there would be no problem trusting me with his precious darling Miranda; well, I wish I had as much faith in myself as he did. If nothing else, she would move back into the house once it was empty, and if she didn't, I bloody well would.

I had planned to have a quiet word to Steve tomorrow about getting her car up and running again. I knew it was out of line, but he couldn't really hold her prisoner for two weeks till he got back from Wahroo. I would have strangled her by then. No, I just had to reason with him, regardless of her being his little girl; he couldn't force her to stay, and that was obvious. As we all knew, as soon as the Mazda was up and running again, she would be nothing but a trail of dust. I smiled at the thought as I made my way to the Commercial door and entered through the barroom.

For a Sunday it was packed; clearly there really wasn't anything better to do on a Sunday night but drink to forget that they lived in Ballan. Not that I could blame them. The dusty nothing that surrounded the town made me almost wistful for Onslow … almost.

Still, you would never have to fight your way to the bar on a Sunday in Onslow. Yet here I was in Ballan, sliding past people, a few young blokes spruced up with their polished RM Williams belt buckles, downing a few Bundys. A pretty little brunette tucked her elbows in and smiled coyly as I slid past her. I had a height advantage over most, and yet I couldn't see Bluey as I pushed through and anchored myself to the bar. I caught the eye of the burly, balding barman, motioned to the VB tap and held up one finger, reaching for my wallet in my back pocket. He nodded with understanding and grabbed a pot glass with his chubby fingers. I was somewhat disappointed there wasn't some buxom beauty swanning around behind the bar—I could deal with a bit of a distraction—and when the barman bent over revealing his hairy butt crack, well, that was definitely not the kind I had in mind.

"Say, you haven't seen Bluey around, have you?" I asked, exchanging money for my beer.

"You won't catch him in here tonight; he and his daughter are heading to Wahroo in the morning for the cattle auction."

Okay, a no would have sufficed.

I masked my smirk by sipping my beer; it was so like a small-town barman to relay a life story.

Steve must have gotten it wrong, unless Bluey was having some kind of romantic rendezvous in town, something I'm sure the barman would know in great detail if I had been emotionally invested in caring.

I all but choked mid-sip when a hefty wallop hit my back.

"Here, son, take my seat: I'm heading."

I turned to see a sun-beaten Farmer John tip his pot glass over on the bar, nod his head at the barman, then at me, as he slid from his stool.

Score!

With much appreciation, I accepted what appeared to be the best seat in the house: my back leaning against the corner wall, my beer within reach from the bar. This was me for the night, perfect vantage point to take in the local entertainment. A rowdy pool showdown with some young boozed-up locals, the typical cluster of primped chicks walking awkwardly in their blistered heels, stollies in hand, and bags under their arms. A group weaved their way towards the ladies' toilets together. Why do they do that? I wondered. Oh, to be a fly on the wall.

After surveying the scene, I soon discovered it wasn't unlike that of any other pub; the smell of desperation was rampant in the local meat market of singledom. Boys with their mates, caked on aftershave, dressed in their Sunday-best denim. Girls with thickly layered mascara, straightened hair and fake tan, all wanting to be noticed. Whispers and glances from the girls, rough housing and hollering amongst the boys. I lazily nursed my beer, motioning for another as I finished off the dregs. With each fresh delivery, I soon discovered that this would be the highlight of my night, and the hairy-arsed barman was going to be my new best friend. Boredom wasn't something I was going to escape easily until I noticed a whispered gathering, and glances my way.

Hello?

A group of four friends all nursing their raspberry Vodka Cruisers with straws were all sniggering comparatively and elbowing their blonde friend. I lifted my eyes from my beer and they all turned in a fit of giggles.

I smiled; would they ever know how incredibly easy it is? You simply get up, walk over and talk to a guy. It was never really more complicated than that and just as I silently mused, two of the pack got up from their seats and walked over to the bar, squeezing in next to me, yet pretending I wasn't there.

"Two more Cruisers, thanks, Merve," called out the blonde, before casually turning to me and acting as if she had only just discovered my presence.

"Hi," she said, accompanied by a high-wattage smile.

"Hi." I nodded my head.

Her shorter, dark-haired friend craned her neck around to see me.

"You're not from here, hey?" she yelled out.

I set my beer back on the bar top with an air of amusement. "Is it that obvious?"

"Um, yeah, just a bit." Short and dark snorted.

"And here I was trying to blend in." I smiled. "Guess it's not working."

The doe-eyed blonde chewed on her straw, and shook her head. "Don't try and fit in, you're much better off if you don't," she said coyly.

"Dude! What the fark!" a voice shouted.

One of the pool players stumbled into the girls in an effort to get near the bar with his mate.

"Shorry, Ladiesh." He tipped his non-existent hat to them.

His mate laughed and said, "Man you are totally fucked!"

"I am a pool CHAMPION!" He lifted his hands to the sky as

if speaking to the gods.

"Yeah, all right, Rory, keep it down," said Merve the barman, as he filled up their empty pots.

Rory dramatically cupped his hand over his mouth. "Shorry, Merve," he whispered … well, as quietly as a drunk could whisper, that is.

The two extra bodies wedged in at the bar only forced to bring the blonde closer, my brows lifting as her hand rested on my jeaned thigh so she could balance.

I offered her my hand. "Ringer."

A crease pinched between her brow as if wondering if I was serious before taking my hand. "Jenny."

She smiled. I smiled. Suddenly my whole evening was looking up, until I overheard the not-so-hushed whispers of Rory the pool champion that snapped my attention.

"Hey, Jools, see that Henry girl's back in town."

"Oh yeah, fuck, what's her name?"

"Miranda." I spoke lowly into my beer as I sipped.

Fuckwits!

"Sorry?" said Jenny.

"Oh no, nothing." I smiled in good humour, my eyes ticked over her shoulder at Dumb and Dumber.

"Miranda!" Rory clicked his finger. "Max's hot sister."

"Ugh! She's not that hot," said Jenny's friend.

"Do you know her?" I asked, causing all eyes to land on me.

"Um, yeah. She's a total fucking bitch."

Jenny winced as if embarrassed by her friend's outburst. "Yeah, we went to school with her."

Rory's mate leant heavily on the bar. "I heard she got some modelling contract in Paris and that's why she left," he said conspiratorially.

"Oh please, everyone knows it's because she was pregnant; everyone knows she was whoring around, that's why she got sent away."

My brows lowered as something stirred within me. Miranda

Henry wasn't exactly my favourite person in the world, but hearing her be called a whore got my back up. I went to say something and felt Jenny's hand back on my thigh.

"The real reason she got sent away," she said lowly, "is because of the accident."

I leant closer, intrigued by what Jenny was saying. "What accident?"

But before she could answer, a shrill burst of laughter sounded from across the room that caused us all to take notice; my eyes shifted towards the sound, the sound that instinctively made my blood run cold.

"Oh, my God. Speak of the fucking devil," said Jenny's friend.

And as there was a shift in the crowded room, there she was, drink in hand, sitting on a sofa. Miranda Henry.

Chapter Eighteen
Miranda

"Hey, who's Jenny Madden talking to?"

I broke off mid-discussion with Tom Hilton to glance over to where Jenny stood at the bar with Ruby Dalton. Whoever she was talking to, the poor soul was probably dying of boredom, I mused to myself, until the one thing that was blocking my vision—a drunk Rory McKenzie and his pool cue—stumbled to the side, and only then did I see exactly who Jenny was talking to.

My heart stopped.

"I don't know, but he looks like a smooth bastard." Tom Hilton slid closer to me on the couch, snaking his arm around me as if claiming his property. "Hey babe, what's wrong? Your beer gone flat?" He laughed.

I watched as Jenny bent her head towards Ringer so she could listen to what he was saying, even though she was as good as sitting on his face, she was so close. My eyes dipped to where her hand touched his leg. She smiled, all coy and sweet, as she tucked a blonde lock of hair behind her ear.

Vomit!

Watching the scene play out before me was enough to make

anyone's beer flat. I had been having as good a time as I could possibly manage at the Commercial. I had looked forward to making a grand entrance, being 'that' girl who had returned home from Paris. I had quite enjoyed the spectacle of old and new faces elbowing one another, more so with the likes of Tom Hilton and his mates, whose mouths sat agape when I had sauntered up to them with confidence that no local girl would ever be able to manage.

"So are you going to stand there and stare or buy me a drink?" I smiled. It had been rather comical watching Tom almost fall over himself to get to the bar and whip his wallet out to buy me a drink; in fact, I hadn't paid for a drink all night and nothing tasted so sweet. I took in the horde that surrounded me, mainly all the boys that were a year above me, the ones I usually crushed on but they didn't even know I had existed until I started coming out to the Commercial on the sly and drinking with them. They were also, incidentally, the ones that had never left town. They were born here and would die here and even though all those years ago when I would have given anything for a young, charismatic Tom Hilton to pay me an ounce of attention, now looking him over in his creased dress shirt, blundstone boots … and was he thinning slightly on top? … seeing him pore over me in such a way definitely had me thinking I had dodged a bullet there.

Pfft, of course, Ringer was cocked up there schmoozing with her, I thought darkly, as I took a deep swig of my beer; he would have experienced the same thrill of walking in here and being 'fresh meat' to all the local desperate and dateless girls. All the ones that had worked their way through the Tom Hiltons and Rory McKenzies, now they lived in hope that some gorgeous blow-in would come to town and sweep them off their feet.

And here he was, the answer to their prayers. I scoffed, glaring into the bottom of my beer glass.

What a joke.

They would be dead wrong if they thought they could tie him down and marry him; at best they would get one night of hot sex in a back alley somewhere, but nothing more than that. I suddenly had visions of Ringer leaving with the insipidly dull Jenny Madden, and something twisted in my gut.

"Do you want another drink, baby?" Tom rubbed my lower back, causing a shiver to run down my neck and not in a good way. I cringed away from his touch, moving to stand and look down on him.

"Don't call me baby." I cut him an acidic look before turning to make my way towards the bar to get my own beer.

I could have been served from up my end, but instead I made my way to where they stood, sliding my way behind Ruby's back and Rory's side.

"One more thanks, Merve," I said confidently.

I knew his eyes were on me, I could feel them burning into my profile.

I glanced over and, sure enough, there he was, a serious gaze fixed on me, a small smile tilting the corner of his mouth as our eyes locked.

"Of all the bars in all the world," he said.

I rolled my eyes. "Of all the clichés in the world."

His smile widened as he brought his beer up to his lips. "Who let you out?" he asked, before taking a sip.

I curved my brow. "Who let me out? Who let you out?" I scoffed.

"I'm my own man." He winked.

My eyes fell to the hand that rested on his leg. "So I see."

Ringer shifted uncomfortably, but I dare say no one was more uncomfortable than Jenny, who seemed to go a deeper shade of red.

Ruby interjected as any best friend would. "So I am guessing you two know each other," she said snarkily; it was more of an accusation than a question.

I glanced around, seeing that I had a rather captive audience. Rory and his mate behind me, even the barman seemed to be lending an ear.

"I know Ringer," I said casually, picking up my beer. "My dad posted his money for bail."

Ringer spat his drink out that led into a coughing fit and a murderous glare.

I wasn't sure what was more comical, his choking fit or the speed in which Jenny ripped her hand away from his leg.

I grinned broadly. "Don't forget to check in with your parole officer in the morning, remember what happened last time," I said gravely.

Ringer cleared his throat, blinking away his watery eyes. "Yeah, I really appreciate your dad posting that money, I know your folks were a bit strapped for cash after the nose job you got for Christmas." He saluted me with his beer.

I laughed, really laughed, because I could hear the inward hitch of breath from Ruby next to me; if she had have had a pearl necklace I am sure she would have clutched it in horror. I could just imagine the spiral of gossip that would ensue from our banter; I could already sense the girls wanting to run to their friends and spill the hot goss'.

I just shook my head seeing the devilish twinkle in Ringer's eyes.

Ruby linked her arm through Jenny's. "Yeah, well, we'll leave you two to catch up then, shall we?" she said, dragging away a disheartened-looking Jenny.

Thankfully, with their dramatic exit, it afforded me a bit more space at the bar.

"You shouldn't break local girls' hearts; all their daddies have shot guns, you know."

Ringer moved to answer but was cut off by a hurried question over my shoulder.

"So, what did you do time for?" Rory McKenzie looked on with a mixture of horror and awe.

Ringer cast me a dirty look before shifting in his seat with a sigh. He looked Rory right in the eye. "I beat someone up with a pool cue," he said in all seriousness.

Rory's eyes shifted comically to the very pool cue he held and he swallowed, nodding in understanding before excusing himself from our presence, his mate dually following without a backwards glance.

I shook my head incredulously. "Wow, Ballan is going to be set alight with rumours tonight."

"Yeah, well, apparently you're a total bitch," he said.

"Oh really? That's funny, because I heard you're a smooth bastard."

"I see." Ringer raised his brows. "By any chance this wouldn't be coming from a group of local lads that are casting me daggers from across the room?"

I followed his eye line to see the murderous stare of Tom Hilton and his minions.

I turned around, rolling my eyes. "Oh please, I went to school with them a billion years ago; they're just having a pissing contest."

"Yeah? Well, I hope they don't cause any trouble; I'm on parole, you know?" Ringer cast me a sly grin as he motioned for two more beers.

"Yeah, well, if a barroom brawl breaks out I can't afford a wayward stool to the face; I mean … hello," I said, pointing to my nose.

"That's true," he said, thumbing out a twenty from his wallet.

'Wait on, I'll get mine." I went to reach for my purse that wasn't there. "Shit. Hang on a sec."

"Too late." Ringer handed over his money.

Crap-crap-crap.

Dread swept over me remembering exactly where I had left my purse. I sighed.

"Back in a sec," I said, before sliding back over to the couch. Excusing myself through Tom and his mates, I reached for my bag that I had sat down next to the couch, but before I could turn, a hand snaked out and caught me by the wrist.

"What, leaving so soon?" Tom frowned.

My eyes fell to his vice-like grip. "Ah, let me go." I half

laughed.

"So what, is this how they do it in Paris, eh? Leach drinks off one sucker and then on to another?" He lifted his chin towards the bar.

"Yeah, that's why I'm grabbing my purse, to scum drinks." I tried to twist out of his grasp.

He yanked me closer, causing me to stumble into him, the smell of beer wafting off his breath. "Well, how about a kiss goodbye, baby? It's the least you could do, seeing as I bought all those leg openers for you."

I cringed away. "Piss off!"

Laughter from his mates turned into catcalls, and the more I struggled, the tighter his hold became.

"Let go!" I cried against the pain, which seemed to only encourage him more.

"Aww, when I feel like it." He laughed.

"You heard her, let her go."

The laughter that surrounded us melted away, as did the smart-arse smile on Tom's face. I followed his glare to where Ringer stood right behind me. All glimmer of any humour he had before had dissolved into coiled anger.

"And who the fuck do you think you are?" spat Tom.

Spud Nelson moved to Tom's shoulder. "Careful, Tommy, I heard this guy served some time for stabbing some bloke."

What? Christ, how gossip travelled.

Tom's demeanour didn't change, but I could feel his grip lighten as if he was actually taking in Spud's words. I took the moment of pause and ripped my arm free of his hold, moving to stand beside Ringer, glowering and massaging my wrist.

The air was so thickly filled with tension and it didn't escape me that Ringer was seriously outnumbered. I grabbed his arm.

"Come on, let's go. They're not worth it." It was like pulling at a boulder, his attention dark and threatening as he refused to tear his eyes away from Tom. Slowly, with a few shunts to the chest, I edged him back.

"Come on, let's go," I warned. Finally Ringer snapped out of his Alpha mode and looked down at me. "You okay?"

I smiled incredulously. "Yeah, of course."

His mood lifted at my words and he stepped aside to let me move past him. We were on the home stretch until Tom scoffed.

"Fucking pussy."

Oh shit!

If I had managed to persuade Ringer to leave well enough alone before, I had absolutely no chance now. I just closed my eyes in dread, and before any of us could stop it, Ringer turned and closed the distance towards Tom in a deadly, determined stride that had Tom visibly shit himself as he put up his hands in peace.

"Hey, mate, I was only kidding, I was just kidding." Tom's last words broke off in a pained cry as Ringer kicked the coffee table in front of the couch with such force it rammed hard into Tom's legs, and with barely enough time to gauge the pain, Ringer dragged him by the scruff of the neck and slammed him down on top of the coffee table, sending drinks and glasses smashing onto the floor. A girl screamed out in the distance and the juke box music died as Ringer refused to let him up, pinned by his fists and his murderous stare.

I knelt beside him. "RINGER, LET HIM GO!"

This I didn't expect. Ringer, who had been laid-back, mischievous, and reserved thus far. Angry and aggressive? Who was this Ringer?

"Not until he apologises," he bit out. He was so wound up I could visibly see the tick in his clenched jaw.

I gently slid my hand on his shoulder. "Ringer, please, my family have to live here," I pleaded.

At my words, I saw the tension slowly melt in his shoulders, and I finally let out a relieved breath when he pushed off Tom.

Tom rolled off the coffee table, coughing and spluttering, his face purple from Ringer's chokehold.

Ringer stood, his chest heaving as adrenalin coursed through his body.

"Did you see that, Merve? Kick this son of a bitch out," rasped Tom.

Merve stood behind the bar, casual as anything as he filled another empty glass and shrugged. "I didn't see anything."

Ringer went to the bar reaching for his wallet. "I'll pay for the breakage."

Merve slammed off the beer tap, casting him a dark look. "Just go."

Ringer nodded a silent thanks to Merve before he grabbed my hand, and without a word, led me through the stunned, silent crowd. Passing a wide-eyed Jenny and Ruby, Ringer pushed through the bar door out into the night. He led a straight, determined line down the street; I fought to keep up with his long strides.

"Ringer, wait a sec."

It was like my words were falling on deaf ears, as he dragged me along as if I weighed nothing.

"Ringer, STOP." I yanked my arm from his hold, finally pulling him up. He stared back at me, confused.

"Where are you going?" I fought to catch my breath, resting my hands on my kneecaps.

"To wait for the fucking courtesy bus," he snapped.

I looked up at him for a long moment, before losing it in a fit of giggles.

His scowl deepened. "What?"

I straightened with a sigh as my laughter finally tapered off and reached into my bag, pulling out a set of car keys that I jangled with glee.

"Ta-da!"

Chapter Nineteen
Ringer

When it came to Miranda Henry everything was a bloody argument.

"Are you sure you don't want me to drive?" I asked for the tenth time. It was the one thing we had debated about all the way up the main street towards the car. We calculated the height and weight ratio, the alcoholic content of our beers, the lack thereof of her barroom brawling, and with all the evidence thoroughly laid out before us—yeah, I was screwed. Miranda was driving, a small victory on her behalf, yet nevertheless bloody infuriating. Especially seeing the twinkle in her eyes and the defiant lift of her chin as she swung the car keys around her finger when she headed towards the driver's side. In that moment, I had cursed myself for not leaving her behind at the pub, and then my eyes dropped to the confident sway of her hips … by this point I had completely forgotten my name. I blinked, shaking my head and looking away; yeah, I was totally buzzed all right—good thing she was driving.

I sighed, opening the passenger door of Bluey's Land Cruiser, momentarily pausing at the thought of what Bluey might do to me if he found me in this situation. Alone, in his car, with Miranda.

I slid uneasily into my seat, my attention snapping to the open driver's door, where Miranda was climbing into the cabin. She settled in, adjusting her seat a little, a shimmering glow from the streetlight above the car highlighting her blonde, tousled locks. She slid the key into the ignition and twisted the engine into life; a smile ghosted across her lips as if she was immensely pleased by the sound. My guess was that driving the Mazda had been like living on a wing and a prayer. As if sensing my roving eyes, she paused mid-reach for her seat belt, all the smugness of her fired-up engine melted away, which kind of made me annoyed because I quite liked the look of it; it suited her, much more than the quizzical look she gave me.

"What?" A line crinkled between her brows as she followed through and clicked her belt into place.

I set my eyes forward and settled into my seat. "No … nothing."

For fuck's sake! Get it together, Ringo.

"Come on, chop-chop!" Miranda smiled broadly, as she tooted the horn for added effect.

You've got to be kidding me.

My molasses-black stare bore straight ahead, fixated on the car's headlights illuminating the first of the many property gates. A cluster of flickering bugs danced in the beams of light; I sat there for a long moment.

No wonder she wanted to drive.

I slowly tore my eyes from the gate and set my deadpanned expression on her as I clicked the latch of the handle and opened the door. Light flooded the interior, exposing me to the wicked grin Miranda had spread from ear to ear.

"Try not to run me over this time," I bit out.

"Oh, I wouldn't dream of it, you have four more gates to open," she quipped.

As I neared the gate, turning my back to the car, Miranda pumped the accelerator causing the car to roar like a lion and me to flinch and spin around. As the rev died down, all I could hear was the maniacal laughter coming from the interior of the car.

Oh yeah, such a fucking comedian.

I tried to reign in some of my dignity by making fast work of the chain and pushing the gate open, standing aside as the car slowly moved through.

I would have thought by the last gate her enthusiasm might have died, but as we jolted to a stop, she appeared more amped than ever as she turned to me, her brow cocked.

"Well, what do you know, this is where we first met," she said, all traces of her humour barely contained.

"Yeah, it was the day I got my first concussion, such happy memories."

Miranda rolled her eyes. "Yeah, well you ripped a piece of my car off so I guess we're even."

We would never be even, never.

"You mean you didn't find it when you went snooping in my room?"

Miranda's eyes widened oh so slightly, but her demeanour didn't falter. "Pfft, I don't know where you put it," she said, avoiding the accusation. "But I can definitely suggest where you *could* put it." She smiled sweetly.

I raised my brows. "Well, that's not the most subtle of suggestions."

"Ringer."

"Miranda?"

"Open the bloody gate."

Had I have known what the lift back to Moira involved, parking on the outskirts of the property and trekking across paddocks at midnight, I would have taken my chances with the courtesy bus.

Snaring my good Levis on the barbed wire fence, I swore under my breath, lifting my knee up to the moonlight to inspect the damage.

Son of a bitch. Second pair of ripped jeans courtesy of Miss Henry. Shit.

I blew out another sigh as I continued to navigate my way through the dark.

"Oh, stop being such a girl, we're almost there, see?" Miranda pointed before her, where a faint glow lit in the distance.

I tried to contain my relief and my breath as I hunched over; Christ, I was unfit, I thought, as I reached for my cigarette pack. Miranda went to move on and paused mid-step, her attention snapping at the sound of my lighter.

"What are you doing?"

I took a deep glorious inhale. "Baking a cake, what does it look like I'm doing?"

"Well, don't."

I couldn't see her face clearly but I didn't need to, I could imagine the scowl of disapproval; I had seen it a thousand times before from the anti-smoking movement.

Her barked order made me enjoy the next inhale even more, as I deliberately blew smoke in her direction, and she stepped away swiping the smoke away dramatically.

"Arsehole." She coughed.

"Relax, I think the surrounding open elements can take my tiny cigarette," I said, studying the lit cylinder.

"Yeah? And one drunken flick and you could start a fire."

"A fire?" I scoffed, looking around. "Set what on fire? Unless dust is flammable, I think you'll be safe, *sweetheart*." I stepped past her, making my way towards the distant glow, whistling a little ditty and ignoring the eyes I felt burning into the back of my skull.

By the time we made it to the last barrier, another wire fence, I reached out to help Miranda over, but instead earned a violent handbag to the chest.

Oomph.

"Hold this."

"Whatever you say, sweetheart."

"Ugh, stop calling me that." Miranda climbed over the fence

with ease; you could take the girl out of Ballan, but you couldn't take Ballan out of the girl. I smiled, watching the much brighter light of the homestead glow around her. Her messy hair and dusty jeans were a far cry from European chic, and more like a farm girl that you would want to take a roll in the hay with. Visions of Miranda Henry laid stretched out on a bale of hay suddenly entered my thoughts and I quickly tore my gaze from her.

Yeah, this night couldn't end soon enough.

I hooked the bag over my shoulder and climbed over the fence with extra care not to rip my jeans farther or injure myself in rather tender regions. I sighed with relief when I had two feet both firmly on the ground.

"Be quiet, just in case anyone's around," she whispered, before taking off with a brisk walk towards civilisation, leaving me behind with a rather fetching handbag over my shoulder. I slowly etched my way to follow her tracks, shaking my head in disbelief.

If only the boys at home could see me now.

Chapter Twenty
Miranda

I tentatively crept along the infuriatingly noisy verandah of the shearers' hut.

Wincing as a pained groan sounded underfoot, I came to an abrupt halt, causing Ringer to slam into my back.

"For fuck's sake, Miranda, what are you doing?" Ringer all but yelled.

"Shhh," I motioned to him, annoyed.

"Oh, for Christ's sake, if no one can hear your shit-box Mazda chugging in the night, no one will hear us tiptoe to our rooms," Ringer said, side stepping around me and making his way to his room.

"Hey, wait," I said, reaching out for the strap of my bag from his shoulder before he disappeared with another of my belongings into the abyss of his room.

I grabbed without thinking how securely he had hold of it, pulling him up short and causing it to catapult upwards and spill its contents onto the decking.

"Shit!" I cried, kneeling on the verandah, working to save things from rolling off the edge, my search made easier as a strip of light illuminated the mess. Ringer had turned the light to his room on; he leant in the doorway looking rather amused.

"Bloody hell, no wonder that thing was so heavy."

"Oh yeah, sure, don't help, will you?" I snapped, scooping up some wayward coinage.

I heard a sigh of resignation before he knelt within my eye line. He picked up a lipstick and a key chain. I saw him mostly in my peripheral vision, but I also saw him pause, pick something up, and move to slowly stand.

My eyes narrowed in question as I moved to stand before him, wondering what he held in his hand that had him so entranced.

Oh. My. God!

In movies, when something flies out of a bag when a girl bumps into a tall, dark stranger, it usually leaves him standing—mortified—holding a tampon, or birth control or something to that effect. But worse than any nightmare situation in a make-believe scenario was Ringer, standing before me with his brows raised in surprise, as he held a long strip of condoms in his hand.

"Had a big night planned, did you?" The corner of his mouth lifted into a cheeky, crooked grin, and all of a sudden I wanted to make my way to the dam and drown myself.

I snatched them from his hand. "You will never know."

"More's the pity." His heated gaze ticked over my face.

"Ha! Not with a thousand condoms," I scoffed, storming to my door.

"Well, you certainly have enough there if you change your mind," he said, smugly leaning out of his door. "If you feel like practising some safe sex, you know where to find me." He winked.

I tried to juggle my bag and its contents in my hands, while I furiously worked to open the door, finally managing it with some rather ineloquent stumbling. I slammed the door without a backwards glance.

I wanted to die.

I had remembered shoving them in my bag, smiling to myself;

after all, you never knew your luck in the big city. And although I was absolutely certain that there would be no one within a hundred-mile radius I would want to touch with a ten-foot pole, you could never be too careful.

I cupped my face, mortified. I lay alone in the dark, but I could feel my cheeks on fire.

Seriously, Miranda, couldn't you have maybe tore a square off instead of shoving the entire packet in?

The look on Ringer's face flashed under my lids every time I closed my eyes. It was a look of surprise and, more disturbingly, heat. I hadn't failed to notice the way he looked at me, as if he could believe that what I had in my bag was a swag of condoms.

Pfft, and why wouldn't I?

I was definitely no virgin, and, sure, it may have been a long, long time since I had slept with anyone, but it didn't mean I didn't think about it, didn't desire it—of course I did. The part of me who had shoved those condoms in my bag did so in case, by some small miracle, I would find a tall, dark stranger to have a moonlight tryst with. Not that I had ever had a one-night stand in my life, I wasn't that kind of girl. I hadn't been that kind of girl to walk around naked either, but hey, what do you know? It seemed that boredom in Ballan made you do strange things, things you would never ordinarily do, like thinking about Ringer lying in the dark, in the next room over. I tossed and turned in my twisted sheets. It was three a.m., and I was wide awake with my strange thoughts, my crazy, insane thoughts that made my stomach twist at the thrill of what ran through my mind.

I couldn't sleep, I kicked at my blankets with irritation; the feel of them grazing my oversensitive skin was too much to bear. I swallowed deeply. It was all too much, far too much, as my mind raced at a million miles an hour. I couldn't, surely I couldn't.

Could I?

It was about going to the one place, with the one person who I was fairly certain would accommodate me. I needed to unwind, to fall apart and lose myself to the bone-melting pleasure that I was certain he could provide. I had seen the way he looked at me, I was no fool. And sure, he despised me as much I did him. But this had nothing to do with emotion or feelings, this was about letting go, about desire and what I wanted right at that moment, what my body craved was for … release. And as I lay there in the dark, staring up at the ceiling, restless with my wicked thoughts, I knew that if I was looking for that much-needed release without the messy emotional baggage that would be attached, then Ringer was the perfect one-night stand. Although the thought of rejection did play on mind, I quickly dismissed it.

I would make it an offer he simply couldn't refuse.

I unbuttoned the oversized white shirt I used as a nightgown, unbuttoning it down to my navel. I slid my knickers off and a thrill shot through me as I felt the soft fabric against my bare skin; my stomach twisted as I ran my hands over the shirt, smoothing out the lines. It was my intention to have the fabric completely crinkled before the night was out—if all went the way I wanted it to. I held a singular foil square in the palm of my shaky hand.

What was I doing?

Before I gave myself the chance to answer, I slid the condom in my shirt pocket.

"You know where to find me."

Ringer's taunting wink and the memory of his words ran over and over in my mind as I crept by tippy-toe towards the door, twisting the handle and opening it slowly, praying that no sound groaned from the unoiled hinge. The screech was deafening in the night, but no more than the creak of the decking underfoot as I froze mid-step, wincing at the sound that seemed so painfully loud.

I listened for a long moment, wondering if the noise I made stirred any movement in the room next door. Was Ringer asleep? It was late enough. He had looked weary and tired before; what if I was the last thing he wanted to see? Which was probably the exact case seeing as he was never happy to see me. Still, maybe a half-naked body in his bed would wipe away his fatigue. There was only one way to find out.

Sneaking along the verandah, I opened the door to Ringer's room slightly, choosing to slide myself in so the light of the moon didn't illuminate anything in the darkened room. I wanted to be a shadow, a shadow he could discover in the darkness and it was dark. I was still able to make out the silhouette of a body on the bed, the bed I was slowly creeping towards. My heart was almost pounding out of my chest, my legs felt like jelly as I stood at the end of the bed; I tried to keep my laboured breathing in check. I stood there for the longest time.

What was I thinking? I had no idea what I was even doing. Yeah, sure, Miranda, come into Ringer's room, seduce him for a quick thrill in order to release some pent-up tension. And how exactly are you going to go about that, genius?

My mind was whirring at a hundred miles an hour; oh God, I didn't know, didn't have a bloody clue of how I would actually go about it. What if I woke him and scared him, he might lash out and punch me in the face, or worse, tell me to get out. No! No an offer he couldn't refuse, remember? And just as the memory of my plan resurfaced inside my brain, a devilish pinch pulled the corner of my mouth. As my inner alter ego came to the surface, it was the same voice in my head that had given me the confidence to walk out of the shower cubicle and grab my towel. I would listen to that voice, she seemed to know what to do—she liked to live on the edge. I slowly sat on the bed, making sure no part of me was touching him, until I reached out. My hand felt the warmth of the blanket as it slid further up his thigh, slowly, teasingly higher, my hand reaching the line of his hip and then across, skimming tauntingly close to the most intimate part of him that caused him to stir in his sleep. He probably thought he was having an amazing dream, a dream that was about to come true as my hand brushed against him, causing him to stir in other ways.

His body's reaction only excited me, encouraged me further, and just as I was about to slide my hand lower, something froze me from my actions. Ringer's hand snaked out and caught my wrist in a vice-like grip. My stomach plummeted, and the horror on my face was well and truly illuminated as he flicked the bedside lamp on, showing him my flushed expression, the hunger in my eyes as I looked down at his mystified expression. His eyes were not bleary from sleep, but narrowed in dark questions, and his breaths were just as laboured as my own. I thought his stare would burn a hole straight through my skull: unblinking, alarmed and truly surprised. I was about to scurry away into the night, mortified, until something happened. His eyes dipped lower, to where my unbuttoned shirt plunged and parted, exposing my nakedness underneath, before flicking back up to me. He swallowed deeply, and his need betrayed him. In that moment I never felt more powerful; it was all I needed to make my next move. Either out the door to die of embarrassment, or make my move right here, right now with Ringer. I chose the latter.

Chapter Twenty-One
Ringer

I was dreaming, I had to be.

Miranda Henry, scantily clad, touching me in the dead of night would never happen in a million years, she had said so herself. Not even alcohol could be blamed. We had left the Commercial hours before and even then she walked a straight line, drove the car with ease. And yet there she was above me, looking like a blonde angel, an angel with the look of the devil in her eyes.

Fuck.

I should send her away; she would thank me in the morning, seeing as she hated me already. She was sure to despise me, and herself more, if this was going where I think it was going. And if this started, that would be it; if this were what she wanted, there would be no going back for me.

I had to ask if she was sure—maybe it was all that she needed to snap her out of this—but as my eyes dipped to her exposed breast from her slipped shirt, I knew I was a fucking goner. If it wasn't then, it was most certainly when Miranda moved, pressing her hand on my chest to lie back down, and then slowly straddled me.

Holy shit!

I could feel the heat of her even with the blanket between us. A blanket that really had to go—even the thinness of the barrier was too much—as I needed to feel her against me. She needed it too as she sat back, shifting the blanket off me, exposing my bare top half and my tented boxers. The way she bit her lip made me want to explode right there and then, but, Jesus, I clamped the urge down. Her doe-like eyes lifted to mine as if asking a silent question as her hands rested on my abdomen; when I didn't move she took that as a yes. That was the key to this. Don't move; don't let her stop. I clearly would never know or understand what went through Miranda Henry's beautiful head, but all I knew was something drove her into my room, into my bed, and if it meant not saying a goddamn thing to make her stay, then I was completely and utterly at her mercy. She broke away from my eyes, running her delicate tongue over her bottom lip that was only a moment before punctured with teeth marks. She moved her hands to slide down my stomach, causing me to inhale for the torture of it on my sensitive skin. I bit the side of my mouth to force silence as I knew where she was headed and that is exactly where I wanted her to go. Her finger hooked into the elastic of my boxers and peeled them down, exposing me to her eyes, eyes that I almost didn't recognise. I had seen the fire in Miranda's eyes before; hell, it was that deep-seeded burning hatred she often looked at me with, but as her eyes met mine, it was a different kind of fire: a burning, powerful need I knew mirrored my own. She never tore away from my eyes, even when she took me in her hand and stroked me up and down in a slow, maddening rhythm. I closed my eyes, reeling from the sensation. She was turning me into a mad man, a man who wanted to beg and cave and do whatever she wanted, but still I was silent in fear of snapping her out of her femme-fatale state, and just as I repeated the vow of silence over and over in my head that I was crushing back into my pillow, the silence was obliterated as I felt her soft, hot mouth on me.

"Miranda," I exhaled. I couldn't help it. My eyes flung open to see the top of Miranda's blonde head moving over me, my hands instinctively folded through the silken folds of her hair, my hands gently guiding her pace. When she looked up into my eyes, I was lost, completely and utterly lost to her, and she knew it too, as a wicked smiled teased her lips as she withdrew from me. She felt the violent rise and fall of my chest as she steadied herself by placing her palms on my chest, so as to manoeuvre herself above me. I let her take control, my hands fisting in the sheets by my side as she took me in her hand and guided me slowly into her mouth again. I groaned, clenching my jaw as my hips lifted involuntarily to guide her. Miranda's breaths blew over my hot skin as she adjusted her pace, and technique.

Holy shit!

I had to think about something else, volcanoes erupting … no, trains travelling through tunnels … no, Demi More making clay pottery … hell, no!

She took me deeper and I was lost in the mad throws of torture and ecstasy combined.

"Miranda." My voice was hoarse, my breathing hard. "You better stop."

Miranda looked up at me with her half-hooded stare, then she moved, running her hot lips up my abs.

"Why?'" She smirked against my skin.

She bloody well knew why.

And I didn't want to do that. There was nothing romantic about this; whatever this was it wasn't for romance or feelings. Christ, I didn't know what it was, other than an absolute surprise, and don't get me wrong, as far as surprises go this was at the top of my list, and just when I thought it couldn't get any better …

Miranda ran a slow trail of kisses and nips up across my chest, the folds of her hair whispering across my skin. She worked her way up to nip and kiss along my neck; my throat swallowing deep, she kissed my Adam's apple. She pressed her lips together as if savouring the taste. She hovered above me, her hair curtaining us from the glow of the lamplight, but I could see the depths of her green-blue eyes. She neared my mouth, tantalisingly close, but not touching, our hot, shallow breaths the only connection. She watched me, really watched me with such intensity until the corner of her mouth lifted.

"Do you want to come in my mouth?"

Holy fucking hell.

She was like no girl in Onslow, and I am pretty certain there was no one like her in Ballan. The way her eyes challenged me, her wry taunting smile, she had completely taken me over, dominating from the first touch until I was a quivering mess who would do anything she wanted. This was foreign territory for me. I was usually the persuader, the one in charge, whispering the questions into the skin of a quivering girl, not the other way around. And although this would seem like every man's dream scenario, something stirred within me, and in an instant, the smile formed on my lips. In one swift movement I rolled, flipping Miranda onto her back and wedging myself comfortably against her; her eyes were wide and her breathing shallow at the unexpected turn of power. I pulled apart her shirt sending a spray of pearl buttons onto the floor; a yelp of shock only made me harder as her wide eyes looked up at me. There she lay, naked and quivering under me; I ran my own tongue and lips over her, this time making a trail up to the crook of her neck, and whispered,

"Ladies first."

Chapter Twenty-Two
Miranda

My world was spinning.

Completely thrown off its axis the moment Ringer flipped me onto my back, the motion had snapped me out of control and it suddenly dawned on me. I had come here for release, but I had also come here to assert some kind of control. I had never felt more beautiful or desired the way Ringer reacted to my touch, to my mouth. He looked up at me like I was a Goddess, and although I knew it was all fuelled by the traitorous parts of his body, it was still what I needed beyond anything. To feel wanted, and, oh, how he wanted me. I could see it even now as he looked down on my naked body pinned under him, his hardness wedged against me, causing my breath to hitch. And yet, this was not how it was supposed to be, this took away my control, my power. I didn't just want to be fucked, that could happen at any time; I could have gotten that from Tom Hilton in the back seat of a car. No, I had wanted it to be different, and I had wanted it to be with no one other than Ringer.

I was seriously fucked up.

My body quivered, not out of desire but out of a new

sensation. Stone-cold reality. I had wanted to sleep with Ringer if he begged me, but not to be just one of his emotionless conquests. I was an idiot to think anything else. Bedding women was probably an extra-curricular activity for him, and here I was trying to be some kind of seductress when I hadn't slept with anyone since my cheating ex-boyfriend. I was way out of my league, clearly. And as the reality slammed into me with such an overwhelming force, I pushed at Ringer's chest with all of my strength.

"Get off me," I managed through the tears that wanted to flow.

"Miranda?" Ringer's brows lowered as he eventually moved at my insistent push. "Are you okay?"

I sat on the edge of the bed, pulling my button-less shirt together to find some dignity.

"I'm sorry, I shouldn't have come here," I said quietly, and standing on my jelly-like legs, I made a direct line to the door, moving to open it. I only managed to pull it back a little before I felt the press of Ringer's body behind me; wrapping his arm around me he pushed the door closed, wedging me against it. His lips were on my temple as his hot breaths blew rapidly against my skin.

"Don't go, not like this," he whispered, his voice pleading. His hand splayed against my bare stomach, his skin on mine burning into me. I closed my eyes, turned on mostly by his rapid breathing and his mouth that rested on my shoulder. We stayed there frozen for the longest moment; I made no effort to move. Wrapped in Ringer's hold, pressed against the door, an excitement twisted in the pit of my stomach. An excitement that spiked as I felt Ringer trace lazy circles with his thumb into my skin. I bit my lip, finding my traitorous body lean back into him. His hand slid slowly down my abdomen, farther and farther until he found the very place he knew would unravel me. He slid his clever, taunting fingers inside me. First one, and then another. A noise I didn't quite recognise as my own escaped me, my head falling back as Ringer kissed my neck.

"Shhh … just go with it," he whispered.

Go with it? There was no way in hell I was not going to go with it, my control was lost to him, but I couldn't have cared less. Above all the psychological bullshit in my own mind, this was what I needed. This was what had me staring up at the ceiling in my darkened room, trying to solve the mysteries of the universe. Well, I had found them within Ringer's touch, the light teeth grazes against my shoulder and the dirty words he whispered into my ear as he brought me towards the cliff I would willingly tumble over. My hands splayed against the wood panel of the door, clawing as I arched back against Ringer, unable to contain my silence I readied myself to fall, to fall with the fierce intense pleasure he had driven me to, and just as I was about to …

Ringer took away his hand.

WHAT?

He turned me around, crushing his mouth against mine, slamming my back into the door. The kiss was deep, claiming, hungry. And just as a thrill spiked through me at what was to come next, he pulled away, pressing his forehead against mine, wincing as if in pain, breathless.

"Go."

"W-what?"

"Go, before I fuck you against this door."

Sounded like a plan.

I blinked in confusion, the pent-up frustration of being so close to the bone-melting pleasure I had so desperately wanted.

"Are you serious?" An incredulous anger was rising in my chest.

Ringer looked down at me, his expression grave. "You don't want this."

It was like he had lit a fuse inside me as my eyes darkened. I pushed him. "Who are you to tell me what I want?"

"Miranda." He sighed.

"Save it!" I said, wrapping my top fiercely around me. "You're right, I don't want this; if anything, you have saved me from insanity."

Ringer's expression darkened. "You already hate me enough, by morning you would hate me and yourself even more if we continued." He looked ... pained. *What?*

I paused in the door I had violently yanked open, looking back with eyes that I prayed would not well up just yet.

"Then why did you stop me?"

And when he had no answer, other than just a poignant stare, I walked through the door and slammed it behind me as hard as I could.

He was right. I did hate him. But more importantly, I hated myself.

Chapter Twenty-Three
Ringer

What had begun as a dream had ended in a nightmare.
With no sleep and a raging hard on that not even a cold shower could fix, I was set for the longest, most torturous day of my life: a five a.m. start for the official handover with a bright and breezy Steve for the day.

"So how did you go last night?"

I spat out a mouthful of O.J at the breakfast table, heading into a raging coughing fit that earned me a quizzical brow lift from Penny Henry. It was a pretty simple question. Still, barroom brawling, and an-almost blow job from your daughter didn't make for friendly light-hearted chit-chat.

"Yeah, it was pretty uneventful," I rasped.

"Ah, I see, so did you get the courtesy bus then?" Steve leant his elbows on the table, eagerly awaiting my answer.

No we stole your best mate's Land Cruiser and drove home under the influence.

Yeah, I was definitely trustworthy enough to be left alone with your livelihood, possessions and daughter. I shifted in my seat thinking about how I would be, stranded there with her for two long weeks.

"Yep, got back just fine." I suddenly found the remnants of the bottom of my O.J glass fascinating.

Penny Henry pushed out her chair from the table, gathering the empty breakfast plates. "I better start packing if you insist we leave tonight," she said, offering a weak smile, as if she wasn't looking forward to the task ahead.

I took the moment of man time to ask Steve an important question; lowering my voice I leant forward.

"Hey, Steve, about Miranda's car."

Steve winced, his head snapping around to where his wife disappeared down the hall. He motioned for me to be quiet and mimed towards the kitchen door. As I had suspected, Penny knew nothing about the car sabotage. I followed a nervous-looking Steve out onto the porch, the door slamming shut behind him.

"Just don't go mentioning that around here, okay?"

"Sorry, I just think that maybe you should fix it before you head. I know you want her to stay but maybe it should be because she wants to," I tried to reason.

Steve looked as if he was a million miles away. "I know I can't make her stay, and she won't, and I have accepted that. I know it seems selfish to expect her to be here, especially when we're essentially the ones abandoning her. I guess I just had a bit of a manic moment seeing her here again after so long. It's brought a lot of things back that I haven't had to think about in a long while."

I wanted to ask what things, but my silence seemed to encourage him to continue.

"You probably wonder why a farmer's daughter is driving around in a busted-up old car anyway."

It had crossed my mind.

"She used to have a nice car, a sporty little red Lancer when she turned eighteen. It was her birthday present from us." Steve smiled at the memory. "Thinking back I think it was probably not the greatest decision. Ya see, when you have a wife and kids, you want to make them happy, you want to give them the things you never had, and living in a household full of girls who can twist you around their finger," he snorted, "what bloody chance does a man have?"

I smiled past the cigarette I had placed in between my lips. "Not a chance."

"Exactly. And besides wanting to give them all you can, you also want to protect them." He broke off, his eyes darkening and going to another place, a haunted place by the look of his lined face. "Four years ago, when Miranda was home and going through that delinquent phase teenagers go through—where everything is boring and parents are the enemy—we tried to lay off a bit on the discipline, thinking that all our rules were actually pushing her away. On the one night we decided to loosen the reigns, it was the one night all our lives would be turned upside down."

The accident.

I had known no more than just the very mention of what Jenny at the pub was about to tell me, but when Steve started speaking through the last night of Miranda leaving the Commercial with her friend, Mel, and driving home drunk and flipping the car, it made my blood run cold.

I hadn't even questioned why she was driving Bluey's car last night, or why she parked it on the outskirts and walked into Moira Station instead of driving it. I was such an idiot. I didn't think to believe that Miranda would be sneaking around in her twenties keeping secrets from her parents, but now I could tell the wounds were still pretty raw.

I had wondered about the tension between her and her parents, about what drove her to the shearers' hut in the first place. It was because even after all this time, all these years, her parents obviously had an inability to let go. Who could blame them?

"You're a good man, Steve, and I know I have only been here for five minutes, but I know you're a great father."

"What kind of father sabotages his daughter's car?"

"One that cares. Besides, I don't think too much sabotaging needed to happen to that bucket of rust," I said.

"You never stop worrying about them, Ringer, no matter how old they get. Her mother and I just can't see where she's going, ya know? She seems so lost; I mean, what is she going to do now she's back in Oz?"

I butted out my smoke in an ashtray on the outside table. "Let her figure it out, mate, and she will. But in order to discover her destination, she's going to need a way to get there."

Steve nodded. "Well, what's say we make that our first mission then? Get the beast up and running."

I slapped Steve on the back. "Mate, we're going to need some holy water and a priest to exorcise the evil from that car."

By lunchtime, we had returned on our quad bikes in a blaze of dust. After fixing Miranda's car we tended to the stock in the far-end paddock. The caretaking was routine and manageable, and with each delegated task, Steve seemed to visibly relax as if mentally he was edging towards a break from the farm for a bit.

We housed the bikes in one of the out buildings and headed around towards the shearers' huts.

"I'm just going to freshen up for lunch," I said, veering off to the shower block.

"No worries, see you in a bit."

Aside from wanting to wash the dust and sweat from the hot summer day, I hadn't really wanted to walk past Miranda's room with her dad. I could see from the shower block that her door was open, and I didn't really know if she would feel comfortable if her dad and I stopped by for a chit-chat. I guess it was inevitably going to happen over lunch, but still, at least she would get the good news about her car, I thought, as I splashed cold water over my face and across the back of my neck. I stood clasping the sink, looking at my sodden complexion, dark circles under my eyes from no sleep, my skin darkened from my days in the sun.

What if she did want to leave? After all, it's what she wanted more than anything, and after last night, I am sure her objective would be to avoid me. I didn't know how I would feel about that; the minute she slammed the door on me last night was the equivalent of throwing iced water over me. She was right, if I thought it was a bad idea, why did I stop her from leaving my room in the first place?

Because I didn't want her to go.

But I also didn't want to sleep with her and have her despise me in the morning, which didn't really matter because, regardless, I'm pretty sure she felt the same anyway.

I splashed more water on my face before it hit me; what if her dad told her how I had helped fixed her car, that I had suggested it? He was probably in her doorway right now telling her the good news.

I grabbed the towel, drying my face, and broke into a jog back to the shearers' huts; Steve wasn't anywhere to be seen but her door was still open. I quickstepped up the steps and strode towards her door and without so much as a pause, walked into her room.

"Miran …" I paused.

The room was bare, more than just her not being there, but all her things were gone. The room had been stripped of bedding, it was a barren shell. I slammed my hand on the door jamb.

"Shit." Making my way up the verandah, my heart thumping in my chest as I went to investigate what I suspected, and to my surprise what I dreaded, I turned the corner and came up short.

Her car was still in the drive.

The tension melted in my shoulders; she was still there, but for how long?

I didn't have time to process the thought before my attention snapped to something else in the drive, something so completely unexpected I had to blink twice, thinking maybe fatigue was playing with my head.

I stared at the unmistakable white Toyota Hilux for the longest moment.

What the fuck was Sean Murphy doing here?

Chapter Twenty-Four
Miranda

"Mum says you have to pack up and move back into the house."

Moira stood in the open doorway to my room, catching her breath, having delivered her message on the run.

"What?"

My heart thundered. Had someone seen me leave Ringer's room in the early hours this morning, or even worse, had he said something? Did he want me away from him after I as good as attacked him in his sleep?

Maybe they found out I went to the Commercial last night?

Had Bluey found out about the car I borrowed off Mel, did they know about the barroom brawl? All these wild scenarios played in my head; I felt sick to my stomach.

"W-Why?" I asked, sitting down on the edge of my bed.

"I don't know, Mum just got off the phone and asked me to tell you to move out."

Oh God!

She knew about the Commercial; it was probably one of the local gossips telling her that I was hanging out with some young troublemaker on parole who had roughed up Tom Hilton last night. The very reason why I hated small towns.

"I wouldn't mess her around either, she seems like she is in a real flap," Moira added helpfully, as she spun out of the doorway and jogged back to the house.

Oh great, this was just great.

My new focus of clearing out my gear from the shearers' huts at least distracted me from the worry of what had happened last night, kind of, sort of, okay … so not really at all. As if I hadn't had enough to worry about with the nervous anxiety of seeing Ringer in the light of day, worried how he would treat me, if he would speak to me, now I had to face off with my manic mother about lying to her last night. It was all too much, too complicated, and as I zipped up the last zipper on my case and lugged my belongings back to the house, I took in a calming deep breath and readied myself to face the music.

I juggled my belongings, struggling to open the screen door, and making my way into the house, I dumped the heaviest of the bags inside the door.

"Oh, Miranda, honey, can you put those in your room, please?" my mum called out as she frantically wiped down the kitchen bench. Okay, so this is not what I had expected, and witnessing my mum in a cleaning frenzy could only mean one thing.

"Are we expecting someone?" I asked.

Mum sighed, rubbing the back of her hand across her brow.

"Max just called and said a few of his friends are going to drop in on their way to Geraldine, and asked if they could camp here for the night?"

"Is Max with them?" Hope lined my voice.

"No, he has to work," Mum said, dunking her mop into a soapy bucket.

So that had been the phone call and the reason behind Mum's panic, and then the penny dropped.

"So his friends will be staying in the shearers' huts?" I asked innocently.

"Well, they're certainly not staying in the house," Mum said, all wide eyed.

"Of course not, we could all be murdered in our beds," I quipped.

"Just put your things away, please. They'll be here for lunch, as if I don't have enough to do." Poor Mum attacked the kitchen floor, which already looked spotless to me; in fact, the entire house was pristine as always, and yet Mum would dust, polish and scrub every inch of it knowing we had company. I gladly picked up my bags and took them to my room, a sense of relief sweeping over me knowing that all this chaos had nothing to do with me, for once. And just as I went to walk down the hall …

"Oh, Miranda," called Mum.

I turned to see her smiling. "Your father wanted to tell you, but he's fixed your car; try and act surprised, okay?"

Yep! Things were definitely looking up.

The one real thing in my favour was knowing all too well that when Bluey Sheehan said he was leaving at a particular time, you could always add a sound four hours on top of that. The Sheehans were late for everything. So in an effort to escape my mother's shouted demands for housework assistance, I gauged the time, and set off to sneak out the laundry door, descending the steps, leaving my mother's shrill voice behind me. I cut across the paddock in the exact same direction I had come only mere hours before, climbing over several barbed fences including the very one where Ringer had snared his jeans. I smiled at the memory until my thoughts drifted to his bedroom. I didn't want to think about how I had acted, how I had tasted him in the most intimate of ways. And the most disturbing thing of all was, even after how the night had ended, the thought of Ringer still excited me. I don't know exactly when I had gone from hating him to … *not* hating him. Maybe it was when he saved my boots from getting wet? Or how ridiculous he looked in my cardigan to prove a point, or his taunting insinuations in the shower block? Or maybe it was the way something dark pressed inside me when I saw Jenny's hand on his thigh at the Commercial? Who knew? All I knew was it was enough to send me into his arms last night, it was enough for me to remember vividly what his mouth, touch and skin felt like against me. But probably the most telling sign of all was I would do it all over again, but with a different ending. That was the only thing I regretted. The part where I left. I now know that if I could have another chance, I would want to stay. I wanted Ringer. Possibly for more than just sex.

I seemed to regret so many things in my short, wicked little life, and one of them was staring right at me: Mel's Land Cruiser. If I learnt anything from last night, I could see that even after all this time I still acted on impulse, and that is where all my troubles stemmed from. I opened the driver's door with a pained screech before sliding into the interior, the keys still in the ignition from last night, the perks of living in the middle of nowhere. Stilling for a moment, I grabbed the steering wheel with a deep sigh. I should never have borrowed Mel's car, and of all the places to go, to the very one place where all my troubles had unravelled four years ago.

"What must you think of me, Mel?" I whispered, recalling the innocent blue eyes of my trusting friend as she made me promise I wouldn't drink and drive. Instead, I had been too hell bent on worrying about my own selfish distractions to concern myself with how leaving Mel in a cloud of dust would make her feel. I sat in her car, clenching the wheel with a white-knuckled intensity as I let the full brunt of guilt wash over me. I didn't move for the longest time; the only thing that snapped me from my reflection was the distant, high-pitched whine of a dirt bike. I blinked, sending a watery trail down my cheeks. I sniffed, wiping them away, and glanced into the rear-view mirror of the car. Sure enough, there it was, a long line of dust approaching my way.

My eyes welled with the flow of unshed tears, seeing Mel come to a stop next to the car. She killed the thrumming sounds of the bike, before flicking out the stand and pulling off her helmet, blinding me with an astonished smile when she noticed me in the car.

"Ha! Looks like great minds think alike." She laughed.

It was all I needed to make my move. I pushed open my door and quick-stepped a determined line around the front of the car. Mel's smile slowly faded catching the sight of my bloodshot eyes before I wrapped my arms around her in a bone-jarring hug. My shoulders vibrated with the heaves of my sobs, as I let the weight that had been lodged in my chest release into the arms of my friend.

"Miranda, what's wrong?" Mel's panicked voice was muffled by my hair. She pulled away, clasping my cheeks, trying to look at me. "Good God, what is it? Are you okay? Is it the car?" Mel's eyes were wide, catatonic almost with fear.

Through my blubbering I managed a head shake, my chin trembling as I looked her, really looked at her. "I'm so sorry, Mel."

Mel's brows narrowed in confusion. "What for?"

I shrugged. "For everything: for what happened, for leaving you, for asking so much of you and never thinking about anyone else but myself."

Mel smiled. "Is that why you're crying?" Her shoulders sagged in relief. "Seriously, is that all?"

My mouth gaped. "What do you mean, is that all?"

Mel sighed. "I am guessing this is all a rather delayed reaction," she said with a wry smile. "It was a long, long time ago, Miranda. We were just young and dumb and in true fashion, young and dumb people make mistakes."

"Then why am I still making them?" I said quietly.

I could feel Mel's eyes on me. "Are we still talking about the car?" she mused.

I straightened my back, shaking off the probing question. "I should never have asked for it, I honestly don't know what I was thinking."

"Well, you obviously weren't." Mel raised her brow. "The question is what, or who, were you thinking about?"

Escaping Ringer.

Oh, the irony: in order to escape him, I had run straight into him.

I changed the subject, or at least tried to keep it in line. "Do you think you can forgive me?"

Mel thought long and hard, which surprised me. I didn't think she would be into making me suffer as it wasn't in her nature, but perhaps that was what I was so used to taking advantage of.

She crossed her arms and tilted her head. "I'll forgive you under one condition," she said.

"Anything," I replied without pause.

"Tell me all about Ringer."

My mouth gaped open as I was genuinely stunned by the question.

How did she know about him? How did she even know his name? And what made her think I had anything to do with him?

I tried for cool and casual. "What about him?"

Mel shrugged. "It's not every day I overhear my dad threatening grievous bodily harm if he so much as lays a finger on Miranda Henry."

"Whaaat?" I breathed out.

Mel chuckled. "So if he has gone against that threat, he must be pretty keen."

I could feel my cheeks flush crimson as I broke away from her knowing eyes.

I heard Mel gasp. "Oh, my God! He so has. Wow! He is either very brave, or very ..."

"Stupid?" I said, lifting my eyes to meet hers.

"Well, I was going to say smitten."

"Oh."

Mel got off the dirt bike, handing me the helmet, but pulled it back at the last second.

"You have my full forgiveness, after you tell me everything."

I swallowed. "Everything?"

"Everything!"

And so I did; well, a sugar-coated version, to say the least.

I had never realised how much of a weight I carried around from the unresolved guilt for so many years. Knowing that Mel harboured no ill feeling towards me, and my stupid actions, made me feel decidedly lighter. And now knowing what Ringer must have endured at the hands of his visit to Bluey had me thinking.

Had that been the reason he rejected me?

Or, like he said, I would only hate him in the morning. Is that what he thought? I guess I hadn't given much of a reason for him to think anything else. I had been such a bitch to him. *But, did he actually hate me?*

I had to let him know the truth. I had to tell him that I didn't hate him, not at all. That in the light of day, I didn't feel any regret, and if anything, if he wanted, well, I kind of wanted to do it again.

My heart thundered at the thought, the realisation that what I felt was something deeper than just using him for my own selfish needs. I had been selfish for far too long and it only ended up in trouble. And maybe where I was headed was for trouble? But I knew that I had to find out, I had to know if, in the light of day, did Ringer regret last night? I had to know. Only then would the last of the weight be lifted from me, and only then would I be able to decide.

Should I stay? Or should I go?

I heard the sound of deep voices echo down the hall. It drew me from my bed and I paused, standing near my opened door.

I heard the shrill laughter of my mother and I knew that was strange. Moira, no doubt, was elsewhere in the house, remaining in the shadows. I made my way out of the room and into the kitchen area.

"Oh, Miranda, honey, come meet Max's friends from Onslow." My mum was all flushed and smiles as she stood before four men all seated around the kitchen island. The one nearest stood, towering over me, and offered his bear-like hand.

"Max is a dark horse, he never mentioned he had a sister. I'm Sean." He took my hand in a manly shake.

"He must be ashamed of me." I smirked.

Sean grinned, stepping aside, as the other moved forward to shake hands.

"Oh, I doubt that; I'm Stan." A blue-eyed boy with a beaming smile.

"Toby." Tanned with striking dark eyes that looked like they housed a million mysteries.

"Chris." The more serious of the group, but his smile was warm and sincere.

Silence swept across the kitchen that soon settled into awkwardness as Sean coughed. "Um, I hope we aren't intruding?"

"Oh no, of course not." My mother waved off his words, which amused me no end; she was so overly accommodating I wouldn't have been surprised if she shipped us all out to the shearers' huts so they could have the house.

"I hope you're all hungry, we're just about to dish up some lunch."

"Sounds great, Mrs Henry," said Stan.

"Oh, please, call me Penny."

Ugh, she was so embarrassing.

"Moira, stop staring," I whispered.

"I am not." She glowered.

I continued to wash the salad at the sink. "Well, get a good look, because they won't be here when you get back. Are you all packed?"

"Nope."

"What? Mum is going to kill you."

Moira looked confused. "Why, we're not leaving till the morning."

Wait. What?

I turned to Mum. "Are you leaving in the morning?"

"Well, we can't just leave Max's friends unattended," she said quietly. "That would be a bit rude."

No, of course not. We wouldn't want to abandon Max's friends, but you were ready to abandon your daughter who had only just returned back to the family home after four years. Not that I would complain, the presence of Max's friends and them staying for the night took the pressure off what I would endure being faced with here, alone with Ringer.

The kitchen door opened and my heart stopped. In walked my dad … alone.

My heart sunk with an edge of disappointment; I wanted to ask but didn't need to.

"Where's Ringer? Lunch is ready," she said, carrying a casserole dish to the table where the boys sat.

"Ah, he's just freshening up," he said, before making his way towards the table. "G'day, you must be Max's mates, welcome." Dad beamed, shaking their hands and exchanging information on the best fishing destination in Geraldine, and the grand tour he would give them after lunch … and did they fancy a beer, blah, blah, blah. I smiled to myself, setting down a basket of bread rolls. Dad was lost in the throes of man talk, poor fella he was, absolutely starved of such conversation with a house full of women; he was definitely making up for lost time. I moved to gather some napkins from the buffet near the door. That's when I heard it open and a figure stood in my peripheral vision.

"Well, bloody hell. Look what the cat dragged in," said Sean, laughing.

My eyes lifted to see Ringer standing in the doorway, shaking his head at his mates with an incredulous grin; it was the kind that exposed his devilish dimple in his cheek. *Oh shit, that man is delicious.*

"There goes the neighbourhood." He laughed, flicking his gaze towards me.

I twisted a napkin in my hand, daring not to move as his eyes locked with mine. Heated. His look pierced my heart which pounded erratically, and I could barely think, paralysed by his presence. I didn't know if I should stay, go, smile, laugh, glare.

But in one mere moment, I didn't need to do anything, because as he neared me, brushing past me, his muscled chest grazing my shoulders at the buffet, I turned my head, lifting my eyes to his to catch his warm smile that made me melt as he winked at me.

My lips tilted, and delight surged inside me at such a simple gesture. It was such a Ringer thing to do, and the fact he acknowledged me and wasn't weird caused my entire inner turmoil to thaw.

It wasn't a look filled with regret, it was full of fire and cheek and I all but wanted to reach out, stop him, and tell him I had no regrets either. Heat flooded my cheeks as I watched him round the table, rubbing Stan's hair and back-slapping his mates. It was like a fire had been lit inside him, seeing his friends again. Watching their boyish exchange and taunts caused strange stirrings in my stomach; it made him, dare I say, more attractive to me, witnessing him in a more natural environment.

I was shunted from my thoughts by an elbow to my side as Moira passed me. "Stop staring," she said smugly, sticking out her tongue.

Chapter Twenty-Five
Ringer

I desperately wanted to talk to Miranda.

But with the change in circumstances, I could see there was no way that was going to happen.

Sean sat next to me at the dining table, piling a mass of potato salad on his plate.

Speaking lowly, he said, "So why didn't you tell us you were heading here?"

I shrugged. "It was just a spur-of-the-moment decision."

"Well, has being away knocked the chip off your shoulder?" He looked at me poignantly.

I could have said what chip? But both he and I knew exactly what he was talking about.

I worked on buttering my roll. "The change has done me good," I admitted.

I could tell Sean was eyeing me with interest, the cogs turning in his big head. "Well, I have to admit," he said, "the view is pretty nice."

My eyes instinctively flicked up to where Miranda sat opposite, listening intently to Stan, who was no doubt boring her to death with fishing stories going by his hand gestures. My mouth curved as I refocused on my dinner roll.

Sean chuckled. "You old dog." He broke into his own roll, and buttered it violently, glancing up at Miranda. "Have you gone there?"

It was a cryptic question, but one I understood perfectly. "No," I lied.

Sean just smirked, as if he wasn't buying it for a second.

"So did you catch up with Bluey last night?" Steve addressed me from the head of the table.

"Ah, no, I didn't run into him." I flinched.

But it wasn't at the question, it was the unexpected sensation of a foot sliding up my calf.

What the?

"Really? I doubt that you could have missed his big ugly mug, the Commercial isn't that big." Steve laughed.

I smiled in good humour, shifting awkwardly in my seat as the foot slid higher. I glanced across the table; Miranda was nodding earnestly and hanging onto every one of Stan's words. I had great pleasure in casually flicking out my serviette and dropping it in my lap. I watched the impressive lines of her poker face, until I grabbed her bare foot with my hand. She never flinched. She was good, very good.

Until I ran my thumb tauntingly along the pad of her foot, only then did I see her brows rise as she squirmed slightly in her seat.

"Ringer?"

My head snapped around to Penny.

"Can you please pass the salt?" she said with a smile.

"Oh, yeah, sure."

I pulled Miranda's foot into my groin, clamping it in place with my thighs as I reached for the salt and passed it to her mum. It's where it stayed for the rest of the meal, until she announced to the table that she had to be excused. And after a long moment, and then a rather obvious look from her that as good as said 'let's go', a slightly flushed Miranda got up from the table and walked out of the room.

I took a moment to process what had just happened. Seeing as last night ended with a murderous death stare and a door in the face, the foot sliding up my leg as a peace offering was … *unexpected.* What was more unexpected was how my heart raced, and my dick hardened by such a subtle touch, how I had … revelled in it.

Fuck, I was in trouble. It was more than what was in my pants telling me what I wanted; no, this was far worse. It was what my head was telling me.

I had known it the moment she slammed the door, the moment the panic surged inside me thinking about her leaving Moira. It was more than just a midnight liaison I was interested in, and the moment her dainty little foot slid slowly up my leg, I knew it. The relief of her not being mad at me, not despising me was palpable. But I needed to know for certain, make sure she wasn't just fucking with me.

Amidst the chaos of the after-lunch clean up where everyone chipped in to help clear the table, I took the opportunity to break away and wander down the hall where Miranda had disappeared. I made it halfway down the hall until the door at the left swung open and Miranda appeared, stopping short in front of me. Gone was the calm poker face from the dinner table; instead, her slightly pinked cheeks deepened and her eyes were wide.

"I see we're not neighbours anymore."

"No," she said, glancing down.

"Was it because of last night?"

Her eyes flicked up, alarm creasing her face. "No! No, I mean, I didn't have a choice. Your friends are staying the night and it was where Mum wanted to put them."

A smile broke slowly, more in amusement at myself for knowing that what I felt was a sense of relief. Relief that she hadn't left in her car, or moved away from me to avoid me, and most of all, I was endlessly amused at what an absolute fucking goner I was when it came to this girl. I wanted nothing more than to step

forward, crush my mouth against hers and never let her go. I felt
the edge of disappointment flare that I couldn't do it. The fact that
my mates were staying the night, and that her family was leaving in
the morning, because if I knew one thing for certain: when I had
a chance to get Miranda alone, there would be nothing cool, calm,
nor collected about it, and that scared the hell out of me as much
as it excited me. I didn't want to need someone, to desire them, and
when I was just about to pull myself away, she stepped forward,
closing the distance between us.

"What are you thinking?"

My eyes bored into hers; I wanted her to know that everything
I said was what I meant. "That I am not a person who likes to leave
things unfinished."

Her brow curved. "Oh?"

I nodded. "I'm very thorough like that."

"Even with the likes of Bluey threatening your nether
regions?"

My mouth gaped.

How did she know about that?

I cleared my throat, shifting on my feet at the memory of
what he would do to me.

But as I looked at the bemused lines of her innocent face I
couldn't help but break into a knowing grin.

"Some things are worth the risk."

"Really?" she asked. I watched the delicate movement of her
tongue run along her bottom lip.

I swallowed. "Really. Whatever it takes to get the job done."

"Well, Moira Station is in good hands then." She laughed,
sliding past me in the hall. I reached for her elbow, stopping her
in her tracks; all amusement drained from her façade and her eyes
flicked from her arm to my face.

"Your car's fixed," I said in all seriousness.

"I know." She blinked, her thick lashes framing the all-
consuming depths of her eyes that flicked over my face.

I could feel my jaw clench; I couldn't force any light-hearted stance about the silence that settled over us. I was so entranced by the intensity of our exchange, I didn't realise I was circling a slow, caressing motion into her skin until her hand moved over the top of mine, tracing the back of my hand with her fingertips. I swallowed deeply, drumming up enough nerve to work up the courage to say the one word that held more weight than anything.

Stay.

And whether it was the silence, or my touch, or the fact she may have somehow read my mind, Miranda broke into a slow, beautiful smile.

"I'm not going anywhere."

Chapter Twenty-Six
Miranda

The house was silent.

And my advantage was I knew every single creak in the house, I had snuck out of it often enough. So the fact that I found my way outside, creeping across the drive undetected at eleven o'clock at night was no brilliant feat. The only unnerving thing about my movements was the direction I was headed in. I skimmed my way against the side of the building, slowly edging around. Grabbing the corner of the verandah post, I swung around quickly, ready to catapult myself up the decked stairs until I slammed into a chest, hard. My scream was quickly muffled by a hand, my heart racing at a hundred miles an hour.

"Miranda?"

The hand slowly fell away allowing me to step back before lashing out and whacking Ringer across the arm.

"What are you doing? You scared the crap out of me," I whispered angrily.

"What am I doing? What are you doing?" he whispered back.

My mouth gaped, as I stumbled at the question.

Sneaking into your room to jump your bones.

No, I didn't think voicing that would be wise, and I don't think I needed to. There was enough moonlight filtering down from the sky that Ringer's smug stance was not lost on me. He crossed his arms across his chest and leant casually on the banister to the stairs.

"You were coming to see me," he said cockily.

"Pfft, you are so full of yourself."

"Deny it," he said, stepping forward, edging me back to where I had come from. I walked back until my back hit the wall of the hut.

"Tell me you're not here for me and I will dissolve into the night," he whispered against my temple.

I smiled, slow and wicked. "Admit that you were sneaking out to see me, and I might just kiss you like there's no tomorrow."

Ringer braced his hands against the wall on either side of my face, caging me in with his biceps. "I admit nothing."

My smile fell from my face. "Well, that's a shame then …"

"Because regardless of why I'm here, or you're here, it's not going to stop me from wanting to kiss you," he said, running his thumb gently along my cheek, causing me to shiver at the sensation.

I lifted my eyes, looking beyond my lashes at his heated stare. "Go on, then," I breathed.

And with no invitation beyond that needed, he closed the distance and claimed my lips, slowly, deeply, thoroughly. My hands fisted into the fabric of the back of his shirt, drawing him closer to me, a sound of approval escaped my lips as he crushed me against the weatherboard wall. He cupped my face, tilting my head gently to gain better access to my mouth. This felt right: no guarded uncertainty or misunderstanding that this was both what we wanted. Ringer's hand skimmed down my neck and slid down, cupping my breast; his touch burned through my top. I leaned into him, encouraging him to touch me; I knew from last night what his clever hands were capable of.

Hooking his thumb into the collar of my shirt, he slowly peeled the fabric across, allowing access as his lips ghosted across my collar bone.

"Is this what you want?" he whispered tauntingly into my skin, before pulling away and looking down, fixing his heated eyes on me.

"Tell me what you want."

I slid my hands over his shoulders and linked my hands together around his neck. "You know what I want."

He curved his brow in question.

I smiled. "You."

Ringer's face sobered into a serious, stony façade. "In what way?"

I paused, considering the question. Suddenly my answer held so much weight. What would he take from it? That I wanted just sex, a boyfriend? I didn't know how to voice it, so I went with what came to mind, thinking he could take it any way he wanted.

I extended on my tippy-toes to whisper into his ear, "In. Every. Way."

I heard the groan of satisfaction as I captured his lobe between my teeth. He ground into me against the hut, his tongue gently delving into my mouth, coaxing me to open for him, in every way it would seem, as his hand slid between my legs.

Okay, so he definitely took my answer as sex; it was just sex he wanted … one night.

I was a fool to think of it as anything else and for that I was suddenly glad I hadn't been more specific, even though I felt the pang of disappointment inside me; what had I honestly expected? That he was going to get down on one knee and ask me to go steady?

Yeah, right!

I broke from his kiss, dazed, breathless but still containing the edge of my frayed senses. "But I think you have forgotten something," I said, looking wickedly up at him, amusement lining my face.

Ringer looked confused for a long moment, but when I raised my brows it was like it was a trigger; I could see the light bulb go off in his mind.

I giggled. Perhaps Ringer had forgotten about the many packets of condoms he's seen in my handbag.

"I guess I will have to go back and get one," I teased.

Ringer caught my arm, stopping me in my tracks. "I've got one in my room."

Oh.

Of course he would have one, didn't every red-blooded male carry a condom? I didn't know whether to be relieved that I didn't have to sneak all the way back into the house, but when Ringer leaned in and pressed his lips against mine, it was like a long-lingering promise that caused heat to brand my cheeks, and he pulled away looking particularly pleased with himself.

'Wait here," he breathed against my mouth, before slowly backing away and making his way around the corner and up the stairs quietly to his room.

I ran my fingers through my hair and straightened my twisted clothes. I could still taste the tobacco and remnants of beer in my mouth and strangely, it left me with the memory of him, causing butterflies to stir in my tummy.

I rubbed my upper arms and paced along the sidewall of the shearers' hut, rampant thoughts circling in my mind.

This is happening, this is really happening.

I had gone from despising Ringer to dry humping him in the shadows. I had gone from wanting to run him over, to wanting to run my fingers through his hair. I had gone from wanting to strangle him, to wanting to wrap myself around him. Considering he had gone from someone I never wanted to see again, to someone I never wanted to leave, all the emotions confused me, but more than that, they excited me. My heart slammed against my chest thinking about what was going to happen when he came back; would he take me by the hand and lead me somewhere? Or press me up against the wall and take me right there? *I really hope his mates are fast asleep.* Would he be hot and demanding or gentle and slow, and Christ I was shaking. Overthinking everything as I walked up and down, chewing my knuckle, my rampant thoughts turning me into a bag of nerves. It was made even worse, not by Ringer's return but by the blinding beams of the outside light that now switched to life and flooded the yard.

Someone *in* the house was coming *outside*.

I dove onto the ground, army crawling under the steps of the shearers' hut. There wasn't much room but enough to shield myself from view, at least I hoped there was. I spied through the gaps in the slats of the stairs only to realise my worst fear. The screen door opened and my dad walked out onto the verandah in his fetching blue dressing gown. He stretched his arms to the sky before yawning and scratching his butt. I didn't know what was worse: this vision, which I would really have preferred not to see, or the sound of an unknowing Ringer, whose footsteps were quickly closing in. He would be expecting to be met with my open arms; instead, he was going to be met with my dad.

Awesome.

There was no way of warning him; he would be in direct sight of Dad opposite the drive and then it was too late: Ringer's foot appeared on the step, pausing as if he had just realised.

"Ringer?" Dad squinted. "Ha, can't you sleep either?"

"Oh … um, yeah."

Ringer slowly descended the steps, his body was rigid, guarded. He casually looked to his right, no doubt wondering where I had managed to go. I would have found it rather comical, the look on Ringer's face, the strained surprise in his voice, oh yes, all really funny if I wasn't wedged under a staircase.

"I just can't help thinking I've forgotten something, ya know?" Dad said, tying the cord around his beer belly and making his way off the verandah and, oh God. He was walking this way. I shrunk down a little.

"Oh, I wouldn't worry, I think we have everything covered." Ringer coolly slid something into his back pocket, and I knew exactly what it was he had in his hand; well, if this wasn't a mood killer I don't know what was.

"Yeah, I suppose," Dad said, thrusting his hands into his pockets and looking up at the moon. Ringer took a moment to glance around, trying to locate me; he flinched to full attention when Dad neared, and then passed him?

"Ahhh." Dad exhaled, perching himself on the middle step to the shearers' huts; the wood groaned under his weight, my eyes widened, but that was nothing compared to Ringer's reaction when he turned to face Dad. His eyes flicked to under the stairs and quickly looked away comically fast, so as not to give my hiding spot away.

"Ever been to Wahroo, Ringer?" my dad asked. I inwardly groaned, lying on my back as Dad settled in to play questions and answers.

"So, what's your old man do for a living?"

"Does Onslow get hot in the summer?"

"What mile per gallon on the Ford do you get?"

Oh God, I was going to be here for hours, trapped in the dirt, awkwardly scrunched up. Of course Ringer wasn't helping, he had pulled up a step and sat next to Dad, politely answering his questions.

Bloody hell, now was not the time for idle chit-chat.

I seriously had to resist the urge to poke Ringer in the spine. And if something bites me in the arse while I am under here, I will blame Ringer. Sexy man or not.

"Thanks for helping me with Miranda's car today, too, mate."

My head snapped up.

Ringer helped him? Aww …

"That's okay, it was nothing."

"It's something that shouldn't have needed to be done in the first place; by all rights, Miranda should have been on the open road if she wanted to, it wasn't anyone's place to stop her."

What?

Ringer visibly shifted in his seat.

"Don't mention it."

"Nah, I mean it, Ringer, what I did was unforgiveable and if

Penny found out, Christ …"

I shifted up onto my elbow, listening with interest.

What was he talking about?

And just as that very thought ran through my mind, the step creaked again, almost as loud as Dad's pained groan as he wearily moved to stand.

He slapped Ringer on the shoulder. "So, for Christ's sake, whatever you do, don't tell the girls that the Mazda was tampered with. We'll never hear the end of it."

WHAT?

Dad chuckled, amused by his own thoughts. "Night, son, go get some sleep."

If it weren't the light of the porch guiding Dad's way back to the house, it would have been the laser beams of rage protruding from my eyeballs.

The outside light flicked off, plunging us both into darkness. I heard Ringer sigh, but I didn't know whether it was in relief or resignation; either way, I didn't really care. All I wanted was to crawl out from my cramped little hiding space. I edged out rather inelegantly; it was a struggle to find purchase to stand since my right leg had gone to sleep. Ringer moved to help me up, but I pushed him away.

"You tampered with my car?" I shouted.

Ringer winced, glancing back towards the house. "Keep it down. No, I didn't."

"But you knew about it?"

"I only found out yesterday," he said, defending himself.

"That's twenty-four hours' plenty of chance to tell me."

"Well, we haven't exactly been on friendly terms."

"You mean before or after you had your hands down my pants last night?" I scoffed.

Ringer crossed his arms, "As far as I recall you weren't wearing any pants," he said smugly.

My face blanched at the memory. I hated him for reminding me of the fact, of my wanton walk into his room last night. It made me feel stupid; it was a feeling that I really didn't need to fuel my rage. I breathed a calming, yet shuddery breath; I closed my eyes, feeling hot tears pool behind my lids. I was suddenly thankful for the dim lighting, thankful that we had been interrupted from making what I could now see would have been such a colossal mistake.

I didn't want to be Ringer's summer fling, and truth be known, now I didn't have to be, I was free. Free to leave this dustbowl of a place, free to leave my traitorous parents, but more importantly, the infuriating boy that stood opposite me, the one that made my heart thunder and my cheeks burn. What had I been thinking before, wanting more from him? He was just a cad like every other man I knew.

"You can't be mad at your dad for caring; yeah, it's extreme, but he had good reason."

"There is no excuse," I snapped.

Ringer plunged his hands in his pockets. "He told me about the accident."

My eyes snapped up to meet his. That one singular sentence sucker punched me, knocking all breath, all clear thought. That night had always been a constant source of shame. It was something I wanted to push to the furthest corner of my mind, and why wouldn't I want to? It was the night that I almost killed my best friend; the scar on Mel's face was a permanent testament to the fact. It was also a huge part of me not wanting to come back and face these ghosts, to be faced with the same distrust from my parents even after all these years. The fact I had even asked Mel to borrow her car last night to escape for my own selfish reasons made me feel physically ill just thinking about it. Even though we had now discussed it, I still felt guilty for my stupid choices. How could I not?

What was wrong with me?

"Is that why we trekked across the paddocks last night, so they wouldn't know?" he asked gently.

I could feel my blood boil; I didn't need him to point out the irony. That the reason I couldn't be trusted was, well … because I couldn't be trusted.

What could I say to that?

My mind was overheating; the more Ringer said the madder I became. I didn't want to see reason or logic; I just wanted to be mad. Be mad at Dad and at Ringer. The incredulous feeling of betrayal was so much easier to process than the reality of my self-loathing. So I did what I did best in these situations.

I walked away.

Chapter Twenty-Seven
Ringer

I closed my eyes the moment the words tumbled out of Steve Henry's mouth. Yep, a definite mood killer.

Miranda stormed past me towards the house.

I inwardly groaned, looking up at the sky. "Miranda, wait." I sprinted after her, moving to block her path.

She glared up at me. "Move."

I stood tall, defiant and crossed my arms. "No."

I half expected her to abuse me with a long line of insults; instead, she did something much worse and far more unnerving.

She smiled sweetly.

My brows knitted together, staring down at the vision of a blonde angel; I slowly let my guard down thinking maybe she was actually coming around? And just as a small line lifted the corner of my mouth, Miranda's smile slowly fell from her face as she let out a blood-curdling, ear-bleeding scream. I leapt to cover her mouth, to muffle the sound that had me jumping out of my skin at the unexpectedness of it. What wasn't unexpected were the lights turning on, first from the shearing huts, then the outside light to the homestead.

Fuck!

I let Miranda go and dropped to the ground. I rolled under Sean's ute in the nick of time, as the screen door burst open and Miranda's dad appeared in just his jocks and armed with a cricket bat.

The sound of feet pounding on the gravel and coming to a halt made me cringe as I saw a gathering of legs appear.

"What's going on?" asked a breathless Sean.

"Sorry, everyone, false alarm, I thought I saw a snake in the drive," Miranda said.

"Good God, Miranda, we thought you were being murdered," said Miranda's mum.

"I'm so sorry, I was just getting something out of my car."

"So there's no snake?" said a yawning Moira, who almost sounded disappointed.

"All right, show's over, folks," Steve Henry announced.

A series of sleepy mumbles sounded as I watched the barefoot shuffles in the dirt as the boys slowly disbanded back to the shearers' huts, and heard the sound of the wire door opening and closing as the Henrys went inside, but none of that held my interest. My gaze was solely fixed on the pink polished toenails and the long legs that disappeared out of view, her thongs flip-flopping up the steps, the door sounding for the last time, and then a moment later the outside light went out, plunging me into darkness.

I held my breath, thinking that the simple motion of exhaling would interrupt my efforts to listen, what for I wasn't sure. Miranda had gotten what she wanted; she was inside now.

I groaned, shifting myself from under the ute, pulling myself to stand, brushing off the dirt from my jeans and shoulders before flinching at the shadow in the corner of my eye.

The shadow chuckled. "You are so fucked."

Sean.

He casually leant against the tray of his ute; his smugness was not lost on me.

I was in no mood for this.

"Don't start." I glowered.

Sean shook his head. "Ain't love grand."

Too many late-night rendezvous are bound to catch up with you; this was clearly the case as I felt the harsh kick to my bed.

"Get up, lover boy! We're heading."

I groaned, burying myself deeper into my wrapped cocoon as I ignored Chris's voice. My attempt of 'ignore it and it will go away' was short lived when my bed started to shimmy violently. I sat up, squinting at Toby rattling the foot of my bed.

"Let's go, Ringo," he shouted.

"What do you need me for?" I croaked.

"Well, that's bloody nice, we've come all this way and you can't even open the gate for us?"

I sat on the edge of my bed, rubbing the sleep out of my eyes. "Get stuffed."

As I slowly pulled myself out of the dregs of sleep I took in the scene before me. My mates, dressed and ready to start their adventure. All bright and upbeat: it was enough to make you sick. Nothing about this scene was right, and the fact it was still dark outside seemed just wrong. I grabbed for my jeans, peeling them on, one leg at a time.

"You may hate us now, Ringo, but wait till we bring back the big one," Stan said, miming casting a fishing rod. I smirked, watching my delusional friend.

I stood, slapping Stan on the shoulder. "Haven't the girls told you size doesn't matter?"

"Oh, ha-ha," said Stan, as I pushed past him to the sink in the corner of my room. Splashing water onto my face, I blindly grabbed for a towel.

"The Henrys must really trust you, Ringer," said Toby.

"Hmm?" I managed past the minty toothbrush in my mouth.

"They've left already," he added.

I paused mid-brush. Well, that was unexpected, I honestly thought Steve would come say goodbye, if nothing else give me another neurotic rundown of my daily chores; he really was keen to get away.

"They trust you, all right," added Chris. "Leaving you here with their daughter."

"Their hot daughter," added Stan. "Seriously, why do you suppose Max never mentioned he had a sister?"

Chris rolled his eyes. "Gee, I wonder?"

Rinsing and wiping my mouth with my towel, I offered a friendly whack to Stan's ribcage as I made my way out onto the verandah.

Sean was relaxing against the verandah post, looking off into the distance with amused interest as he sipped on a cup of tea. I collapsed into the chair outside my door, working to scrunch my socks up to put on my feet.

"What are you looking so pleased about?"

"Not so much pleased as intrigued; you might want to check this out." Sean nodded towards the house.

I got up from my chair, moving to stand next to Sean who had a better vantage point and view to the driveway. I followed his eye line and froze, my eyes narrowing.

There she was.

Dragging her ridiculously oversized duffle bag, struggling to lift it into the boot of her car.

I could feel Sean's eyes watch me with interest. "Seems like not all the Henrys trust you."

I didn't really know what I wanted from Miranda, and it wasn't just sexual frustration of two nights in a row of teasing. But, I know that I didn't want her to leave. More so, I didn't want her to leave me.

Was I really willing to chase after her? Willing to ask her not to leave?

I watched as Miranda gently pulled down the boot and pressed on it lightly. She was creeping around so as not to draw attention. Well, she had my attention all right, and as I watched her dart back quickly into the house, my mind was made up. She may have not wanted to see me, or hear me, but you don't always get what you want.

Chapter Twenty-Eight
Miranda

By the time I heard the house stir into life I had made up my mind.

And once I had, I wasted no time in getting up and ready; I wanted to do it before Ringer and the boys made it over to the house.

I needed to clear my head, to think about what I almost did last night, what I had done the night before. I was becoming someone I didn't wholly recognise anymore. I wasn't so much as angry but confused. I knew it as much when I walked into the kitchen, I had the full intention of blasting my dad for messing with my car, but when I was met with a giant bear hug from him, all the resentment melted away, and I could feel my chin tremble like I was a small child.

"Well, we're all packed and ready to go." He was so excited, I didn't even have the heart to tell him I planned to leave too. I think he knew.

He pulled back from his hug and looked down on me, smiling with warm affection. "I checked the water and oil on your car, she's good to go."

"Well, we better get moving before the hungry hordes expect a cooked breakfast." Mum laughed. "Miranda, I have left notes for Ringer for any household stuff, and our number is on the fridge."

Whoa, she wasn't kidding, there were Post-it Notes everywhere. On the fridge, the pantry, the remote controls, and the TV.

"Mum, I think Ringer will know how to operate a kettle," I said, flicking the bright yellow square.

"Well, just in case," she said, wrapping her arms around me. "We'll see you when we get back, be good."

Oh, dear Mum, always in denial.

"What? We're not saying goodbye to the boys?" Moira pouted, incredibly put out with no opportunity to view some man candy before she left.

"Nah, let 'em sleep," Dad said.

"Miranda, there is cereal, fruits, toast and juice for when they get up; make sure they have something to eat before they go."

Ha! I hoped there were Post-it Notes for that, because I hadn't planned to be here when they came up for breakfast.

I gladly herded them outside with the last of their bags to the ridiculously over-packed car; they always over packed. I glanced towards the darkened shearers' hut, grateful that there were no stirrings of life ... *yet*.

In true Dad style he had to warm the car up for what seemed like all eternity; I wrapped my arms around myself in the coolness seeing as the sun had still yet to pierce the sky. Each minute that passed my anxiety grew.

"Well, drive safely," I said in an attempt to hurry them along.

Mum wound down the passenger window. "Oh, I can't help but feel like I have forgotten something," she said, her expression troubled. "Miranda, can you make sure I turned the iron off?"

"I will."

"And can you make sure the boys don't make a mess in the kitchen?"

"Sure."

"Oh, and don't forget to tell Ringer about the pot plants; Steve, did you tell Ringer about the pot plants? I didn't put a Post-it on the pot plants."

I half expected her to ask me to check the attic for Macaulay Culkin; instead, I just bent down and pecked my mum on the cheek.

"Go! It will be fine." Mum seemed taken aback by my affection, a rare moment that hadn't been exchanged between us in some time. It was a nice way to part. Unlike my sister, whose elbows appeared propped from her open window in the back seat.

"Don't do anything I wouldn't do." She wiggled her eyes in a hubba-hubba motion. There was just enough time to whack her outside the head before Dad pulled into gear.

"Burn rubber, eat my dust," he chanted. It was something about Dad behind the wheel of a car that evoked terrible Dad humour.

I just laughed. "Have fun." I stood back, waving, finally breathing a sigh of relief watching them circle and exit out the long, dirt driveway. I cringed when Dad tooted, my eyes flicking towards the huts.

Still in darkness, good.

When Mum and Dad's car was no more than a speck in the distance, I bolted inside the house, through the kitchen and down the hall into my bedroom. I had all my stuff packed and ready by my door; I had been showered and dressed for hours, waiting for the perfect timing. And now with my family gone, never had there been better timing. I didn't have to suffer the endless questions of where I was going. What I was doing? I had no real clear plan, other than to go see my brother, Max, which was a start.

I dragged the biggest of my bags across the freshly polished floor before pausing at the door. My heart plummeted to my feet.

There was a light on at the shearers' huts.

Damn!

I was on borrowed time. I kicked the screen door open, pulling my bag out after me. Not wanting to put my back out, I dragged the big bulky weight behind me, leaving a very obvious drag mark in the dirt. I worked to open the boot and then, rather awkwardly, manoeuvred the bag into the car. My heart pounded, I closed the boot oh so gently before racing back into the house for my last bag. I dared not look behind me, to see what light was on now. I just had to move quickly and quietly and get the hell out of there.

I shouldered the last bag and managed a quick glance around the kitchen; even in my hurry to leave, a small spike of emotion rose in my chest. I clamped it down. I wasn't sure when I would see this kitchen again.

Don't be silly, Miranda. You have never been whimsical about home, don't start now.

I left the lights on inside and made my way out the door, ensuring it didn't slam behind me. I crept down the steps, rounding my way around towards the car. I could almost breathe a sigh of relief the closer I got to the driver's side.

Almost there.

But just as I closed the distance I was brought to a jarring halt.

"Forget something?"

I closed my eyes; the sound of his voice caused my stomach to twist. I dropped my bag; my shoulders slumped in resignation as I turned to face him.

Oh crap! Why did he have to look so good?

There he stood, hair all tousled, yet perfectly imperfect from his sleep. His trademark navy T and navy Levis made my heart race; he was so sexy. I didn't want the sight of him to affect me like this; it's only lust, I told myself. Don't be fooled into thinking it was anything else. But then I made a huge mistake.

I looked into his eyes.

His deep, soulful hazel eyes, that always seemed to alter in colour depending on how the elements hit them. And with the sun only just piercing the sky, his eyes were flecked with an intense lightness that made me want to forget everything and just walk to him. Hold on to him.

But then that familiar cocky smile tugged at the corner of his mouth and I slammed down my rampant hormones. My brows lowered; it was so much easier to hate him with that smile on his infuriating, yet highly kissable, mouth. I double blinked, snapping my traitorous mind away from such thoughts, and straightened my spine.

"You can't go," he said seriously.

His voice was warm like melted butter and I tried to ignore the butterflies that tickled my insides when he spoke. I defiantly lifted my chin, hoping my silence would urge him to elaborate.

If you ask me to stay, I will. I need you to ask. I don't know where I stand with you.

Ugh! Shut up, brain!

"You see, there's something I have been meaning to give you," he said, slowly taking a step forward, then another.

My chest tightened as he stood before me, so close I could smell the mint on his breath, and the intoxicating richness that was just him.

I swallowed. "Well, hurry up then," I snapped.

My urgency was more out of the danger of being completely drugged by his presence, folding to his words and charm. I could feel my resolve melting, and what was worse was the cocky gleam in his eyes that showed me he knew it.

"I just wanted to give you something to remember me by," he said, slowly closing the distance. I instinctively closed my eyes, waiting for his lips to brush against mine. So when he gently took my hand instead, and turned my palm upwards, I was surprised. I was distracted by the fact there was no kiss, and by the other fact he had placed something in my hand. I opened my eyes; I slowly lifted the object Ringer gave me. There, lying in the palm of my hand …

The door handle to my Mazda?

"Are you fucking kidding me?" I said, the incredulous words flying from my mouth.

Ringer mocked concern. "Oh no, you're disappointed?"

156

I shook my head, words failing me.

Ringer straightened. "Wait a minute, what did you think you were getting from me?" he asked, amusement lining his features.

My urge to throw the stupid handle as far as I could with rage was paramount, but seeing as I really did need it, I just crushed my fingers around it with a white-knuckled intensity instead, as I glared up at Ringer.

"Nothing! I want nothing from you," I said, turning to my car door. Ringer grabbed me by the arm and spun me around so fast my head was in a spin. He pushed me up against my car, all humour lost in the heat of his eyes as he cupped my face with his hands.

"Nothing? Really?" he asked calmly, his breath whispering across my lips; my chest heaved at the unexpectedness of his touch.

No, not nothing, never nothing, it would always be something with this infuriating man. He made me forget my demons by simply challenging me in ways my heart failed to understand, let alone my head. My head that was reeling from such a simple question.

"Say you want nothing from me, say it like you mean it, and I will walk away." His thumb skimmed teasingly over my bottom lip.

I looked at him for a long moment, loving him, hating him; around and around again my emotions spiralled in a mesh of insanity, till the final twist settled in my mind and with a resounding force.

I can't stay here. The guilt will eat me alive. My parents' censure is too overbearing. Ringer probably won't stay, anyway. Not for me. What am I thinking? There is no reason to stay.

I snapped my head to the side, refusing to look at him.

I sensed the moment his shoulders melted; he pressed his head against my temple staying there for a long moment, his fingers gripping me so fiercely I knew there would be marks indented in my flesh. The heat of his skin was like a furnace scolding me with his touch, and just when I thought I couldn't take anymore, he let me go, turned, and walked away.

Chapter Twenty-Nine
Ringer

Miranda's silence was the equivalent of punching a hole in my chest.

I wasn't prepared for that when I had made my way across the drive fresh from a series of back slaps and 'go get her' well wishes from the boys. Rejection had not been at the forefront of my mind.

I had been certain that even past the death-like stares, I could feel her body react to me. I should have just fucking kissed her instead of playing stupid games. *But, it seems I was wrong about her. Fuck.*

Her hair smelt like vanilla, her skin so soft under my hands, I didn't want to let her go. I wanted to grasp her so tightly and never *not* know what it felt like to touch her skin. To have her by my side. I savoured the memories of her, before working up enough courage. I finally broke away.

Walking a resolute line back to the huts, I was determined to pass them as far as I could go, to save listening to the sounds of her beat-up Mazda, to hum and moan out of my life, and into the distance. *Away.* From. Me.

But only a few steps into my journey, I felt the sudden thud of something hitting me between the shoulder blades. I turned around, my eyes dipping to where something had fallen.

What the?

My incredulous eyes lifted to where Miranda was standing by her car. From the very vantage point she had just turfed the door handle at me. I bent down to pick it up, examining it with a questioning look her way.

Tears welled in her eyes; she looked mad as hell. I didn't know whether I should comfort her or run.

She shook her head. "Why can't I just hate you?" she bit out in a sob.

My heart raced as I slowly stood. "Well, I would like to think it's because I am so irresistible?"

Miranda's watery eyes looked up at me as I moved to stand within touching distance. "You're an idiot," she said.

I smiled; somehow the insult was like music to my ears. "They say opposites attract."

Miranda sniffed. "So what does that make me?"

"A genius."

Miranda rolled her eyes.

"Any girl who could nearly run me over, flip me off, tell me to eff off, drench me in cold water, stomp on my foot, push me in a dam, rip my *favourite* jeans, make me carry her handbag, attack me in my sleep, force me to hide under a car ... and yet, still manages to make me fall in love with her?"

I was met by a catatonic stare of disbelief, and then like some form of magic, as my words slowly sunk in, a small smile tugged at the corner of her mouth.

"Well, I must be a genius then," she said.

This time with no gimmick, I took her hand, laced my fingers with hers. "You're more than that. You're the most beautiful, infuriating person I have ever met in my life, and you may not want anything from me, but I want everything from you."

Miranda shook her head ever so slightly. She sobered and said on a whisper, "But I have nothing to give."

I pulled her into my arms. Only when her hands fisted into my shirt did I let the sensation of hope flood through me. I cupped her chin to lift her face to mine. "You're more than enough." And before she could argue the fact, I silenced her with a kiss, robbing her of all breath until she melted in my arms.

The sound of catcalls and cheers sounded from the shearers' huts. There stood our own little personal cheer squad; Miranda broke our kiss, laughing and blushing crimson.

"About bloody time." Sean jumped off the deck and strode towards the house. "Who knew *The Bold and the Beautiful* was alive and well in Ballan."

Stan poked his head out from one of the rooms. "Is it over?"

"Yes," threw Chris over his shoulder.

"Oh, thank God, I'm starving." He followed the others down the steps.

With each passing mate there was a hard slap on the back, Chris's the hardest of them all. "Hurry up, lover boy; I like my eggs sunny side up." He winked at Miranda.

Miranda raised her brows at me. "They are leaving, right?"

I sighed. "Even if I have to open every bloody gate myself."

Epilogue
Ringer
Three weeks later

The irony was not lost on me, as I stood outside the women's changing cubicle in Onslow's only women's fashion boutique.

Oh, how my life had changed.

Miranda's head poked through the opening of the curtain. "Ringer, can you grab me a navy of the same, please?"

Off I would go without a care in the world, skimming the clothes racks. I could see the smug, knowing eyes of the shop assistant lady watching me, but I didn't care. Against my better judgement, I was happy; even though the idea had been to merely drop in to replace the cardigan I admittedly ruined back in Ballan, it had escalated into a fashion parade. Not that I minded, having permission to run your eyes over your girlfriend's attire was a bonus; I mean, you had to look at the bright side. The curtains flung back and Miranda stepped out wearing a red knee-length, figure-hugging dress; she moved from side to side in the mirror.

I cleared my throat, trying to distract myself from my devilish thoughts. "So when do Steve and Penny hit town?"

"Tonight; they're picking Moira up from her girlfriend's house on the way."

"Look out Onslow." I laughed.

Miranda sighed. "I can't wait to see them." Biting her bottom lip in deep thought, she studied her reflection. "What do you think?"

I stood behind her, meeting her eyes in the mirror. "I think we need to get out of here so I can show you what I think."

Miranda's blush almost matched her dress.

We left Carters, with bags hooked over both of our wrists. Miranda pulled me up short. "Thank you," she said, brushing her lips against mine.

I looked down into her greeny-blue eyes that sparkled with appreciation.

Christ, I was a goner.

"RINGO JAMES?"

My blood ran cold; paused mid-step, I slowly turned around, only to be faced with a living nightmare.

Sean Murphy swaggering down the street. "I thought it was you." His eyes flicked to our bags. "What are you two up to?"

"Oh, we just smashed Carters." Miranda held up her bags with glee.

"You don't say?" Sean's brows rose.

I discreetly mouthed: *fuck off*.

I straightened, feigning innocence, when Miranda turned to me. "Ringer said it was the place to go."

"It's the only place to go," I mumbled under my breath. At least Mrs C didn't set us up with an account.

"Well, don't let me stop you." Sean slapped me on the shoulder. "Don't forget to take your woman to Total Bliss for a beauty treatment." He flashed a knowing smile.

I couldn't help but smirk as I watched the smug bastard walk across the road.

Miranda elbowed me. "What's wrong?"

I tore my eyes away from Sean's retreating back to face her questioning eyes.

I could see now why my friends' lives had changed so dramatically as a result of having the love of a good woman. Miranda hadn't told me she loved me, but I know she does. She shows me with her body, but those eyes tell me the real story.

"In all honesty?"

She nodded, worry etching her brow.

I kissed the worry lines, feeling them melt and smoothen under my lips; drawing back I looked earnestly into her beautiful face and smiled.

"Absolutely nothing."

If love is friendship set on fire, wait till you read Adam and Ellie's story.

You see there's this boy.

He makes me smile, forces me to listen, serenades me out of tune and keeps me sane, all the while driving me insane. He's really talented like that. But for the first time in since, well, forever, things are about to change. The question is, how much am I willing to lose in order to potentially have it all?

Acknowledgements

Much love to my amazing husband, Mick, for being the beautiful part of my reality and supporting me in all I do; I know it's not easy but I wouldn't want to share it with anyone else.

I am blessed with such a talented hard-working team; these ladies always go above and beyond for me. A special thanks to: Sascha Craig, Marion Archer, Anita Saunders and Keary Taylor.

Many thanks to my formatters Karen Phillips, Emily Mah Tippetts.

Always grateful for the love and support of my friends and family, especially Mum, Kevin, Dad, Daniel and Leanne.

My fellow authors for their inspiration, support and friendship: Frankie Rose, Jessica Roscoe, Lilliana Anderson, Keary Taylor. I adore you ladies and would be truly lost without our daily chats.

To my fierce 'Team Duggan' warriors, for your unwavering support and enthusiasm. For always spreading the word and fighting the good fight to help put the *Summer Series* out there for the masses. I feel incredibly privileged to have each and every one of you on my team and in my life – thank you.

A special thank you to Marion Archer from Making Manuscripts. For being the most lovely, helpful editor any author could ever hope for. I cannot thank you enough for your support and guidance, but most of all your friendship. You will never know how you have changed my life as a writer; you give me the freedom and time with your amazing turnovers and attention to detail. I feel truly blessed to have found you. (Love you, Bette.)

To all the bloggers, reviewers, readers who have enjoyed and shared the *Summer Series*. For taking something away from the story, for loving and embracing the characters. In a world that is often dark enough, it has been an absolute pleasure injecting it with a bit of sunshine.

About the Author

C.J Duggan is a Number One Best Selling Australian Author who lives with her husband in a rural border town of New South Wales, Australia. When she isn't writing books about swoony boys and 90s pop culture you will find her renovating her hundred-year-old Victorian homestead or annoying her local travel agent for a quote to escape the chaos.

The Boys of Summer is Book One in her highly successful, Mature Young Adult Romance Series.

*While each title can be read as a stand-alone story, you will likely enjoy the journey with these characters from the beginning.

The 'Summer Series'
The Boys of Summer (December 2012)
An Endless Summer (July 2013)
That One Summer (December 2013)
Ringer (March 2014)
Forever Summer (July 2014)

Follow C.J on her website: www.cjdugganbooks.com
Sign up for C.J's newsletter.

This paperback interior was designed and formatted by

www.emtippettsbookdesigns.com

Artisan interiors for discerning authors and publishers.

Iris Seidenstricker

Saving My Skin

BoD - Books on Demand

Iris Seidenstricker

Saving My skin

My Way to Cure Atopic Eczema
with the Simplest Method
in the World

BoD - Books on Demand

All information in this book has been researched and compiled by the author with the greatest care. Nevertheless, errors cannot be completely ruled out. Please note that this book is not a self-help guide but personal experience report. The author recommends in any case the visit of a dermatologist, a physician or an experienced alternative practitioner and excludes any liability for health and personal injuries.

Original Edition 2017
1st edition 2020
www.bod.de
The work is protected by copyright.
We reserve the right to make use of all or parts thereof.
© 2020 Iris Seidenstricker
www.seidenstricker-coaching.de
Title of the original edition: „Ich bin dann mal die Haut retten. Mein Weg aus der Neurodermitis mit der einfachsten Methode der Welt".
Cover picture: Shutterstock
Cover design and typesetting: Iris Seidenstricker
Production and publishing: BoD – Books on Demand, Norderstedt, Germany
Printed in Germany - ISBN 978-3-750499362

Contents

There's a Life Without Atopic Eczema

Ways are created by walking them.
Franz Kafka

I wake up, a quick check: nothing burns, nothing itches. Not a single spot on my body that feels wet or hot. The fingers don't stick together, I can bend them without the skin tearing with nasty pain.

Through the open window the fresh morning air blows cool into my face. What a great, wonderful start to the day!

Atopic eczema—also known as atopic dermatitis—is a long-term type of inflammation of the skin. It is an agonizing, stressful illness, often difficult to bear and it is an incurable condition. But writing a book about the fact that after 45 years of living with this disease I now feel very comfortable in my skin? What for?

There's already so much literature on this subject. And you can exchange ideas in internet forums or on special platforms about how to live with atopic eczema, the most common chronic skin condition worldwide. And how it can be treated.

In Germany, Austria and Switzerland it is assumed that 10 to 20 percent of the children and two to four percent of the adults are affected. In the USA, 13 percent of all children have atopic eczema. According to recent studies already seven to ten percent of the adult population suffers from it.

In the past 60 years, the number of cases of this illness in the industrialized countries is said to have quadrupled and, according to forecasts, they will continue to increase in the future. Hardly any other disease shows this rate of increase. However, it is not entirely clear whether there are actually more cases of atopic eczema than before or whether it is simply diagnosed more often because the perception of doctors and patients has changed. Today atopic eczema is taken very seriously and people with this symptom seek hope, help and healing both in conventional medicine and in alternative healing methods. As a result, they are being discovered increasingly and actively courted by the pharmaceutical and cosmetics industries.

Meanwhile, pharmacies and drugstores offer a wide range of creams, ointments and lotions for the special skin needs for sufferers of atopic eczema. According to a consistent opinion of doctors and scientists, consistent, permanent and daily care with everything that increases the fat and moisture content of the skin is the be-all and end-all for atopic eczema.

When I meet someone after a long time, I often hear that I look so different, even more relaxed and—how beautiful—so young …

New hairdo? New job? Or maybe a new love?

Neither.

But it's true, I look different. When I tell them what I did, they are stunned. And they can't believe that the mere decision to omit all the creams from one moment to the next is one of the essential reasons for my relaxed appearance.

My skin, which had been severely inflamed for decades and marked by atopic eczema, was able to perform the miracle of complete regenerating out of itself within a few months.

Zero Ointment, Zero Cream

I, who learned from an early age to "cream, cream, cream" my skin to keep itching and dermatitis relapses at bay, have not used any skin care at all since four years now. My face, my neck and my hands, where the atopic eczema has always been the strongest, are very happy and thank me with a healthy and stable skin.

"Have you gone completely mad?" I'm sure many dermatologists would have said if I had told them about my project "zero ointment".

"Your skin produces less sebum than a healthy one and also suffers from a lack of certain fatty substances. The binding of water is reduced and perspiration is likely to be reduced. All these factors lead to a disrupted skin barrier, which makes your skin dry and more susceptible to infection and more permeable to pollutants and allergens. If you want to avoid this, you have cream your skin with fat-containing ointments. This is the only way to improve the protection of your skin".

The dermatologist would think for a moment and then would say with utter conviction: "And creaming, you can truly believe me, is still the very best method to prevent relapses."

I know all of it. Not to cream completely contradicts what the medical, cosmetic and pharmaceutical industries recommend for the protection and care of the affected and irritated eczema skin. Not to mention that the care for your own skin is good for body and soul. Ever since my childhood I have therefore also supplied myself uninterruptedly with creams and fat ointments. Until my suffering for more than ten years became so unbearable despite constant creaming that I had to look for another way to save my skin. Paradoxically I finally found it in total ointment and cream abstinence.

Courage, Patience and Trust

For as simple as my ointment-free way sounds and as little as it costs—nothing at all in fact in contrast to many other atopic eczema therapies—it was not easy. On the contrary: it was stony and laborious. I needed infinite courage, patience, hope and trust to hold this path by and go to the end.

Courage, because I didn't know if this way would really lead me to the healing of my skin. Hope, because I had already tried so much to heal or at least alleviate atopic eczema, and nothing helped in the long run. Patience, because it only went forward in tiny steps, which often felt as if nothing would change or as if everything would get even worse: itching, new heat, smouldering. And I needed the trust that my body has powerful and extremely effective self-healing powers and that these would also be active after all. And above all I needed people. Who also believed in this way and gave me their confidence when mine just faded away.

I can only talk here about my own experience with my own inflamed skin, of what helped me and what didn't. That doesn't mean it has to be the same for others. How often did I run excitedly to the nearest pharmacy to get the wonder ointment XY. Because someone in an Internet forum passionately reported to have finally found the one and only solution for his or her atopic eczema. Most of the time my skin burned already at the first contact with the new ointment or it has itched unbearably. Having lost another hope, I set out again in search of the miracle product, the true "Holy Grail", which would finally give me a healthy skin.

Captive of the Skin

Atopic eczema is a disease that can not only rob your strength entirely, but also your self-confidence and, again and again, your joy of life.

Atopic eczema has shaped or influenced my development, my career decisions and my relationships. It influenced my daily routines it was the reason for my capriciousness. I have shunned people, said goodbye to them when the others were still celebrating or were just beginning to do so. And my appointments were made long in advance, hoping that the skin would calm down in the meantime. Of course this rarely happened. At the last moment I often cancelled the appointment because I didn't want to show myself. Almost my whole life I felt unwell and sick in my skin, unsightly and unsafe. It was a boundary that separated me from others and made me lonely. Because the skin locked me in a prison and put me under strict "skin arrest" over and over again.

During a lecture in a skin clinic, a dermatologist spoke about the fact that despite a skin disease the joy of life should be maintained. "Above all," he appealed to us chronic eczema patients, psoriatic and allergy sufferers in the audience, "don't withdraw. Mingle with people, take part in social life. Enjoy!"

I got angry. Someone with healthy skin—at least that's what he looked like—called on people who were marked by their sick skin to take life easy.

I've never liked advice. But advice from someone who obviously had no idea what sort of agony and massive restriction atopic eczema can mean was completely off the mark. How can you enjoy life with a skin that you constantly want to rip off your body to free yourself from it?

I know people with atopic eczema who, when they come home from work, first scratch themselves bloody with a brush or shower with almost boiling water. Because the pain of the injured skin or hot water numbs for a short time the unbearable itching that feels like a thousand mosquitoes biting at the same time.

How can you have a desire for people and community when your own skin sticks to your face like a thick, hot, mask of dried mud and you have neither the strength to look at yourself nor the strength to endure the looks of others?

"Have you ever had a really heavy sunburn? In your face, too?" was my standard question when someone actually wanted to know what atopic eczema felt like. Most of them had experience with sunburns. "Okay" I said then, "and you're sitting in the sauna and can't get out. You are locked in the sultry heat, it gets hotter and hotter, your skin burns and you don't know when the door will open again. That's exactly how my face feels now."

I wouldn't be upset about the clinic doctor's call today. On the contrary, I agree with him. Because even if I'm not well, that doesn't mean that I have to sink into suffering and make my life completely dependent on atopic eczema. That is what I was doing for years. Work, relationships, hobbies, eating, sleeping—I subordinated everything to the disease and yet tried to remain efficient and functional. Because I wanted a "normal" life. And this meant an almost constant struggle.

12

In 1891 the French dermatologists Louis Brocq and Lucien Jacquet suspected a connection between chronic eczema and mental processing and called it "neurodermatitis".

In the 1930s a connection between neurodermatitis and allergies was established and the term "atopic dermatitis" or "atopic eczema" was added as a new technical term.

Atopic eczema manifests itself through inflammatory skin changes in the form of eczema, severe itching and red, swollen skin areas. The skin is dry and sensitive, but the appearance of atopic eczema can vary strongly from person to person. Why someone suffers from atopic eczema has not yet been found out exactly. Scientists have identified genes that might have something to do with it. But it is not the genetic material alone—atopic eczema also occurs without hereditary predisposition. It is therefore not a hereditary disease, but nevertheless a hereditary tendency to fall ill with these symptoms.

It is now assumed that psychological factors and environmental influences provoke the outbreak of atopic eczema. External factors are allergens such as pollen, animal hair, the house dust mite or food components, diet, the climate or mechanical stimuli.

As with all illnesses, the psyche plays a decisive role: depending on the condition you are in and how you cope with stress and the strain of the illness, atopic eczema can improve or worsen. More about this in chapter 4.

Body and Mind

"We can never get out of sadness if we constantly feel our pulse," Martin Luther recognized 500 years ago. And puts into words what neuroscientists—the researchers who deal with the structure and function of the nervous system and the brain—can impressively prove with their research: body and mind are one unit. We are what we think we are. We think what we feel. And we feel what we are.

> *If I am constantly concerned with my skin, with how it tortures and impairs me, then all my feelings and thoughts will focus only around my skin and the impairments I feel through it. Doing so I just make bigger and stronger what bothers me.*

Of course, I can't feel well with acutely inflamed skin. Inflammation robs you of vitality, you are tired, cold or perhaps you feel like having a fever. You're just sick. Then to expect only what you want to expect of yourself and otherwise to provide a space of retreat and protection is part of the care you can and should do for yourself during an eczema episode.

But there are also phases of the disease that makes it possible to participate in life. Which, however, requires a decision. Which you can meet against the disease—"I'm going out the way I am now"—or in favor of the sickness—"I don't see any other way and continue to suffer".

Atopic eczema is a joker for all the things, appointments and tasks you would like to spare yourself. You always have an excuse. And that is just one of the many advantages it offers.

Children, in particular, draw attention from it, and adults may be able to take a rest only because of their inflamed skin. You have been in need of rest and recreation for a long time but you never admitted it. Or others finally show consideration for you, which they would not do without the disease. And if you only have to take care of your skin, there is neither time nor energy left for all the other small and big daily topics and problems that are also there. But who could blame you?

When I looked at the benefits of atopic eczema because I began taking on a new perspective, I understood for the first time what kind of advantage I had taken from it.

Learning from Atopic Eczema

The gain from illness is a tremendous power. You have to force yourself to give it up. I had to learn a tremendous amount over the years to take away from atopic eczema the importance it had had for most of my life. Strategies in dealing with stress, for example. Or to listen more to my gut.

I had to learn to accept, to value and to support myself. And finally I had to find the form of nourishment that is equally good for my soul and my body. But above all, I had to understand that no matter what I look like, I can trust people.

I have always found this to be quite a challenge, because fears and experiences inherited from our ancestors also play a role here. In early cultures people kept away from people with skin anomalies and deliberately excluded them. It was like a death sentence to them, because by themselves, far away from the clan, survival was hardly possible. Perhaps this primal fear of rejection, which is deeply anchored in our subconscious, prevented me from showing myself to people.

Today I experience daily how my feelings and thoughts guide my life. And how important joy, gratitude and inner peace are for my health and therefore also for the condition of my skin. However, I cannot afford to wait for the good feelings to fall into my lap. If I want to feel comfortable, I have to choose it. And then do something to get this feeling.

Even very small things make my positive feelings flow and thus strengthen and balance my immune and hormone systems. Gratitude for example. All kinds of things like bird chirping in the morning, the cool air on my skin, the person of my life at my side, the delicious breakfast. For my work, which I can shape with my ideas, my creativity and according to my schedule. Joy is part of it, laughter, enjoyment and relaxation. As well as to have people around me and to enjoy the precious time I can spend alone with myself.

I have learned slowly and by many painful setbacks that health and the certainty to feel well in my skin are not static states, which from now on—after so many years finally reached—I can have for eternity. That's always been my vision. How I would have loved to have had the very last flare up of atopic eczema once and for all. But it wasn't like that and it doesn't work like that.

Fact is I've never felt better about my skin than today. But can I know what the future holds? The thought of the future has always worried me in the past. Today I agree that I have no idea what's coming. Because in the meantime I am confident that I will be able to cope well with all the tasks and challenges that life will give me.

I have come to understand and accept that my skin will always respond to feelings, to the influences of the surroundings and to what is happening in my life. And above all the way I deal with myself. Just as I sometimes have a cold or a headache, drink too much coffee, have too much chocolate or too little rest, my skin is redder or drier, my finger itches or there is a scaly spot on my chin. But that's nothing compared to the time when atopic eczema dominated my life.

I feel healthy today. In the same sense as the World Health Organization (WHO) defines health: "Health is a state of complete physical, mental and social well-being and is not merely the absence of disease or infirmity."

Healthy Skin

45 years of atopic eczema. The work on this book has allowed me to relive all the gravity and tragedy of the last decades. How much strength it took me to endure the atopic eczema again and again. And even more, because I rejected and hated it. And I wished for nothing more than that it would finally disappear.

> *My friend Ferdinand, a teacher, told me about one of his former pupils who had severe atopic eczema from an early age. He bravely fought his way through his school days, which were interrupted by many hospital stays. Shortly before the end of his studies he took his own life. Although I had not known this young man, I was shocked by the news of his death. Because I know how much energy everyday life with atopic eczema costs, how unhappy and desperate you are again and again and how hopeless everything often seems to you.*

"Put up with it," a doctor told me, "that you will be dealing with atopic eczema all your life. If things go well and you take good care of your skin, you can relieve the symptoms. Then you have already achieved a great deal. But there is no cure."

Oh no, there is a cure! At least for me without any skin care at all. Or just because of the renunciation of the daily repeated application of ointments and creams. Right there, my atopic eczema stopped. Healthy skin is no longer a rare exception, it is my daily life now. And every day an amazing wonder for me.

I still experience my "new" skin as an unforeseen redemption, I am certainly relieved at least a hundred times a day that nothing is hot, nothing wets, burns, and my face has clear contours. Because there are no inflammations that lead to swelling. Countless times during the day I indulge in the happiness that my skin feels like "nothing", that I enjoy fresh water on it, I go outside and come back inside without feeling temperature differences and itching and looking in the mirror doesn't cost me any effort anymore. On the contrary: I'm happy about what I see!

Of course, the small and big challenges of my life are still there, and new ones are constantly being added. In fact, dealing with a skin that is no longer a "problem skin" is also one. But now I am in a position to tackle and master them without the existential burden of atopic eczema. I am always happy about that and I am deeply grateful for this.

And this is exactly why there is this book. Because I would like to encourage all those who suffer from atopic eczema to continue to search for their own way and not to give up hope that one day you will feel good again in your skin and in your life. Even if it is often very difficult or sometimes even seems impossible—in the images and feelings we connect with our hope, a secret and powerful energy flows and pushes us step by step towards our goal.

As different as we all are, as different and intertwined are the ways that lead there. Some atopic eczema sufferers have been healed by faith in their God. Others swear to raw food and don't eat grain. Yet others benefit from eating cooked meals according to the teachings of Traditional Chinese Medicine—they predominantly eat warm meals with cooked grain. All ways work, all have already contributed to making people feel better or even get healed. But probably there is no way that works for all.

Ointment Abstinence—The Decisive Step

I know from my own experience that the constructive and untiring efforts to tackle atopic dermatitis always open up new perspectives that move us forward. By trying interesting suggestions and plausible therapies, you get to know yourself in such a thorough way as it would otherwise hardly be possible.

Some things may have to be tried several times because the body reacts differently in each phase of life. And the willingness to follow a certain way is sometimes greater or smaller, depending on life situation and healing progress. It took me three attempts to not cream until I was really ready to follow the strategy "zero ointment" and to throw away all the ointment tubes and cream pots I had stowed into the box in the attic.

This step was the decisive one to save my skin. The suitable nutrition, the loving contact with my body, constructive, good thoughts and effective stress management were and still are also part of it. Because recovery is always a holistic, ongoing process and in my opinion you can only succeed with it if all aspects of life are included.

My journey to healthy skin, the feeling of well-being in my body and the joy of my life was a decade-long search with highs and lows, full of setbacks, hope, disappointments and suffering. Until I finally discovered the hidden, narrow and barely walked on way of total ointment and cream abstinence.

In the following chapters I will tell you about this way and the many paths that all led me a little further to my feel-good skin.

P.S.
Please excuse the sometimes somewhat bumpy translation. I translated "Saving My Skin" myself with my non-professional knowledge of the English language as best as I could.

Chapter 1

Survival. Somehow.

External crises are the opportunity
to pause and become aware.
Viktor E. Frankl

My face is glowing. My skin tightens and burns, my left eye feels swollen. In the right cheek pulsates a sharp pain, sticky-wet warmth crawls up my neck. The bedroom window is wide open and I can hear the wind in the trees. But I don't feel the cool morning air. Just the sultry heat on my face.

Is it the toner dust? Or the printer's ozone? I was in the copy room a lot yesterday. Paper jam, toner empty, new toner cartridge inserted, waiting for printouts.

Or was it the tomatoes in the sauce for lunch? Or maybe the raisins in the salad? I hadn't eaten any for years and I avoid grapes consistently. How stupid to eat raisins with this skin condition. Or maybe I should finally do without my breakfast apple. Too much fruit acid …

The right calf is on fire, it feels like bloody scratches. And there's that diabolical itch in the little finger again. I rub until the skin surface is rubbed down and lymph flows. A hot, sharp pain. But at least the itching is gone. My sultry neck's on fire, too. I'm palpating it, the big scab is gone. I must have scratched it up at night. The gloves I've been wearing again at night are lying somewhere in my bed. They're no good either, they make it even easier to rub the skin down to the raw flesh.

I'm tired to death, my body feels heavy and leaden. It's only three thirty in the morning. I could still lie in bed. But I have an appointment at 9 o'clock, I have to get up. I need the time to physically and mentally prepare myself to go among people today with all the visible and invisible misery of atopic eczema.

I reach for the fatty ointment on the bedside table, smear the skin around my mouth and force myself out of bed. I sneak past the large corridor mirror into the bathroom without looking at me. The light is off, the gleam of dawn is bright enough to find toothbrush and toothpaste. I don't want to see myself in the mirror. How I feel is enough to know what I look like.

For months now I have been living again with dim light and without mirrors. Like countless times before in my life.

> *Every mirror is different. Some are soft, some are*
> *hard. Some a little blind. Some sharp and ruthless.*
> *A lot of people don't even notice the difference. I*
> *recognize immediately those who mean well with me.*
> *They are those who do not mercilessly show every*
> *redness, every crack or scratch and every swelling.*
> *Mirrors can be an elixir of life, but they can also kill*
> *the courage to live. If I want to survive, I have to*
> *know and to use the "merciful" mirrors. And even*
> *those I have to avoid every now and then.*

A look at the alarm clock. Almost four hours to deadline. Perhaps the skin will calm down a little before then.

I wash my face carefully. The water bites in the rubbed areas. I cool the left eye with a washcloth, which I touch in a way that the damaged fingers do not come into contact with water. Somehow it penetrates into the injuries, nevertheless.

Taking a shower? No way. I do not want to endure water in the many cracks and wounds of my injured skin.

As a child I was put in bathtubs with sea salt during my holidays on the North Sea island of Borkum. I screamed my head off and refused to get back in those creepy tubs. How should children at all understand why they should suffer the torture of salt water in addition to their already so painful skin? "It'll be over in a minute," the adults always said. That was right, the burning and biting passed, the atopic eczema doesn't.

I cream the skin around the mouth again. The feeling of tension eases a little, the heat on the face increases. With my head bowed I leave the bathroom. This is the safest way to escape an accidental glance into the hall mirror.

A short meditation on the living room carpet. Pray that the skin cools down, that by nine o'clock I won't feel it at all. That I have an easier, more relaxed day today. That a miracle would happen and I would not look so terrible at the meeting between all the other healthy looking people. Not so red anymore, so swollen, not so inflamed and so blotchy.

Our skin is our largest and most versatile organ. It releases warmth and fluid, with it we perceive touch, feel if it is warm or cold, whether something feels good, bad or painful.

In addition, our skin protects our entire body and draws the line between inside and outside. Which also makes it a contact organ with other people. Tender touches, abuse and pain hit it first.

With our skin on our face and body we also show ourselves to others. It reveals our inner condition, whether we are excited or stressed, happy, worried or afraid. This has to do with the fact that the skin and the central nervous system have the same developmental origin—both are formed in humans from the same predispositions.

In our language now it becomes visible how much the skin reflects our feelings. We blush with shame or excitement and fade when we are scared and afraid. Fear makes us sweat on our foreheads, our whole bodies shudder and we get goose bumps.

Who is insensitive, has a "thick skin", those who are sensitive and delicate have a "thin skin". Something is "no skin off of our nose" or we "escape by the skin of our teeth."

And sometimes we have to save our skin for that.

I'll light a candle in the kitchen, the perfect light for me. I get an ice pad, put it in the washcloth and hold it carefully against the thick eye.

My gaze falls on the cream pack that someone had put on my computer keyboard without comment yesterday when I was not at my desk. An expensive cosmetic organic cream, "skin soothing". I asked my colleagues if one of them had put it there. They shook their heads. Later I went to Sabine, who also suffers from atopic eczema. "How encroaching" she indignantly said. "I would never dare to do such a thing."

I nodded. But I don't know what to make of it. Did someone *really* see me? Is it compassionate? Nice? Or is it just the inability to recognize personal boundaries?

I'll put the cream away. No experiments today.

An apple, a banana and porridge. Add a pot of hot water. I haven't had coffee for a long time, because I read that coffee is supposed to irritate the vegetative nervous system. My body and my entire system are irritated anyway, they don't need any more excitement.

My scalp itches. I scrape and dandruff falls to the floor. In the past the scalp skin was rarely affected and I was very happy about it—at least no dandruff in my hair and on my clothes. But that had been once …

Actually, I wanted to go to the hairdresser tonight.
I'll cancel the appointment. For the third time. The
way I look, I cannot bear to sit in the light in front of
a mirror, to be looked at and not be able to escape
my reflection.

I eat the porridge with my right hand, the left one holds the washcloth against the eye. The cracks in my face burn, my mouth hurts with the smallest movement.

I wonder what someone would think who could see me here in the candlelight at the kitchen table, with a washcloth, a thick eye and a scratched face. I remember what the brother of Natalie, a girl I met many years ago in a clinic where she was also treated for atopic eczema, said to her when she was a teenager: "You could play in the movie 'Ben Hur'. In the valley of the lepers."

In former cultures, lepers had to live apart from society. Maybe that's where my diffuse fear of people comes from. That I'm rejected by them because of my difficult appearance and my skin. I feel as excluded as the lepers had been. I feel like living in a valley, far away from the others with the beautiful, pale, cool skin. And a carefree life.

When I get dressed, my legs burn. I bend down and see only now the broad and long scratches at the calves. It's as if a predator had pulled its claws along it. But it was only my toes that gave in to the nightly itching without restraint. I take a deep breath and disinfect the scratches with pure alcohol.

The alcohol will dry out the skin even more, I know that of course. But it's better to bear the burning and kill the bacteria than to have wounds that get infected. In that case I would have to endure the itching still longer, of course.

As a child, when I couldn't stand the itching any longer, I held my breath and poured Grandma's Mountain pine spirit on the scratched skin. I could have screamed. But I clenched my teeth because I knew the terrible pain would soon pass. And with it the even more horrible itching also.

Whenever I was with others, I always pay attention to their skin first. Healthy skin almost makes me jealous. Why must I of all people have a disease that is so visible? Why is it so easy for others? Why is it so natural for them to get up in the morning, wash, feel good and start the day full of energy? What a luxury to complain about one or even three pimples!

Half past six in the morning. I don't have to leave until eight thirty. I am endlessly tired and want to go back to bed, fall asleep and not feel anything anymore. But I am not allowed to lie down now, so that at least the eyes get a little bit better. Lying down again won't work for the better. The body must be moved or straightened so that the water responsible for the swelling can flow out of the body. I slept sitting up at night so that I don't look so puffy in the morning.

I'm thinking of Kathrin, whom I also met in a clinic. She had had atopic eczema only since adulthood, it came completely out of the blue and showed itself in massive form on her face. Whoever Kathrin met in the hallway, in the dining room or in the care room, she immediately pulled a photo out of her pocket and said "Look at that! That's how I really look!"

In the bedroom I stand in front of the open and full wardrobe. What to wear? I need a business look, but the white blouses don't work. The contrast with my blotchy face is too big. I'm not comfortable in white with my injured skin anyway. Not to mention that the collar immediately becomes bloody.

Turtlenecks don't work either. In the narrowness the neck becomes even warmer, the itching stronger and the scabby areas rub up.

I need something with a big neckline. Which is also difficult because you can see the scratched neck so clearly.

I search a little more and finally choose a dark blue blazer. Not ideal because of the dandruff either, but it's appropriate for the occasion. Plus a blue plaid blouse and my favourite jeans.

Maybe the new elegant sweater of blackberry color, too?

I'll take it off the chair. A really great color, just perfect with the blouse. But the material? I'm not sure. Virgin sheep's wool and wool in general are a problem for many atopic dermatitis sufferers, but not for me. But today this wool blend doesn't feel good.

Is it the color? Or the wool? Rather unlikely, I also have the sweater in dark blue and I like it. However, a sales lady told me some time ago that manufacturers change suppliers every now and then. There could also be other materials in the fabrics or wool blends, although exactly the same composition is in the label. This sweater probably originates from such a production. I'll hang it back over the chair again. No experiments today.

My skin feels unbearably tense. I grease again with my fat ointment. It doesn't really help. In the meantime I even have the feeling that the constant creaming of fat worsens the inflammation even more. But I can't stand other creams and something fatty has to get on my skin. Otherwise the never pausing tension, burning and itching will drive me crazy.

It's getting me down to looking like this. So inflamed and attacked. So unappetizing and unattractive. Ugly. That's not supposed to be my face, it's a distortion, a mask.

Some people ignore what I look like. Some react irritated, some just want to be nice and talk to me about it.

"You're not doing too well again, do you?" a boss once said compassionately. I just nodded and left the room as quickly as possible because I could hardly hold back the tears. He caught me at my sorest spot.

"But it's not disfiguring with you," a colleague said, and it was meant to sound encouraging. No, it's not? I do feel disfigured. I'm always afraid of being rejected because of my looks and my skin. In every contact there is the danger of getting hurt even more than I already am.

I am tired of having to endure myself, tired of constantly thinking about whether I want to expose myself to the gaze of others or whether someone will refer to my skin. I'm physically tired from the inflammation. I want to be alone, not to see anyone. And I don't want anyone to see me.

Seven thirty. I have to get out in an hour. I don't know how to survive the day with all the appointments. But I've always somehow managed it. And it has also become evening again and again. I'm already longing to finally close the door behind me and be alone in the shelter of my dimly lit apartment. Where I can hope anew for an easier next day.

The focus of the classical treatment of atopic eczema with orthodox medical methods is the therapy of the skin.

Applying care products several times a day should stabilize the skin's barrier function in order to reduce its sensitivity to irritations and allergen penetration. A variety of ointments, creams and lotions are available for this purpose, which are applied differently depending on the type and the severity of the symptoms. Medical oil baths or oil showers are another possibility to care for the skin. In the acute phase, in addition to the traditional treatment with topical steroid ointments, warm or cold compresses with black tea, healing clay and other anti-inflammatory active ingredients such as oak bark or potassium permanganate are frequently used.

Not You!

"Not you," my teacher said in gym class at elementary school, holding me back by my shoulder as I tried to climb up the wall bars.

"Why not?" I asked surprised.

She pointed to my scratched and scabbed hollows of the knees. "We don't want anything to tear there."

"Nothing will happen," I said defiantly, shaking off her hand and immediately climbing up the wall bars.

Apart from the fact that the atopic eczema was often visible, it did not yet shape my entire experience as a child. And I didn't let it restrict my freedom of movement either. The skin was bad at sometimes long periods of time, but then it was healthy again for a while. When it was itchy, I scratched, my mother creamed me with ointments or smeared medical tar on the acute spots. Mostly arms, legs and neck were affected, the face only rarely. Almost always I was scratching somewhere. "Don't scratch," the adults said, but I ignored it. Itching and scratching belonged together and were something quite normal for me.

That I was teased by other kids about my skin rarely happened. Once upon a time there was the helpless attempt of my playfellow Michael, who, when he was angry with me, tried to annoy me with "Pimple-Lisa". In fact, I really didn't have a single pimple. But it still bothered me. I complained to my mother about Michael right away. She gave me the advice to simply give him a suitable answer next time.

"And what could that be?" I asked helplessly.

"For example, he doesn't always smell like a perfumery."
Michael still sometimes peed his pants.
A few hours later, however, he and I drove our cuddly toys and dolls in his handcart through the area. In the most beautiful harmony again.

I never used my so well prepared answer for him. For one thing, because Michael didn't say anything about my skin ever again. Secondly, because I didn't mind his pee-pee at all.

The first time I noticed that the atopic eczema began to bother me was when I was dealing with horses. I was a passionate horse lover and urged my parents until I got riding lessons. The skin was itchy even during the brushing of the horses, in summer it was especially bad. After a riding lesson Miriam, the wife of the riding instructor, took me aside.

"What happened there?" she asked frightened, pointing to my neck."

"There was a branch", I mumbled, brought the horse into the box and cycled home. Only there did I see what Miriam had meant: almost one third of my neck was an open, oozing wound. During the riding lesson I had severe itching under the chin strap of the riding cap and rubbed it continuously with the back of my hand. It had been burning like hell, but I didn't think it was such a big wound.

I never told anyone that my skin always itched when I was with horses. Because I didn't want to admit it. But above all because I was afraid my parents would forbid me to ride horses. As often as possible I was with the horses and ignored that being with them and working in the stable did me no good.

During my riding holidays at the Baltic Sea I made friends with Claudia. Shortly afterwards I visited her for a few days.

When we put on our pyjamas and I creamed myself, Claudia's mother came into the room. Horrified, she stared at my legs. They were completely inflamed and scratched after two weeks in breeches and riding boots.

"It's not contagious," I said unmoved, "and it'll go away soon."

I explained to her why my legs looked the way they looked.

"Can't anything be done now?" Claudia's mother asked worriedly, "That must hurt!"

"Sometimes I use a steroid ointment," I answered, shrugging. "But this isn't bad enough for that."

A few years later I stopped riding. I couldn't take the itching, the dust in the stable and the horse hair anymore. Admitting this to me was a long process, but the constant itching and my hot, thick face had become too high a price. I was a teenager now. Even though my parents supported me and showed me that the most important thing were "inner values"—I wanted what all 13-year-old girls want: to look good.

Kill the Lights!

In school, for example from the seventh, eighth grade onwards, I always sat at the light switch whenever possible. So I could turn off the light as soon as it dawned in the morning. Nobody understood why the light went out all the time. But not being exposed to the bright neon lights and the looks of the others for a few minutes longer and to hide in the twilight was a relief for me.

Even later I looked for the place in the seminar rooms and libraries at the university that was the least lit. And in my office I always turned off all the lights as soon as it was bright enough outside. The worse the skin, the darker and blurrier my surroundings should be. Not always to the delight of my colleagues.

During puberty, my atopic eczema became a real psychological burden. The time when I wanted to experiment with my own style and have fun with friends was pure stress.

I was very proud of my long hair, which I could rarely wear open. My hairs tickled and immediately caused itching when they fell in the face. But when I tied it in a ponytail, you could see the scratched neck even more clearly. I couldn't use make-up, to fool around with others or to spend a few days in a scout camp didn't work either—my skin dampened all light-heartedness.

The risk of atopic eczema increases under chronic stress. On the other hand chronic eczema often means also chronic stress and can be a heavy burden as it massively impairs self-esteem.

Many people with atopic eczema are ashamed of their skin. They hide it under long sleeves and trousers even when it's very hot and they avoid all things and activities that lead to showing their skin, such as in swimming pools. This can be the beginning of a vicious circle, because mental stress intensifies the symptoms, and this in turn puts strain on the psyche.

And vice versa: A calm, self-conscious and satisfied psyche has a positive effect on the symptoms of atopic eczema. Read more about it in chapter 4 "What I can do today".

I gave private lessons and whenever I came home from my student Sven my eyes were burning and my skin itched extremely. It took me a long time to find out what the connection between tutoring and itching was. And then I couldn't figure out the cause. Until I was tested positive for cats in an allergy test. Then it was clear: The itching came from Sven's cat, which always purred around my legs when we were working. We moved the tutoring to the library and from then on I strictly avoided every contact with cats—although I liked them very much.

I hardly ever visited friends overnight. And if I did, I didn't like it very much. And I hated school trips.

A three-day bicycle tour in beautiful early spring weather became the purest torture. There were flowers blooming, the sun was just popping out of the sky. I had this terrible itching, felt my swollen face pulsating nonstop and I wanted nothing else than sitting alone in a dark room with a cool washcloth. And not having to ride with the others anymore.

I felt infinitely lonely and isolated in the group of my classmates. Although I was there, I could not participate in the fun that the others had. But I pretended nothing happened. As I always did. And the others did the same. What else could I have done? What else could they have done?

I did my duties, I was there when I had to be somewhere. But as soon as there was a way to escape, I did it and hid myself.

On a picture in my photo album I sit with a wash-
cloth in front of my face in the hobby room in the
cellar in the monkey swing. It was an afternoon when
friends of my parents, who had known me since my
child-hood, came to visit. I had an extreme eczema
attack and a red, swollen face. I didn't want to sit at
the coffee table with them. But as I looked I had also
no desire to meet with girlfriends. So I went into our
hobby room in the basement with a washcloth and a
bowl of acetic clay, which was sometimes good for
decongesting. I insisted that no one would come
down. My mother tried to change my mind, but I
stuck to it: I didn't want to see anyone and nobody
should see me like that.
I remember it very well because my brother came
down sometime and said that the visitors had gone.
He asked me why I had acted like that again. I have
no idea why he had his camera with him—in any
case he took this photo showing me with the
washcloth. For him, I must have been very strange
with my incomprehensible behavior.

Years later, my brother himself once had an abominable allergy
to his face. After that, he understood my situation much
better.

Rescuer in Distress

When things got really bad, I used a steroid ointment. My
mother made sure that I only applied the cream in an

emergency, when there was no other way. From painful experience with her own skin, she knew how quickly you became addicted to steroids and what dangerous side effects that could have.

My classmate Andreas also suffered from atopic eczema. But we never talked about our skin. Once he came to me and said that he had been to a healer a few times and that he was much better since. He almost stopped taking topical steroids and suggested to come along with him.

We went to the healer in the Netherlands, lined up in the queue in his living room and walked past him several times. The healer, a man of about fifty, put his hand on my head, muttered something and after ten seconds I was ready and it was the next one's turn. I did that three times. It helped Andreas, he said, but it didn't work for me. So I didn't go there a second timed.

Ina came up to me in the break of an orchestra rehearsal. I had ridden my bike to the music school, it was spring, everything was blooming and I was sitting behind my desk with a bright red, throbbing face. Ina and I didn't know each other well, but we recognized each other's special skin. She also suffered from atopic eczema.

"My dermatologist's new ointment is just great," she said and showed me a small cream pot. "Why don't you go there sometime?"

Indeed, her skin was really phenomenal. So healthy! And Ina was much more affected than me. Her hands were already marked by "elephant skin", with grey, coarse and thickened skin surface. Fortunately mine hadn't those things. Luckily my skin always recovered well during the time without atopic eczema attacks. Except in the crook of the arm, the hollow of the knee, and the neck. However, over the years, my skin looked much too withered for my young age.

My mother took me the farthest when she heard of a good physician or promising treatment methods. So we also drove to Ina's miracle doctor in the neighbouring town. He prescribed a brown ointment, which was mixed in the pharmacy and smelled pleasantly like tar. I liked its strong medical smell, and the very first time I smeared it, my skin became calmer. The ointment worked so well and I was so excited about the healing of my skin that its improvement couldn't go fast enough for me. I applied the cream several times a day and could watch my skin recover. I felt transformed, I was so cheerful and carefree! During an eczema attack, I withdrew, was always in a bad mood and was grumbling at everybody, because everything was too much for me. But now, after a long time, I finally felt really well again in my skin!

Life at school and at home was also so much easier. Not only me, but also my family was more relaxed. I found myself really handsome, even pretty, made funny photo series, made plans for the next holidays and arranged to meet up with friends again. The skin was no longer a boundary over which I had to laboriously climb to be with others. With my symptom-free skin it was suddenly possible to do something spontaneously and not waste a single thought on my skin.

It sometimes felt really strange and even scary that my life could be so carefree.

Cortisol is a hormone our body produces in the adrenal cortex and which we urgently need so that everything functions in our body as smoothly as it should.

This is because cortisol controls the metabolism and serves in particular to defend against exogenous influxes. With the help of cortisol, the body can also adapt to stress and strain situations. Cortisol is used as an artificially produced hormone in the form of steroid creams with people suffering from atopic eczema. For many patients and doctors it is the remedy of first choice in acute attacks, as cortisol quickly and effectively suppresses skin inflammation. But—and this is the problem—it only suppresses. In my opinion this is a blessing and a curse at the same time: a blessing because it finally makes a human life possible again. Curse, because after stopping using steroids the symptoms come back all the more violent and one can get into a vicious circle. In order to feel better again, you lubricate steroids, but you must take a higher percentage level to achieve the same effect. If you stop it after a long term use, the symptoms reappear more quickly. This is the "Topical steroid withdrawal", also known as red burning skin and steroid dermatitis.

Topical steroids can also have severe side effects. One is the so-called "parchment skin". The skin becomes thin, appears almost transparent and is prone to injury. Even a light push, rubbing or tearing off of a plaster can lead to wounds that are very difficult and that heal extremely slowly.

When the cream pot was almost empty, we went to the pharmacy to have the ointment mixed again.

"You'll need a prescription for this," said the pharmacist, "there's a steroid in there «

"That can't be," my mother replied perplexed, taking the pot in her hand and looking at the label, "there's nowhere to be found anything about steroid."

"Right," said the pharmacist and nodded, "it's not mentioned separately. But one of the ointments used for the mixture contains it."

So for at least four weeks I had been using this steroid cream daily like a normal skin care cream. I would have had to reduce it slowly to drop it off after such a long period of time. But since there was hardly anything left of the ointment and I didn't want a new one anyway, this topic had taken care of itself. The consequence was that I got a mega-slide, a so-called "topical steroid withdrawal". And for a week, I refused to go to school.

In the Labyrinth of Food

When I was a child, the knowledge about the connection between atopic eczema and nutrition was already present, but not yet widespread.

I drank freshly squeezed orange juice without caution, ate mandarins, grapefruits and the wonderfully juicy lemon cake of my beloved grandma. And even better was her nut cake made with hazelnuts from her own garden. We also loved to nibble hazelnuts in the evening on the sofa while watching TV.

I mixed delicious spritzers with the juice from grapes that my grandfather grew on the garage roof, picked gooseberries and currants in white, red and black from the bush. And we ate kilograms of kiwis that my wonderful may grandfather grew in front of the sunny garage wall. And of which in some years, amazingly enough, he harvested buckets of them.

I didn't notice that my skin itched, reddened or felt more uncomfortable after these fruits, foods and drinks. It was itching all the time and I always had a rubbed-off spot somewhere. It was not until I was a teenager that an alternative practitioner told me that orange juice and citrus fruits were not a good choice for atopic eczema. That the skin after sauerkraut became red and itched terribly, I noticed at some point myself, when I began to pay more attention to my nutrition.

I started avoiding certain foods. I no longer ate chips on parties—because of the paprika spice—and avoided alcohol.

Because I didn't want to look more swollen the next morning nor did I want to feel worse than I already did. Remarks like "you've been partying late again?" I've heard often enough anyway. But I hadn't been celebrating, I just had atopic eczema.

My diet has changed over the years. I haven't eaten and drunk many things for years because I know that certain foods and substances—such as alcohol, citric acid, cinnamon and hot spices—are not good for me.

A few years ago I gave up sugar and coffee for weeks on end and fed myself as low in histamine as possible. Since there was no improvement, I gradually suspected almost every food and finally ate only rice and potatoes. When they also came into consideration as "perpetrators", I experimented with kinesiology. At some point I even used a pendulum to see if I could tolerate what I wanted to eat.

What a mess! What oscillated to the left yesterday, swung to the right the next day, or the pendulum said "I don't know" by not committing itself to one direction. Could that really be?

I gave up this kind of food testing, ate only cooked vegetables and tried again to avoid sugar. With very little success. Because my skin was so frustrating and everything was so exhausting, I kept comforting myself with sweets.

Chocolate again! And I know it's no good right now. The histamine content in the cocoa, the sugar, all the other ingredients … As much as I need chocolate at the moment, the bad conscience of having eaten it harms me immediately and destroys the pleasure.

Kinesiology is a kind of allergy test. Muscle testing is used to detect blockages in the body or the psyche and their causes.

Kinesiology is based on the idea of traditional Chinese medicine that the body consists of numerous meridians. These meridians are energy pathways that influence the life and well-being of a person.

Traditional Chinese Medicine, or TCM, uses this energy to address and heal individual body regions. Acupuncture in particular works with this knowledge.

Kinesiology assumes that disturbances in the energy flow of the body lead to changes in muscle tension. Such changes should be triggered by allergens. In a kinesiological test, the eczema patient holds his arm up, in the other hand he holds a possible allergen. Now the therapist presses on the raised arm. If the muscle tension clearly decreases, the substance is classified as suspicious and as a possible allergen.

In my opinion kinesiology belongs in the hands of experienced therapists who know the chances but also the limits of the method. Because the results of the tests often do not match those of conventional allergy tests. However, if allergens are overlooked, this can be very dangerous: Trusting in the compatibility of food, one ingests a large amount of it—which in the worst case can lead to an allergic shock.

Skin Diary

November 17
Face totally inflamed, hot and tense. Kinesiology test.

November 18
Skin super-hot and red. No figs, no Brazil nuts, no oats, itchy neck. Coffee with chocolate. Skin in the afternoon slightly better, later again more heat.

November 20
Food tested with pendulum. Mainly kinesiological results confirmed. Skin still inflamed, slightly worse than yesterday. I ate some cheese. Skin extremely red, puffy, warm. Is it the cheese?

November 21
Skin clearly inflamed. No coffee, no chocolate. Wet chin again. Skin recovers a little in the afternoon, softening. No longer the noticeable redness, hardly any feelings of heat and itching. Jogged, then skin good! Evening: Neck recovers, left side still very rough and injured, neck better. Back: No itching, skin seems to get better there.

November 22
Scratched a lot last night. Why? Skin seemed to get better in the evening. Sheep's cheese for breakfast. Pendulum said it was okay. No coffee, but far too much chocolate. Another weeping wound to the chin at 12 noon. Neck completely injured. "Permanent shower" without cream after showering. So hard! Skin in the afternoon very red, extreme tension and heat.

November 23
Very poor sleep. At night violent itching, weeping encrusted
areas on the neck and décolleté in the morning, neck very bad,
NO chocolate, no cocoa today, cabbage, fish, salad, potatoes.
In the afternoon green tea and rice waffles. Face warm, but no
heat. Skin very scaly, also on forehead. Feels better in the
afternoon, though. Neck, too. But there are more wound spots
on the fingers. Petroleum, sulfur and three zinc tablets.
Vitamin B.

November 26
At night itching again, in the morning open spots on the chin.
Overall, however, the skin feels better after washing, especially
around the eyes. Neck again "dry". Neck also much calmer.
On the décolleté totally dry and constantly itchy areas.

December 3
Eaten chocolate again. Stupid. But there was no other way, I
had to do it. Skin very restless.

December 4
No chocolate, no coffee. Lots of millet. Skin still extremely
restless. No candy at all, just gum. Is it because of that, too?
Rice wafers with rice syrup.

December 7
Skin better, in the afternoon even felt "almost" normal,
because there was hardly any heat on the face. Neck very
scratched. Cracked and swollen fingers, it itches insanely.
In the evening I ate white flour baguette with cream cheese. I
hope it works out okay.

December 9
I woke up puffy, not feeling well. The cream cheese?
Weeping spots on the chin, itching. Rice milk, agave syrup,
cream. Weeping spots again in the afternoon. I ate fish.
Décolleté completely inflamed. Since December 3, no
chocolate, no sweets, no cake.

December 10
Woken up totally swollen again, the swollen feeling was taken
away all day long. Arnica in the afternoon. After sleep swelling
was gone, I felt better. Neck better, too. In the evening
pumpkin-potato puree.

December 11
Fingers almost healed, can even be bent again without tearing.
It's also better on the clavicle. Woke up without a lot of
swelling, no itching. Skin looks better, but is red and scaly.
Décolleté seems to calm down—after repeated showers. Back
very dry, but calm. Neck and throat, too. Cashew nuts in
muesli, soy yoghurt in the evening.

December 12
Skin around the eyes and mouth a dandruff covered surface.
Tried not to give in to every cream impulse. It's almost
impossible. I want to cream all the time. No bread for two
days. I'll have waffles and millet.

December 13
The mouth burns all the time. Two ribs of white vegan
chocolate. I need it sweet! New cream taken from the
pharmacy. The skin immediately burned extremely and tense.

December 22
After I thought that it would get a little better, again severe
deterioration, especially around the mouth. The skin is red and
burns extremely. I ate butter and eggs, but no sweets.

December 23
Skin on alarm, warm and slightly swollen. Three teaspoons of
buckwheat honey in the morning. Mouth region totally
inflamed. Lunchtime pizza at the Italian restaurant, without
cheese and tomatoes. In the afternoon gingerbread and a
chocolate heart. After that more heat on the face. Jogging.
Although better body feeling, but the skin burned in light-red.
The inflamed mouth is driving me crazy!

December 24
Another Christmas with burning skin. I am tired, have no
desire on a hot, tense Christmas Eve and holidays in "skin
arrest". Out of pure frustration I've eaten far too many
biscuits and Dresdner Stollen today. How will it ever get better
like this?

Not a Single Quiet Minute

At school, atopic eczema was my constant companion, but I also had periods without fallback. Like that wonderful summer holiday in Greece, when I completely forgot the eczema because it had completely disappeared.

That changed with the beginning of my studies. I wanted to be a journalist, had just moved to Cologne and had rented a room from an old lady far outside of the city.

The musty-sweet smell of the apartment had already affected my stomach and my mood during the room inspection, and I should have listened to my gut feeling. But I ignored the signals of my body and my soul, they only disturbed me in my usual way of thinking and acting: reasonable and consistent. I wanted to study, the semester began and I didn't have the time to look for another room. So I rented the room. It should only be a short term solution anyway, until I had found a nice shared flat in the city.

When I moved in with Mrs. Gnauserich, a massive episode of atopic eczema began which lasted over four years and which was only interrupted for a few weeks by two stays in hospital.

... and Yet

The new world of the university, life in Cologne and constant moves with a completely inflamed, never calming skin demanded more of me than I admitted and my strength allowed. I also had a job on a television channel and one at a perfumery. Not down in the store, though, but up in the warehouse. Sure, with my skin I didn't belong in the perfect glossy world of beauty and aesthetics. I would have just irritated the customers.

Nevertheless, the colleagues—all top groomed, good-looking and perfectly made-up women—were to my surprise full of understanding and helpfulness. Hardly a day passed by when I didn't receive a kindly recommendation or information for my sore skin. One had heard from a friend that this cream from the luxury company XY is incredibly great—also with atopic eczema. Once creamed and the eczema has disappeared. Really!

I was provided with samples and advice. And once I actually applied a cream, out of a mixture of deepest despair and extreme hope—because the product promise was just as grandiose as the praise of the perfumery employee. The next day I was so swollen, red and stained that I didn't want to go out.

But I overcame myself and walked out. To university. To the jobs. As I did later in my professional life. Only when I had such a severely inflamed face with open areas and the inflammatory processes put me physically out of action I did stay at home. Apart from that, I always went to work and even had an increased performance, because in addition to all the other requirements I also had managed my skin.

A dermatological clinic was out of the question for me at the beginning of my studies. I wanted to prove to myself and everyone that I could get my life in order with university and jobs. Even if every single day was an exhausting overcoming and I tormented myself from minute to minute towards the evening and its end.

It was too hot or too cold inside. It was too stuffy or
it smelled too intense. Every environment, whether
car, room or nature, felt hostile. My face was glow-
ing with heat, especially when I came out of the cool
winter air into closed rooms. I wanted to open the
windows right away or get some fresh air. My
inflamed skin just couldn't balance the temperature
differences—the heat piled up inside.

In summer I couldn't stand the heat, the brightness paralyzed me. Summer meant everybody else showed her or his skin and enjoyed life outside. I didn't. I was excluded from swimming in the nearby lake, from picnics, wearing dresses and cycling tours. So rainy summer days became my favourite ones.

Once on Christmas, when the heat slowly crept into the face, the Christmas tree became a scapegoat. I was invited to friends and was looking forward to this evening. The Christmas tree had an intense smell of fir. Panically I opened the window and put on gloves to decorate it. The itching on the hands and my hot face had to come from the resin of the branches and the fir smell. Sure, I could have asked someone to do the decorating. But I didn't want to be hypersensitive for once, I did not want to confuse the agreed procedure again because I did not feel well. But that didn't work. Something was always suspicious of hurting my skin. The fabric of the bed sheet, the detergent, the candle with the fragrant aroma. The cat in the house or the just painted wooden floor in the guest-room that still smelled of fresh varnish.

There was always something that wasn't right.

If you suffer from atopic eczema yourself, you may know the nicely meant recommendations and advice you are given again and again.

Even in the subway I was asked if I wanted to try mare's milk, mink cream or urine—the niece was completely healed with it. Or you get a tabloid newspaper with a report of a miracle cure under your nose.

Depending on my constitution, I have found such encounters to be intrusive. Sometimes, however, when my despair was strong, I also saw it as a hint of fate to follow up on the clue. If someone who knew the topic of atopic eczema or another chronic disease from his own experience gave me a tip or a recommendation, my openness was much greater right from the start.

In the Light

In one of my student jobs at the television channel I was on duty for a current program. It had been a week with an extremely strenuous skin, but that day I felt so much better. In the semi-darkness of the bathroom mirror I noted with pleasure that I looked really "normal" again.

The presenter was supposed to announce a feature film, so two cinema seats were pushed into the studio as a backdrop.

51

"Iris and Bernd, can you please sit there and play audience? It looks better if the seats are not empty," said the director at the rehearsal. Sure, nothing easier than that. And how wonderful that it was today of all days! Because I looked so rested and my spirits of life were just awakening again.

We had to go to the make-up room first—you can't do anything on TV without make-up. I was skeptical because I never put on make-up and my skin was still very sensitive despite the improvement. But once ... and today, when my skin looked so great ... that would certainly work.

So I went to the make-up room, opened the door and at the same moment someone shouted "Oh my God! I'm not gonna touch that!"

Who was screaming? And whom did he mean? I risked a look in the mirror next to the door and was terrified: A fire-red, inflamed face with white spots looked at me, scaly and with countless scabby scratches. In the cold light of the make-up room the whole extent of the last months which I had not wanted to admit revealed itself. My strategy of taking a look at me just in dim light, if at all, had spared me the truth.

The presenter, who had just been powdered, stood up.

"I guess that's not such a good idea," she said kindly, because I stood there thunderstruck. "I always get pimples from the thick make-up they use here. And this, even though my skin is usually completely insensitive."

The make-up artist who had been screaming was probably completely overwhelmed with the responsibility of putting make-up on such an irritated skin. I can well understand that. But for me it meant a cut in my life planning: it was the beginning of the end of my dream to become a journalist.

Measured by the decades of duration of my illness, actually only rarely someone who was not close to me made a remark about my appearance. Like the teacher in the grammar school, who welcomed me after six weeks of clinic with the remark: "I thought you have been treated in a health cure!"

And there was also the innkeeper where I waited as a student. When I put on gloves to wash glasses at the counter to protect my attacked hands, he said: "That's not possible here. The guests will think you have something contagious."

I lost the job.

But most of the time the comments were compassionate, benevolent and also funny. Like that of my friend Paul. We sat together in a workshop about the organization of trade fairs.

"If exhibits are not too damaged and scratched," the lecturer reported, "they can still be sold at the exhibition price."

Paul, sitting next to me, chuckled.

"What's the matter?" I asked quietly.

"Nothing," Paul whispered, chuckling on.

"Come on, say it."

"Oh," Paul grinned and put his hand on my arm amicably, "You couldn't be sold later."

> *I always found it amazing that just when I was feeling better, I heard comments like "Man, that's bad again" or "You could use some rest too—which a participant during a stress management seminar said to me. But when my skin was vibrating, when I noticed the first swellings and my face was getting hotter and redder, I often heard "But you can't see anything."*

Of course, I have always perceived much more about myself than others. And I have also recognized the atopic eczema in others, while someone who hardly knows the symptom has not noticed anything at all. Apart from the visible signs in the physiognomy—pale or reddish dry skin, deepened skin lines on the hands, the double eyelid crease under the eyes—I perceive atopic eczema sufferers above all through their charisma, which is different from that of people who do not have this skin peculiarity, even without acute atopic eczema. It is a special mixture of distance, sensitivity and strength.

The Entire Dimension

As a freelancer and trainee, I did interviews for radio stations and newspapers, wrote articles and reports during my university studies. All the time I was facing people with an arm's length of distance, just the microphone between us.

Although I conducted my interviews with self-confidence, it became more and more unbearable for me that my interviewee looked directly into my inflamed face. Every morning every second I hoped for a healing miracle. But what if it never happened?

> *With every interview I did with my eczema face, I said a little more goodbye to my certainty of becoming a journalist. Just before the exam, I gave it up forever. And suddenly I looked into an empty future with nothing more than a degree in my pocket. What was I supposed to do now? Becoming what? I didn't have a "Plan B", I had always planned to*

become a journalist. The atopic eczema not only
robbed me of my quality of life and joy, but also
prevented me from pursuing my dream job and
having a career perspective. It was only in retrospect
that I really became aware of all the consequences
that my special skin had for my life. But after a while,
I realized more and more that this could be a huge
opportunity from a professional point of view. There
was probably still something much more suitable for
me than journalism.

Theo, a friend of my family and a passionate railroad enthusiast, summoned me in the last three month before the school leaving examination: "Girl, work for the German Railways!"

Slowly I began to understand what he meant. That a quiet, unagitated profession might not be such a bad idea for my unstable skin situation.

But working for the German Railways? I couldn't do that! I always wanted a lively, interesting job! But I didn't know at all at that time which jobs were possible at German Railways. I had never thought about career opportunities in other professional fields.

Later on I found my dream job after all. I worked as a public relation manager for many years. I met journalists, authors, and booksellers, I visited trade fairs and events. Every day it was interesting, exciting and challenging. It was exactly "my" profession and I loved this work very much. Whenever I felt fine with my skin, I enjoyed being able to organize the complex publicity around authors and their books. But when I wasn't feeling well, every contact became a big burden. On the other hand, I could not imagine doing something different professionally. Here, too, my skin brought me to my limits and I had to rethink my professional future. A very painful process. But the only choice I had.

Today I work as a coach, trainer and author. All my professional experience, my acquired abilities and personal development processes flow into this activity. It couldn't have been better and my motto "Who knows what it's good for" has once again been impressively confirmed.

By the way: When Theo saw me later and I wasn't feeling well, he always sighed and said: "Oh girl, if you'd only had decided to work for German Railways." A phrase that has made a career in our family as a dictum and still provides cheerfulness. When Theo is there, he laughs with us.

Despair, Consolation and Hope

A slight improvement was actually also there. But it had only been a calm moment before an even bigger storm. The following weeks were characterized by hot, wetting, burning and swollen skin.

There was no joy, no freedom, no ease. In the evenings I fell into bed, when I woke up in the morning I still felt exhausted and hopeless. Every day I thought that it couldn't get any worse and that I had reached the lowest point. I could hardly stand it anymore. But when I had just set up myself at the very bottom for "survival, somehow", I slipped even further into the depths. It was like a never-ending fall into a basement shaft with no floor. Would it go on like this my whole life? Did the atopic eczema belong to me so much that it would be there forever on such an agonizing scale?

I had a quarrel with God with whom I had a relationship since my childhood. Did he even exist when he made me suffer like this? Why had he given me such a ghastly, visible disease? I would have loved to trade it for another one. One that would torture me the same way, but that weren't as visible!

I knew, of course, that such thoughts were completely absurd. But I was so unhappy. And so angry! So much that I insulted this god, who apparently didn't care about me at all, and wanted him to leave me alone. But when it got dark inside me, so dark that I was afraid for my life, then I found my way back to him.

I read the Bible and rediscovered the story of Job. I was impressed by this man, who had the strength not to lose his faith despite the trials God had imposed on him. I wanted to do that, too! To understand atopic eczema as a task that I could solve with God's help. And at some point this challenge would be a thing of the past.

On such nights I often read the story of the healing of the leper, which I had marked with a post-it note. In ancient times, also skin diseases such as eczema, acne or vitiligo, the "white spot disease", were described as leprosy. Those who suffered were forced to die socially, i.e. they were expelled from their family and their village. Often for religious reasons: the leper is cursed by God and his illness is the punishment for his sins.

In the biblical story, a man who is marked by his skin disease comes to Jesus, throws away all the judgments that people have made about him (and perhaps also his own

judgements about himself) and asks Jesus with all the strength of his faith: "Lord, if you want to, you can heal me."
Jesus stretched out his hand and said, "I will, be thou clean." And "straight away the disease went from him, and he was made clean."

> *How much desperation in that man's picture was.*
> *How much strength might it had cost him to still hope*
> *that the impossible of becoming "clean" could be*
> *come true at all and that he could be part of society*
> *again. Finally it became true because his faith was*
> *as solid as a rock. I was also hoping to wake up*
> *tomorrow morning with a healthy skin. Since faith*
> *was such a mighty and unbelievably great power.*

I have never experienced spontaneous healing myself. But in regard to atopic eczema I have heard about it several times.

"It will disappear with the years", said the doctors of my childhood. And also later as a teenager I heard: "As an adult you will have gotten rid of it."

Unfortunately this was not the case with me, my atopic eczema remained. However, many atopic eczema children are actually symptom-free later. And there are indications that atopic eczema can disappear completely or at least diminish even in advanced age with adults.

Klaus, about 50 years old and also a patient in a dermato-logical clinic, told that he woke up symptom free after ten years of extreme atopic eczema. But after several healthy and easy years the skin inflammation reappeared just as suddenly as it had disappeared. And was more powerful than ever before.

Ready for the Clinic

At some point, I couldn't take it anymore. I couldn't go on, I surrendered. When I knocked at heaven's door God was usually not at home. And I knocked frequently.

I wanted topical steroids again. The vow to abstain even in the worst acute eczema no longer applied. The last time I had used a steroid cream was when I was a pupil. But after that I didn't want to experience again the wonderful, but unfortunately only borrowed, freedom from symptoms and the guaranteed flare-up after stopping the medication. Better to honestly get through an eczema attack and then also enjoy the time afterwards without the constant fear that it would only be a question of days or—if it goes well—weeks, when the next eczema period would begin.

But after twelve months of persistent atopic eczema in my first year of college, my resistance was broken. I went to the dermatologist, got a high-proof steroid cream and—devil stuff!—immediately after the first application I felt much better. What an unbelievable relief! And how long had I not allowed myself to have that?

I watched with fascination how the skin recovered from hour to hour. And how the normal shape and colour of my face and also my usual energy returned with the decrease of the swelling. The interest in people, in the world and in myself awakened again. I couldn't look in the mirror often enough, met fellow students in cafés and was all in love with that great emotion of feeling alive and free again.

It took me just three weeks to look healthy again. After almost a year in which I looked at myself exclusively in my small pocket mirror.

How I felt alive again! I made plans for the next weeks to meet girlfriends and spend the night there. I hadn't done that in ages. On the one hand because of the bed linen, which I perhaps did not tolerate, on the other hand because of the inevitable traces of blood, consequences of the nightly scratching attacks. Besides, I always looked the worst in the morning. So I didn't go anywhere if I couldn't get home from there the same night.

I was so confident that after the recommended gradual stopping of the steroid the skin would keep in its good condition.

I was perfectly happy for a few days—until the first red spots appeared on the face again and my skin slowly but steadily became warmer. Until I finally woke up one morning again with swollen eyes and glowing skin. And I lost my nerves.

I ran into the bathroom and frantically applied cream to my face and neck. No, I didn't want to give up this carefree life which had only just begun after an eternally long time! I didn't want to get locked up in the skin prison again!

Over the next few days and weeks, I smeared the cream on my skin several times a day, knowing full well that it was completely crazy. But I also knew that I wouldn't be able to get away from the steroids on my own—I hung on the steroid cream tube like a junkie on his drugs.

Now there was nothing else I could do but go to a clinic.

Chapter 2

Globules, Ointments and Clinics

Who knows what follows a single moment in life?

Johann Wolfgang von Goethe

I have tried countless diets, Schüssler salts, probiotics and Traditional Chinese Medicine (TCM) to soothe my skin.

I drank liters of whey, took trace elements and vitamins, evening primrose oil and borage seed oil. I was with healers, was irradiated, was acupunctured, was tested from inside and outside and I got desensitized.

I bathed in salt from the Dead Sea, in apple vinegar, in whey, in olive oil and I made alkaline foot baths to neutralize my body. And of course I tried countless creams and ointments.

Normally, I'm not susceptible to the promises of advertising. And certainly not to those of the cosmetic industry. But during an atopic eczema attack, when my skin and my mental balance lost their equilibrium and nothing helped, I was prone to it.

The promises of healthy, beautiful skin on the so attractively designed boxes and bottles, the scents when I smelled product samples—I wanted to have all the valuable natural things that seemed to be captured in these products to benefit my injured skin. Just as the Spanish mystic Teresa of Ávila once said: "Do something good for your body so that your soul wants to live in it."

New Cream, New Happiness

Like yoghurt fans who passionately study the latest yoghurt creations in the refrigerated shelves of supermarkets and try them at home, I looked around the cosmetics departments of drugstores full of curiosity and expectation.

I was the perfect customer for the pharmaceutical and cosmetics manufacturers because, I was always looking for a new product. And if the ointment XY only slightly alleviated the dryness of the skin or perhaps even the itching instead of causing even more discomfort, I was already happy.

Only a few years ago the term "atopic eczema" was almost exclusively to be found in connection with products from pharmacies. Now it is written on the labels of the cosmetics industry as well. They provide complete product lines for people suffering from atopic eczema—from pure care for healthy skin to alleviation for problematic skin and acute dermatitis attacks.

There are creams and emulsions, skin-soothing and regenerating care masks, creams with micro-silver additives, anti-itching sprays and lotions. Many of them contain uric acid or valuable ingredients such as organic evening primrose and jojoba, omega-6 fatty acids, vitamins and organic shea butter. Often skin soothing herbal or antibacterial active ingredients are added. Everything was developed for the purpose to stabilize the skin condition, to make it more resistant and to improve the quality of life.

Skin contact is vital, our life begins with it. Newborns are therefore put immediately and as often as possible on the bare chest of a parent. This is called "kangaroo care".

For premature babies, cuddling increases their chances of survival and helps them to develop faster into healthy infants. It helps parents to cope better with the strains of childbirth and the upcoming challenges.

Brain researchers assume that our first skin contacts are stored in our emotional memory and contribute significantly to our basic confidence. It is this wonderful feeling that makes us trust ourselves, others and life and that we are capable of bonding.

Every time we allow ourselves to be embraced, cuddle up to a familiar body or cream ourselves with our favourite cream, our body remembers the first beneficial and protective touches and releases the hormone oxytocin. Oxytocin is also called "cuddle hormone" and is a real all-rounder: It stabilizes the cardiovascular system and ensures that wounds heal better, it keeps our immune system fit and it gives us the incomparable feeling that we can rely on ourselves and the people around us.

The attention we give to our skin is therefore not only important for our physical health and a good body feeling. Through the loving care of our skin we also strengthen and develop our self-esteem.

I also regularly took a look around the shelves for baby and child care, where I almost always discovered something new.

It is estimated that every fifth child in Europe and every tenth child in USA suffers from atopic eczema, twice as many as 30 years ago. In the past, there were in Germany mainly medical ointments and classics such as "Nivea", "bebe", "Kaufmann's Kindercreme" or "Vita Horm" as skin care for children. But nowadays there is a wide range of creams and lotions for the special needs of children with atopic eczema in the baby care departments. I noticed that the manufacturers were expecting me also there, because some of them recommended their product either right at the front of the label or in the description on the back with the information "also for sensitive adult skin".

It was difficult for me to choose between "itch-relieving and low-irritant for tender baby skin", "tender and intensive care" and "ultrasensitive care oil". So I just tried everything that promised to be soothing.

Some creams felt good even after one minute on the skin, some I had to wash off immediately. Because they itched, burned or left an unpleasant feeling. I always had some tissues and a water bottle with me for such experiments.

I can understand that parents of eczema children place their hopes on product messages such as "protective", "caring" or "antipruritic". And that they use new creams with the conviction that they are doing something good for their child's inflamed skin. But perhaps this product feels very uncomfortable, because it burns and causes heat sensations?
I am depressed by the idea of how much discomfort is caused by creams, that a baby or small child has to

endure on its skin. As an adult, I can decide for myself whether to re-apply a cream—even if it may not feel good at first—because I want to believe in its promise of relief. A baby or a little kid can't do that.

Magic of Globules

Of course I have also been on naturopathic and there in particular on homoeopathic recovery paths.

Mrs. Friedrich was a classical homoeopath in the neighbouring village, people were enthusiastic about her spectacular healing successes. That's why my mother made an appointment for me with her.

After a detailed anamnesis, Mrs. Friedrich suggested a change in diet—especially less, preferably no more sugar and no more citrus fruits—and an autohaemotherapy. While she was still explaining how it would work, it was clear to me: not with me! I was scared to death of injections.

So there was no autohaemotherapy, instead she gave me three globules. I should let them melt slowly in my mouth—"don't chew it!"—and see what happens. I had to come again in three weeks.

The next days I watched attentively, but it happened … nothing. We drove again to Mrs. Friedrich and I got some other globules. Once again I noticed no decrease of the itching or an improvement of the eczema in the bends of the arms and back of the knees.

We didn't go to her any more. But many years later, when I was absolutely convinced of the possibilities of homeopathy, it was Mrs. Friedrich who could impressively help my father with his health problems.

What Does Itching Mean in French?

When I was 16, my mother and I visited her friend Eva in Geneva. The two had not seen each other for more than twenty years and I was very curious to see how Eva, of whom my mother had told me so much, would be.

How much I would have liked to get a break from atopic eczema for the trip, but there wasn't one. Shortly before this event an eczema attack began again and I boarded the night train to Switzerland with a hot face and steroid cream in my luggage in case it got even worse.

With Eva, it was as if we had always known each other. She realized that I did not feel well in my skin, I tried to explain "itching", but did not know the French word. That didn't matter.

"There are very good products for your skin," said Eva and took me to her "Pharmacie Homéopathique."

Despite my explanation that I had already tried so many things before and also homoeopathy, she did not let me stop her from parking the car in the second row of a busy street in Geneva and jumping into the pharmacy. There she quickly bought a bottle with the inscription "démangeaison".

"Three times a day five beads and don't chew, just suck," Eva said as she gave the little bottle to me in the car.

Homoeopathy is an alternative medical treatment method that has been used for over 200 years by doctors and non-doctors for acute and chronic illnesses.

The name consists of the two Greek words "Homoion" (= similar) and "Pathos" (= suffer).

Homoeopathy is based on a law of nature that similar things are cured by similar things. It can therefore also be described as stimulation therapy, which aims to activate the self-healing powers of the organism or to steer it in the right direction.

For example, if you bathe your ice-cold feet warmly, you will freeze more than before because your body cools your feet down again. However, if the feet are exposed to strong cold for a short time, the body heats them up afterwards.

In this way, a homoeopathic remedy can cause certain symptoms in a healthy person. However, if a sick person has similar symptoms to those caused by the medicine in the healing process, this medicine should be able to cure the disease.

Homoeopathy always considers a person in his or her entirety, including mood, lifestyle and biography. Disease is therefore not seen as an isolated event that affects only one or more organs—as if, for example, only the stomach were sick—but as a signal of a disturbance of the entire organism.

I nodded, I already knew that. I sucked the beads and had unforgettable days in Geneva. Perhaps also thanks to the beads with the beautiful sounding name "démangeaison". At least I don't remember my inflamed skin so much as the many beautiful experiences we had together.

With my wonderful new friend Eva at my side I was highly motivated to improve my French. When I went back home I continued to suck the globules diligently. But I noticed no change in the skin for the better.

At some point I looked up the word "démangeaison" in my dictionary, which sounded so magical and that had become deeply rooted in my vocabulary. Meanwhile I could pronounce it better than many other French words.

It meant "itching."

On Your Own Way

After some attempts with homoeopaths, which did not bring the longed-for success I so desperately needed, I started to deal with this treatment method myself. I put together remedies in low potencies according to homoeopathic remedy pictures that I had found on respectable homoeopathic pages in the Internet. To my own surprise sometimes with phenomenal success.

Once I came home from a conference with a tremendous eczema attack. I hadn't been feeling well before, but I really wanted to attend the meeting and stay with my friend Franziska, whom I hadn't seen for many years.

I somehow survived the conference, Franziska picked me up in the evening and we drove to her house. When she showed me the guest room, I froze: on the windowsill sat a big and magnificent black-brown tabby cat.

"This is our Oskar," Franziska said. "You like cats, don't you?"

"Yeah, sure," I said and swallowed, "but they don't have to sleep in the same room with me."

Since I always kept forgetting my allergy to cats, I hadn't thought at all that Franziska could have a cat. There was a movie going on in my head: Shouldn't I be going to a hotel? But I didn't want to be complicated again. And I was so looking forward to being together with Franziska. Maybe my allergy wasn't even there anymore? Some allergic reactions just - disappear. And since I hadn't had any contact with cats for a long time, I might not have noticed that.

"Oscar is out at night anyway," Franziska calmed me down and as if on cue, the tomcat jumped from the windowsill and strolled elegantly out of the room.

I tried to forget Oskar as best I could, and I concentrated on not showing my discomfort in my excited skin. Probably the many meetings and conversations I had on the conference were still vibrating in it.

Franziska and I talked a lot that evening and said good night late. But before I went to bed I looked in every corner of the room and also under the bed. Oscar was not there. Relieved I lay down in bed, prayed that the next day I would be able to leave the sultry skin prison. Please—just for a short time!

I woke up before the alarm clock rang, recognizing that I couldn't open my eyes properly. The skin on my face was pounding and glowing

I looked at the clock, it was only half past five. I groped into the bathroom and since I didn't know the way, I needed light and pressed the button next to the door. Three lamps went on and I looked right into my reflection. Oh, my God! It was even worse than it felt! I had completely swollen eyes and a red-spotted, swollen face. Totally shocked, I poured lots of water on my face, hurried to take a shower, got dressed and grabbed my things.

In the kitchen I wrote a message for Franziska and put it on the table. When I put on my jacket in the hall, I met Tobias, her husband.

"Do you have to leave this early?" he asked in surprise.
I stammered something about preparations I had to do for an early appointment and left in a hurry.

It was Saturday. This weekend should have been so different. I actually wanted to stay with Franziska until Sunday, because we hadn't seen each other for so long. But now I was sitting on the train on my way home early in the morning. There was a very important business meeting on Monday and I had to be fit.

I had hoped so much that my skin would recover by the end of the week—with all the nice appointments and meetings. The opposite was the case now. And the day after tomorrow was already Monday! It was an agonizing thought that I had to attend the meeting in my present condition.

But I gave myself a jolt. If I found the right globules and if I had absolute peace, the skin might still calm down during the next 48 hours.

Back at home I didn't even unpack my things, but opened the notebook immediately. I feverishly searched homoeopathic sites on the Internet for a remedy that corresponded to my symptoms in a high degree and to my emotional condition.

I came across the homepage of a homoeopath who explained in detail how she treated patients in an acute eczema episode: with a certain remedy in different potencies. This was not quite in the sense of classical homoeopathy, because it was a general and not an individual medication. But for me it sounded plausible and almost perfect for my situation.

By now it was evening. I looked at the watch, the pharmacies were already closing. I left everything behind and drove to the nearest emergency pharmacy and—hurray—they actually had the two remedies I needed right now. I immediately took five globules. I got hot ears and my face felt like being just before the boiling point. I knew there could be an initial worsening and hoped that my reaction was one. Because in that case it was the right homoeopathic medicine and it would work. And really: After only one hour I felt better! There was an inner relief, the heat on my face no longer determined my entire perception and the pressure of suffering was no longer quite as intense.

On Sunday I woke up fresher, took the remedy again and on Monday I went to work—visibly worn out, but I had much more energy than the days before. And my skin calmed down more and more over the next days.

Over the years, I have had similar experiences with homeopathic remedies several times. But the success never lasted. As a result, I was constantly searching for more suitable globules, cheering sky-high when I thought I had found them, and grieving to death when they failed to fulfil the hopes I had placed in them.

I became a regular customer of a pharmacy that had many homoeopathic remedies on stock or could quickly obtain them. From that time comes also my considerable collection of unusual and exotic medicines, which I fortunately do not have to try any more.

"Atopic eczema is a clinical picture that can often be treated surprisingly simple with homoeopathy," writes a doctor on his homepage.

Well, I haven't had that experience. But I also found a possible explanation why homeopathy sometimes can't work.

"When a man beats his wife, I can give her arnica for the bruises and she will feel better," my physician once said when we talked about the possibilities and limitations of homoeopathic remedies in low potencies. "If she's beaten by him again, she can take Arnica again. And she will be relieved again. But she will always get bruises if she doesn't finally decide to change her life situation."

Unfortunately, homoeopathy could not deliver lasting relief for me because I did not change anything about its causes. Without knowing it, I kept throwing fuel into the inflammation. And kept the eczema fire burning.

Permanent Shower and Raw Food

On the constant search for the "Holy Grail"—a medicine, a cream, vitamin cure, diet or any other healing therapy—my journey also took me several times to clinics. The weeks with sea or mountain air, sun and relaxation did not bring any lasting relief or even healing, but always new insights. And fresh energy. For a short time I saw again how my life felt with a healthy or at least healthier skin. And how pleasant encounters with people could be, to whom nothing had to be explained.

Although my eczema skin had hardly really disturbed or repelled anyone and although my partner never had any problems with it, I was ashamed of my appearance. To be in a clinic means being in a place where many people with similar experiences were and visible skin diseases were the norm rather than the exception. And this was always a great relief.

It's Not the Skin That Is Sick

The continuous atopic eczema and my steroid addiction during the first two semesters had brought me to the "Klinik Lahnhöhe", whose therapeutic approach plays a key role for my well-being today. My friend Jan's mother, who was very interested in healthy nutrition and alternative medicine, told me: "I'm not a physician, but I don't think your skin is sick. Something in your body is probably imbalanced and your skin reflects this. With topical steroids you can suppress it and ointments can relieve the symptoms. But as long as you don't get to the root, you will probably have to deal with relapses of atopic eczema over and over again."

She gave me the books of Max Otto Bruker, a physician who studied the connection between nutrition and chronic diseases. On the bus on the way home I began to read immediately "Our food, our destiny" and had almost missed the stop to switch to the train, because the content tied me up so much. Although Bruker wrote in a tone that was rather old-fashioned to my ears, I was fascinated by his view of atopic eczema and his completely steroid-free method to permanently curing it.

The focus of his therapy was an animal protein free wholefood nutrition. Almost exactly what we call vegan today and what has become absolutely established among the numerous nutrition styles. But in the 1980s and 90s this form of nutrition was hardly known in Germany. Or just something for weirdos. This diet seemed to be extreme and strange.

Now, during my studies, when I was looking for a way out of the topical steroid spiral, I remembered Jan's mother and Bruker's book. I bought it, devoured it again, and regained hope. There was a way to healing! And if nutrition were such an important pillar in the recovery process, my atopic eczema would soon be a thing of the past!

Full of hope that I would finally be able to heal my skin, and firmly convinced that I would never have to touch steroid ointments again, I used the summer break of the university, traveled to Lahnstein and checked in at the "Klinik Lahnhöhe".

Max Otto Bruker already recognized the connections between nutrition, health and civilization diseases in the sixties.

To maintain and restore health, he developed his own nutrition therapy, in which he essentially followed the inventor of the wholefood nutrition Werner Georg Kollath and the Swiss physician Maximilian Bircher-Benner, the father of "Bircher-Muesli".

According to Bruker, everything that has been industrially preserved or treated should be abandoned and a large part of the food should consist of raw vegetables. At the center of his diet is fresh grain porridge, a muesli made from freshly ground cereals, nuts and fruit. As fat he recommends cold pressed oils, butter and cream. Vegetable protein is preferred to animal protein in his diet, fruit juices, fruit teas and milk are completely rejected by Bruker. The more severe the disease is, the higher the proportion of pure fresh food should be and the more consistently animal protein should be avoided.

Bruker's form of nutrition or parts of it can be found today in nutrition styles such as low carb, vegan or raw food. Many people swear by the health benefits they get by pure raw food and do not eat animal protein.

A lot of Bruker's theses have now been scientifically proven, some have been refuted. I am still absolutely convinced of many aspects of his diet because I have experienced their beneficial effects on myself and seen them in others.

Had I known beforehand what awaited me there in the next weeks, I probably wouldn't have done it. But so I moved into my room, unpacked my suitcase with my last strength and fell into bed—relieved to be in a place where others knew better than I did what could help my skin.

That's Not Possible!

"No more topical steroids from now on," said the doctor the next morning in the first consultation. I swallowed. I had firmly assumed that I could slowly wear out the steroid cream. And—even worse—I should not use my creams at all anymore. What a shock!

But that was not all—I was also prescribed "permanent shower".

"What's that?" I asked suspiciously. The permanent shower sounded like a lot of water. Like too much water.

"There you lie on a flatbed for half an hour and a moving shower jet runs over your body," the doctor explained.

"And I don't apply cream after that either?"

I must have misunderstood something. It couldn't be that I didn't cream my skin after those amounts of water. It was completely dependent on the fat coming from my cream tube.

"Exactly. From now on, no more creams at all," nodded the doctor. "It is best if you leave all the creams you have brought with you in the nurse's room."

I protested. I needed my ointment at least after the permanent shower! And also in the morning when getting up. That was the least care I had to do for my skin!

But the doctor didn't let me negotiate with him.

"Absolut abstinence form ointment and cream is important so that your skin can recover from the constant application of cream and can start its own fat production again. The water application activates also the self-healing powers of your body and the vegetarian diet with the high raw vegetable content will support your entire regeneration process."

Since the doctor seemed to know what he was doing and I had nothing to lose except my catastrophic skin condition, I gave up my resistance. With a heavy heart I left my creams behind and entrusted myself to the clinic with their peculiar methods.

Water leaches out the skin. Especially people with atopic eczema notice how dry the skin is after contact with water.

According to the common opinion of dermatologists, people suffering from atopic eczema have to re-grease their skin after each intensive contact with water—but of course also several times a day as a daily basic care.

"The best method to reduce relapses" was once recommended by a dermatologist to a listener with atopic eczema during a German radio broadcast on eczema treatment.

Desert Period

It was clear that the topical steroid withdrawal would not be a Sunday stroll. I had already stopped taking steroids several times and a steroid eczema had always followed—even if I had only creamed steroids for a few days. But I had never smeared steroid ointments in such a long period of time as in the past weeks. What followed now, however, exceeded everything I could have imagined with my lifelong eczema experience in my wildest imagination.

My face swelled up into a hot ball. I could hardly see out of my eyes and I could not open my mouth without the skin over my lips and the corners of my mouth bleeding immediately.

The neck was a completely wetting surface and felt as if I was wearing an iron collar, which I had just taken out of the fire. The skin felt extremely stretched, it burned and glowed.

The only relief during the day were the thirty minutes under the permanent shower. The water etched hellish in the beginning, but it quickly subsided and then the best time of the day followed in the warm, humid air of the shower cubicle: half an hour of pure well-being! I couldn't remember the last time I felt this good.

However, it was quickly over again. If the water dried after the shower, I got my usual skin feeling back: my skin felt too small, too hot, too burning and it was itching like crazy.

My face became harder every day during the first 14 days, it was peeling, the skin burst and cracked. Bloody crusts were formed. I avoided looking into the mirror. But one day I gathered up all my courage and dared a look. I hardly recognized myself: Never ever had I looked so bad!

Surprisingly, however, I was not ashamed, although in my

Like the well-known "water treading" the "permanent shower" is one of the naturopathic procedures of the famous Sebastian Kneipp.

Sebastian Kneipp was a Bavarian priest, a famous hydrotherapist and the eponym of Kneipp medicine, which is one of the classic naturopathic methods. Kneipp's best-known methods, apart from water treading, include washings, wraps, steam baths, compresses and mud packs, various forms of baths and the permanent shower. In the case of chronic and acute health problems, it—like his other methods—should have a harmonizing, activating and soothing effect on the regulatory mechanisms of the organism. Kneipp's hydrotherapy methods strengthens the entire immune system.

The "Klinik Lahnhöhe" offers a wide range of physical therapies according to Kneipp. They also use the knowledge of anthroposophical medicine, homoeopathy and phytotherapy—the healing, alleviation and prevention of diseases with medicinal plants.

My stay at the "Klinik Lahnhöhe" took place a long time ago and in the meantime a lot may have changed in their treatment methods. However, the psychosomatic and naturopathic approach is still there. I also like to remember the wonderful walks and hikes that you can take from there into the - beautiful nature of the Middle Rhine.

opinion I was now really disfigured. For the first time in my life I felt deep compassion for my skin and for myself. And I didn't care what anybody else thought. What we have been already through, my skin and me! And what we both just went through again!

Compassion for myself was completely new to me and I became increasingly amazed to realize that the energy that I had always directed against me was now unrestrictedly available for the recovery process.

For me it was a whole new experience to see how much strength the rejection of my strongly hated skin used up and how much energy flowed when I just let myself be like I was.

After a long time I finally dared to believe again that my skin would recover and I would really get healthy.

I've always been considered self-confident. I certainly am. But it was also a learned role that I could slip into when I needed it or when I thought it was expected of me. And which had proved to be extremely effective when it came to mastering everyday life as well as possible.
When I graduated from high school, a teacher patted me on the shoulder. "I admire," he said, "how you've managed all this with your skin over the years. So strong and brave." He was right. I've been in theatre companies and orchestras because I thought I had to. And I often had a big flap. But that was the role. In reality I was rather introverted, insecure and preferred to be alone.

Today I know that above all I rejected myself. I did not stand behind me and did not stand up for myself. I didn't even know what that meant at all: to stand by oneself. Not to mention that I didn't know how it felt. I had no idea what my body and soul needed to feel good. I was a stranger to myself.

Added to this was the constant comparison with my healthy fellow students, who were bursting with energy and enjoying their studies and also their lives to the full. I felt even more paralyzed by their lightheartedness. Because every day they showed me what I didn't have and probably never would have. And the thought of continuing to live a life like the one I was leading horrified me.

New Skin!

The first few weeks in the "Klinik Lahnhöhe" were are hard time. I began to doubt whether I would ever be able to move my limbs and joints again without tearing my skin.

After three weeks I woke up in the morning and accidentally twisted my neck, which I had kept as stiff as possible until then. I waited for the pain of tearing, but … nothing happened. I turned the neck a little further. This was also possible without difficulties. Very surprised, I palpated my neck with my fingers. Incredible! Between the scabs was new, smooth skin! This strange "zero cream method" really worked!

That was the turning point, from then on my skin condition steadily improved. The other patients with atopic eczema also benefited from the tough and unusual therapy, which consisted of showers and the strict vegan diet.

Thomas, who was very ill at the beginning of his stay, ate only raw food for several weeks. He was so enthusiastic about the healing effect that he didn't want to touch a cooking pot in the future.

I had been planning for a long time anyway to skip dairy products and to test whether my skin would then calm down. But my passion for curd cheese, yoghurt, cheese and kefir was always so great that I never managed it for more than a few days when I got back home. In the clinic, on the other hand, it was easy for me to do that.

Only the knowledge that this diet would do my skin good motivated me to continue with it. Even on trips to the next bigger city I resisted the culinary temptations that appeared in every corner of the City Center.

Today I eat 90 percent vegan, which is to a large extent still a result of my good experiences with the kind of nutrition in the "Klinik Lahnhöhe". However, since food and eczema are a very special and also very important topic, it will be dealt with in more detail in chapter 4.

In total I spent six weeks in the "Klinik Lahnhöhe". My neck recovered completely, my arms healed, the swellings in my face disappeared and my skin became softer and paler with every day. But towards the end of my stay I had increasingly used an olive oil paste, which the clinic offered for extreme skin tears. I used it to lubricate the surfaces around the mouth to relieve the extremely unpleasant feeling of tension. These were exactly the areas that had also improved significantly in comparison to the previous months, but which were still red, scaly and slightly inflamed.

A Bad Conscience

Richer in valuable experiences and encounters, but above all: freed from topical steroids, I went home with visibly soothed skin. Only to find myself in the middle of a new attack of eczema after one month. This time—and this was the good thing in all the bad things happening—only the face was affected, but again I still felt extremely stressed again. With this new attack a permanent feeling of guilt came into my life.

After the clinic I quitted following the new diet. Now that I felt so much better, I didn't follow Bruker's diet as strictly as in the weeks before. I felt an enormous desire for everything I had abstained from for six weeks, I ate cheese and white bread again, enjoyed kefir, buttermilk and yogurt.

I was firmly convinced that I alone was responsible for the deterioration of my skin, and reproached myself severely. Because I was not in control of my diet and could not manage to avoid the things that were not good for me. This was the purest stress for my soul, which naturally also manifested itself in the condition of my skin.

Looking back, I know that my diet was in parts responsible but not completely. There was a variety of causes that promoted the first eczema attack after my stay in the clinic. I creamed my face again, I came back to University into a stressful flat-sharing community and a very exhausting study period. In addition, I constantly put myself under pressure with the question of what I was allowed to eat and what I was not. I realized that I would not be able to keep up with the new diet that I had experienced as so healing at the "Klinik Lahnhöhe". There were just too many foods I liked and I just couldn't manage not to eat them. I was very much afraid that the beautiful skin would remain just a small, much too short episode. And so it was.

Ointment Dressing and Rotating Diet

There were times in my adult life when I felt really good about my skin. The atopic eczema flared up from time to time, but also subsided again. Until a few years ago another attack did not want to come to an end.

For years my Bepanthen cream—which is a very fatty ointment—was there when my dry facial skin stretched and demanded cream. The cream was my care and life insurance, I always stocked some large tubes in the cupboard. And several small tubes with Bepanthen were spread over all my bags. When I left the house and realized that I didn't have the cream with me, I went back to get it. If I was already too far away to turn around again, I quickly bought a new tube on the way.

Not that Bepanthen stopped an attack of atopic eczema. But it did make it more bearable. The cream made me feel like I was providing my skin with what it needed most: fat. All the time. When I woke up in the morning, my first grip was to

Bepanthen on the nightstand. In the evening, just before falling asleep, it was the last. And in between I opened the tube countless times.

In my search for a new homoeopathic remedy, I came across the expression "addictive, unhealthy skin".
I was amazed how exactly this description applied to what I felt: my skin was addictive, fat-dependent.
I had never heard of or read about addictive skin.
But if any skin was addictive, it was mine.

Rien Ne Va Plus—Nothing Works Anymore

At some point, Bepanthen no longer worked. The skin itched immediately after applying the cream and became even redder than it already had been. A dermatologist suspected an intolerance to wool wax or the active ingredient Dexpanthenol. "It doesn't happen so rarely," he explained, "that the skin no longer tolerates something that it has tolerated well for years." He recommended a similarly fat ointment with no active ingredient and I was able to cope with this new cream for a quite long time. Whereby well meant that I could endure the life with my always latently inflamed skin to some extent.

But after a while also with this ointment the skin suddenly reddened and itched already during application. Now it got complicated. Because everything I tried, either stretched, itched, burned, or all at once. My skin on my face became more and more inflamed. At some point every morning I woke up with a red and swollen face and in a flaky and weak state. I tested one cream after the other and finally discovered one that put me in high spirits for two weeks. Because the feeling of tension in my facial skin was released and that just felt super. There it was—the miracle cream! I floated through the day and once again understood how much my attitude to life depended on the condition of my skin and the right cream.

For two weeks I was convinced, now finally—finally!—to have found the "Holy Grail" with this cream.

But on the 15th day the face itched. I continued to cream myself. The 16th day it was tense. I continued to cream myself. On the 17th day, the skin turned red and burned as always.

I put the cream away and I started from zero again. But ... where was zero?

> *I abstained from eggs, sugar and fruit. I renounced cereals, coffee and tea and everything sour and hot. In order not to further promote the itching, I no longer ate dairy products and food that contained a lot of histamine. For a few days had only rice, carrots or potatoes. Or potatoes with carrots. Or carrots with rice. But the fire in my face kept burning.*

Bake a Cake!

I have avoided appointments or postponed them very far into the future, always hoping to look then better and have fresh energy. I noticed that I always adjourned my life to a time with healthy skin. A future which I wished for, but which perhaps would not come for a long time, perhaps never. But should this be my life? Pull back, hide and wait? No!

I gave myself a jolt. "If my soul is all right, my skin is all right," I said, buying butter and eggs, baking a cake and inviting girlfriends whom I thought could handle my skin condition.

And of course they were able to do so! As much as my skin was *the* subject for me, so little was it for my girlfriends. The only one who had a problem with me was … me.

Suddenly I understood how much I was narrowing down myself with my limited view of myself.

I had to learn to see the world and myself anew.

Holger, a long-time friend, once said: "You always count atopic eczema, two, three, four, five, six, Iris. Count Iris, two, three, four, five, six, eczema!"

I remembered that now. I began to incorporate rituals and mindfulness exercises into my day. They helped me to stop thinking around my skin all the time. So I could learn to recognize my thoughts that have locked me into atopic eczema with all its agonies and replace them with new ones. If I caught myself trying to hide, I said to myself, "Get out and meet people! I'm sure you'll have some wonderful experiences."

And so it was. I almost forced myself to get out of the old ways of thinking and to give myself the chance to make new experiences as often as possible.

But even if I went new ways with more conscious thinking and became more alive again—my skin was completely unimpressed by my efforts.

Becoming Honest

At a seminar on stress management I worked for the first time together with my colleague Frederike. We liked each other very much, but I had no idea whether we would make a good team. It was a big group with 26 participants and I arrived with hot and sore skin at the venue. Ideal conditions for a seminar day would feel different. But I was accustomed to appearing in front of groups with my eczema appearance. How often I had mastered similar situations.

Lately I have always been very honest with my skin story. In the introduction I said right away that I had an eczema attack. This made me feel relieved and I felt much freer towards the seminar participants.

It turned out to be a great seminar. I relaxed with every hour, the cooperation with Frederike turned out to be a real stroke of luck and the feedback of the group was accordingly good.

When Frederike and I cleaned up the pinboards and packed up our materials after the seminar, she told me that she had also suffered from atopic eczema.

"That was some years ago," she said, "but at that time this ointment helped me." She reached into her pocket and took out a small tube of cream. "I always have it with me ever since. You can try it if you want." Frederike handed me the cream tube.

"Thank you," I said, took it and had to swallow. Because of her gesture and openness, but also because I had been so honest. For years I had been avoiding to talk about it in a professional context. For me private matters especially sensitive ones like this did not belong to the workplace. Now, however, I made the experience again: The more naturally and openly I dealt with my skin condition, the more I was in contact with myself and with other people. It was exactly this quality of being together that brought new energy to flow and—what was especially beautiful—made me feel joy again.

The exclusion I always feared was mainly through myself. Not through the others. On the contrary, the seminar participants signaled: "Eczema, okay. So what?" They saw my personality and my performance as a whole, my atopic eczema played no role at all for them. On the contrary I defined myself only through my skin and experienced myself almost exclusively through it.

And Now?

For a few years I had not been to a dermatologist because the doctor I trusted no longer practiced. He had mainly given classic homoeopathic treatments, but had not been afraid to prescribe steroid creams once my hands were completely inflamed.

My resolution, however, never to use topic steroids on my face and neck again, had been carved in stone since the hospital stay in Lahnstein. Just once I had to make an exception. But that was already more than seventeen years ago. I hadn't creamed my neck and body since the clinic either. There my skin had been healthy, soft and stable. Only the face was almost always in a state of emergency. There are only few photos from these years, because I hated to be photographed.

At this point all my resources were exhausted, I hoped that there would be a breakthrough in dermatology since my last visit to the dermatologist a few years ago. That something completely new had been developed after the eternal topic steroids and the youngest hope carriers Pimecrolimus and Tacrolimus, which came on the market at the beginning of

2000. I had at once tried out Elidel and Protopic with great hope. But my skin quickly got used to the active ingredient. And since the side effects could be severe and the creams were even suspected of causing skin cancer, I refused them.

Nothing New

"In your condition," said the dermatologist, who gave me the next possible appointment, "I can only offer a topical steroid ointment. Or you may try it with Protopic or Elidel. It's all we've got."

I shook my head. "Out of the question," I said decisively but very disappointed. My hope for new, more harmless, but effective active ingredients for the treatment of atopic eczema had just disappeared into thin air again.

The doctor opened his medicine cabinet and looked for some samples of cosmetic lotions and ointments.

"Maybe there's something in it that helps," he said and handed me some packs. "Especially the creams with urea are quite good. You may also try it with black tea compresses. The tannic acid alleviates inflammations."

Nothing new, no miracle cure. Instead, the old-fashioned and well-tried black tea compresses. Many sufferers of atopic eczema actually have good experiences with them, I also had tried them several times. Under the compress with the lukewarm tea it was always quite acceptable. But after that the feeling of heat and tension in my skin increased extremely.

Pimecrolimus and Tacrolimus are natural products of microorganisms (fungi) that have been developed for prevention or treatment after an organ transplant.

They're supposed to prevent the rejection of the new organ. The same active ingredient is available in ointments form for the treatment of atopic eczema.

The active ingredients Tacrolimus and Pimecrolimus were celebrated as steroid alternatives. In the meantime, however, disillusionment has set in: For the U.S. Food and Drug Administration (FDA), the side effects were reason enough for a warning against skin cancer that could result from Tacrolimus and Pimecrolimus. In Europe other therapy methods must have been exhausted before Tacrolimus is prescribed.

New Clinic, New Luck

Disappointed, I cycled home from the doctor's office. I sat down on the sofa with my laptop and googled "Spezialklinik Neukirchen". Years ago I had already read something about this clinic, and while surfing in atopic eczema forums I came across it again and again. I actually wanted to avoid a further stay in a clinic after I had been to the North Sea Island Borkum just four years before. In the ocean climate—always outside by the sea, with a lot of relaxation, ultraviolet irradiation and super nutrition—my skin recovered quickly. But after one, two weeks at home my skin had been back to its old condition.

I could no longer bear the thought that I only had a break from the atopic eczema and a new attack was guaranteed to come back. I finally wanted to find keys for my eczema. I wanted to know what I had to do so that I was no longer its prisoner.

Neukirchen's therapy concept included comprehensive diagnostic procedure that absolutely met my need to finally find the causes of atopic eczema. The doctors there treated without steroid creams, and holistically. Nutrition also played a central role in the recovery process.

I ordered information material and was torn back and forth. Should I really go there? The clinic ratings on the internet ranged from "catastrophic" to "the best place ever".

But what did I have to lose? Except for the umpteenth time, the hope of not finding the key to healthy skin there either. So I called the clinic.

"We won't have a vacancy for another three months," said the lady at the other end of the line.

Hallelujah, good news! Maybe I wouldn't have to go to the clinic after all? Because what could not happen in three months? Maybe I would finally experience one of those fantastic spontaneous healings, for example with the help of hemp oil, which I had been eating for several weeks. Or by leaving out apples and eggs, which I tried to do just as well. Or through the new homoeopathic therapy. This time not with self-medication, but with an experienced doctor at my side, who had prepared a well-founded anamnesis.

But what had not happened in the months before did not happen in the following weeks either. On the contrary, my skin got worse and I became more and more compulsive about what to eat. So I checked in at the "Spezialklinik Neukirchen" in the deep Bavarian Forest.

Testing and Hoping

Apart from the fact that the clinic building looked old-fashioned in comparison to those I already knew and that the rooms were sober as in a hospital, I felt in Neukirchen at the right place at the right time. I had the good feeling that with the help of the extensive diagnostic procedures the doctors and all the people working there really cared about what triggered the permanent inflammatory process in my body and didn't let it come to rest.

When I think of the clinic, the first things that come to mind are the small and large masked figures. They walked along the long corridors, wearing head bandages with slits for the eyes, nose and mouth and they were dressed in striped shirts and pyjama-like trousers. The clinic provided these clothes for the duration of the stay, so that the patients' own clothes were protected from the ointments that were applied two or three times a day in the nursing room.

On my way there, I passed many "before and after" collages on the walls where patients had documented their progress in healing. There were shocking skin diseases to be seen. All the more fascinating were the photos in which the skin had completely healed after weeks or sometimes months in the clinic and the faces were beaming with joy and relief.

In addition to atopic eczema, the "Spezialklinik Neukirchen" also treats diseases such as psoriasis, chronic fatigue syndrome (CFS), allergic asthma, acne and autoimmune diseases.

The clinic offers a comprehensive and holistic diagnosis and therapy procedure, which requires a great commitment on the part of the patients to participate. In the case of atopic eczema steroids are completely avoided. Instead they use antibiotics and antiseptic drugs. In addition to daily application of cream, nutrition is one of the main pillars of the therapy, which is put together individually for the patient according to his test results and other diagnostic procedures.

Neukirchen is small and quiet, it lies on the border to the Czech Republic. The village offers ideal opportunities for beautiful mountain hikes and excursions.

For the first time for so long I had the hope that with this concept of new creams, physical analysis and nutrition everything would finally also become fine for me.

There were always mothers with their babies or toddlers not having a single spot of eczema-free area on their entire small bodies. The mothers learned from the nurses how to apply the ointment dressings correctly and how to wrap the tiny hands professionally in "boxer gloves" so that the children could not scratch themselves bloody. The small boys and girls, who already knew what a boxer was, walked proudly through the clinic and showed their little fists around.

*Two-year-old Amanda never played. Like many of
the very young ones there, she had never experienced
what a skin felt like without burning, aching or itching. I will never forget her sad and serious look of
her inflamed eyes, her impressive patience, but also
the irrepressible rage with which she endured the
cream and bandage procedures three times a day.*

I was prescribed zinc oxide paste, antibiotic and antiseptic
active substances, which were each mixed into a cream or
ointment base. I highly appreciated the fact that the clinic
offered many different cream bases to try out, so that each
patient could find out what he or she could cope with and
what the skin did not like at all. The range of creams also
included expensive products on an alkaline basis, the costs of
which are normally not covered by the German Health
Insurance Funds. Active ingredients such as hibiscus and
incense, which has an anti-inflammatory effect and which the
ancient Egyptians used to disinfection, were also used in the
treatment concept. However, I found it difficult that most of
the creams and ointments in the clinic contained parabens
and paraffin—preservatives and mineral oils that are thought
to promote allergies and trigger atopic eczema.

Eating in Rhythm

The meals were simple, tasty and a joy to eat in the morning,
at noon and in the evening—if you appreciate fresh vegetables
and fruit prepared as naturally as possible. They were based on

the rotating diet, an alternative method of nutrition with the aim of healing intolerances and preventing new ones.

All patients worked with the clinic's nutritionist to develop an individual nutrition plan, which was then compared on the basis of experience with consumed foods and the results of the tests. The plan was constantly updated by observing the physical reactions. The results of the food intolerance tests were of burning interest to me. I could hardly wait to finally see if my body really had problems with certain foods. If so, I would avoid them in the future. If not, I could finally eat again everything that I had blamed so long for my skin problems.

The rotating diet is particularly useful if it has already been determined which foods are not tolerated or cause allergies. But it is also suitable for finding the triggering substances.

The compatible foods are consumed at intervals of 4 or 7 days. This means that what you eat today is only eaten again after 4 or 7 days.
Allergies and intolerances strain the intestines and the entire immune system. However, the body gets a great chance to recover from these stresses and the immune system is also strengthened by the interval between food intake. Symptoms and the complaints can thus be reduced and brought to an end.

"Since I have only been feeding Sascha according to the results of the food intolerance test, his atopic eczema and allergies have greatly improved," Irina, a young mother, said enthusiastically at lunch in the dining room.

Elke, who was in the clinic for the second time and also sat at our table, nodded thoughtfully. "It came out last year," she reported, "that I'm allergic to wheat. Therefore, I switched to quinoa and bought everything there was with quinoa: Quinoa bread, quinoa burger, quinoa muesli, quinoa flakes and quinoa wafers. I ate it puffed, baked, cooked, steamed and fried. With the result that I am now allergic to quinoa. And I have to find out anew what I can eat now."

Even though it was quite clear to me that test results were always just a flash, they gave me the orientation I needed so badly at the time. With the results in my pocket, I finally had clues as to what I could eat and what was not good for me.

The constant and so gruelling helplessness on the question of food selection now belonged once and for all to the past. And if I stuck to this diet, which tasted good to me and also corresponded to my way of cooking, if I ate my favourite sweets—as hard as it would be —only rarely, ideally not at all, then everything could finally become good.

In Neukirchen I was convinced by how consistent the clinic was in the implementation of its therapy concept. I could try out things there that were rather difficult for me at home. Like drinking a different herbal tea every day, which supported the skin-health. Or that I could daily enjoy the meals, which were prepared so creatively according to the rotation principle, and feel their calming and strengthening effect on body and soul.

A test is always just a snapshot. Our body changes constantly as well as its ability to react to certain substances.

A doctor had told me once about a patient who immediately had his airways swollen at the slightest bite of tomato. On holiday in Greece he ate once a piece of tomato and was very frightened. But nothing happened. He was very astonished and ate another tomato piece. And also this time the expected reaction failed to materialize. A phenomenon for which there are many scientific explanations: On holiday body and soul are relaxed and have a completely different tolerance to react to allergens. Or the tomatoes the man ate at home were burdened with pesticides. Or it was another kind of tomato. Or... or...

Good in Bad

In the peace and seclusion of the clinic, I began again to think about the significance of the atopic eczema for myself and my life. Could the skin perhaps not heal because I was unconsciously convinced that the eczema had grown together with my being and me? And that it would always remain so?

I began to wonder what I received by the eczema. There must be a psychological reason also, it had to give me something that I couldn't get by other means. As much as I wanted to get rid of the eczema, I needed it. Because it allowed me to satisfy wishes and needs for which I had no other strategy. Because it allowed me to satisfy wishes and needs for which I had no other strategy. For example, to skip the last lesson at school. Because I was not feeling well in my skin, but also because I didn't feel like it anymore and knew that the teachers were indulgent with me.

In the Grammar School, I even had an attestation for sports, because my skin did not tolerate sweating. The free hours, however, I have tolerated wonderfully.

With the atopic eczema it was no problem to be in a bad mood or to withdraw. Everybody understood. But without it, I wouldn't have known how to do it.

Since I could think, the eczema belonged to my system. I didn't had to develop any other methods of dealing with myself. It was one thing to make me aware of the benefits I had gained from atopic eczema for decades. But to see how I used them to give me advantages ... that was a very hard lesson.

The "gain from illness" refers to the benefits you could derive from an illness.

If you are ill, you can avoid unpleasant situations such as exams or appointments that can cause difficulties or that you are afraid of.

The gain from an illness could be that you suddenly receive from the environment the attention or support that you miss in a healthy state.

Often the gain from illness is an unconscious process. If you want to get healthy, but suspect that you need your disease, an honest analysis of the benefits of the sickness can be a significant contribution to recovery.

In the course of the last years I had learnt to clearly say what I wanted and what I didn't want. And also to stand by it. This didn't have to take over my skin for me anymore.

But nevertheless atopic eczema still had important tasks. The more vehement it was, the more I took care of myself, allowed myself to rest and listened attentively into myself to find out what I needed. It didn't leave me another choice.

I had to take care of myself in healthy times and to satisfy my needs in such a way that I felt good on the one hand, but on the other hand I could sometimes do without their fulfillment. For example, when something as important as keeping company with others required me to renounce my need for withdrawal. That was a real challenge. And there was still much to do.

All Is Well. Is All Well?

At the end of the three weeks stay in the "Spezialklinik Neukirchen" I felt so good and looked more relaxed and healthy than I had in ages. Again richer in experience, hope and energy and with a big bag full of creams and ointments I travelled home.

But also with a rotating diet, without gluten—because of the high allergy potential, without coffee—because of the acidity, the many bitter and irritating substances and the caffeine—and finally even without rice cakes—because of their high degree of arsenic and acrylamide—the atopic eczema flared up again. The familiar spots around the mouth first tinged slightly, almost imperceptibly, then flickered more strongly, finally burned, turning red and igniting. With the ointments from Neukirchen the eczema could still be controlled a little bit. I smeared myself through my complete range of pots and pans. But after four weeks nothing worked anymore.

I was stunned and felt devastated.

My last great hopes, the diet, the new ointments and creams no longer worked. The eczema showed once again that it could not be controlled, let alone cured. And my old trauma of being powerlessly at the mercy of arbitrariness and merciless rule broke out again with all its might.

It maybe sound strange but from my today's perspective but I'm so grateful it came to this. Otherwise I might not feel so well now and wouldn't have so much healthy energy. And I couldn't have written the next chapter—the amazing turning point of my story for the good.

Chapter 3
Saving My Skin

*I don't know if it'll get better if it's different.
But it has to be different if it's gonna be
better.*

Georg Christoph Lichtenberg

In the next weeks I managed my daily life with my last tiny bit of strength. I tried again and again at intervals of a few days the ointments from Neukirchen, either as pure care or with active ingredients. But my skin consistently rejected them. I also made another attempt with the once so reliable Bepanthen. But here, too, no negotiation was possible. Thousands of times I tried everything that lay in my cream - drawer and what drugstores and pharmacies had on offer: ointment after ointment, cream after cream, lotion after lotion.

But nothing gave me the slightest feeling that my skin was relaxing. On the contrary: The constant trying out of new creams irritated my skin even more.

Creams didn't help, but without ointments it was also unbearable. I didn't know how to deal with myself anymore, I was at a loss what to eat. Whether I renounced sugar, grain, milk, cheese and kefir, apples, eggs, green tea, coffee and rice waffles or not—it made no difference.

In German there is the saying "it's to get out of your skin", which means something like "it was enough to drive you up the wall".

In Madagascar there is the fish scale gecko. This gecko species can shed its skin when attacked. His dandruff then separates completely from his body, the gecko literally drives out of his skin and escapes. Afterwards the skin and dandruff regenerate very quickly. Not that I wanted to swap with a gecko. But this mechanism... enviable.

I reduced my professional and private appointments to the bare minimum. The calm was relieving, but it didn't improve my skin condition. Desperately searching the internet again for suitable, promising homoeopathic remedies, I wandered again through the forums for atopic eczema. Perhaps someone had actually found the "Holy Grail" of healing in the meantime.

Yet Still a Miracle?

Before Christmas I drove to Munich and ordered a new cream in a pharmacy on December 22 in the morning. I had read an advertisement on the train and had regained hope. When I bought the cream with advance payment, the pharmacist told me about a customer who had also suffered a long time from atopic eczema. But whose skin was now in a wonderful state thanks to this ointment.

I just loved to hear it. Maybe there was a Christmas miracle for me this year?

I have wished for nothing more than to get a break during the Christmas holidays from the fact that everything was always hard and difficult to bear. I wanted to feel the desire to meet friends and enjoy the sweetness of life in the form of Christmas cookies and Dresdner Stollen. I just wanted to feel "normal" again. Or at least a little better. Just a little, just a tiny bit better...

Full of hope and with joyful expectation, I picked up the cream at the pharmacy in the afternoon, wished Merry Christmas and hurried out. On the sidewalk I opened immediately the cream tube. The cream smelled good and had a pleasantly greasy lubricating factor when I tried it on the back of my hand. Nothing happened. Great. But also not surprising, since the skin on my hands was fine and mostly didn't react at once. So I applied a small amount of cream under my right cheek. What I felt shortly afterwards was enough to hectically pull the water bottle out of my bag and wash off the cream panically.

The spot on my cheek was still burning sharply when I was already sitting on our sofa again and understood what had happened on the sidewalk less than 20 minutes ago: My hope of having "skin vacation" at this Christmas Eve had burst once more like a soap bubble.

Have you ever heard of the stewardess disease, also known as clown eczema, perioral eczema or mannequin disease?

The stewardess disease is a non-infectious inflammation that is ring-like around the mouth. The skin there becomes drier and scaly, it stretches, forms inflammatory pimples and red nodules. One reason for this is too much care. For those affected, however, it seems logical to use even more creams and cosmetics to improve the skin's moisture and fat balance. In the long run, however, this aggravates the symptoms as the skin cells become dependent. Or they even develop an allergy to one of the ingredients of the product through the constant application of it.

It has been scientifically proven that this eczema can occur when cosmetic products are frequently changed or constantly tried out. Perioral eczema has become known as a stewardess disease because flight attendants are the prototype for this skin disease. A well-groomed appearance is part of their job, they can easily come into contact with many cosmetic articles in duty-free shops and constantly try out new ones. The dry air in the airplane also leads to the need to want to apply cream permanently.

But of course, perioral eczema cannot only affect stewardesses—it can affect anyone who loves skin care and cosmetics and enjoys trying them out.

On Zero Again

Outside, it was beginning to dawn. I stared at the trees whose outlines were barely visible. "The greater the expectation, the deeper the fall," it kept going through my mind. I just fell very low at that moment.

Apart from the short period in and shortly after Neukirchen, I hadn't had relaxed skin for more than a year now. In the years before I had felt better every now and then but never really well. What was it that kept this inflammation going on and on? What did I do wrong?

Didn't I do what I could? I paid attention to the right balance between tension and relaxation. I had reoriented myself professionally. Of course, that was a big challenge that also brought stress. But it felt right and good. Writing books and working with people in coaching, seminars and workshops was absolutely fulfilling for me.

I meditated, had a happy relationship and made sure that my thoughts were as positive and strengthening as possible. But why had been there only an occasional short respite from atopic eczema every now and then for so many years? Periods that were far too short for my skin to heal and recover.

As a little girl I had atopic eczema without drinking coffee or stuffing myself with chocolate and other sweets. I ate oranges, mandarins and lemons or dishes that were spicy. Things that I consistently avoid to do today. But no matter whether I had eczema as a child or not—my skin was creamed. Because on the advice of dermatologists the skin

always had to be well cared for. From an early age
on I smeared ointment onto my skin day after day,
month after month and year after year like butter on
a sandwich. Except for the time in Lahnstein. Six
weeks without creams, during which the skin all over
my body had completely recovered.

I stopped for a moment.

Was the permanent inflammation of the face perhaps connected with decades of creaming?

I had already had this suspicion once in summer and tried to get by without cream. Instead of getting calmer, the skin became crazier by the hour. I tortured myself through six endless days, then I gave up. The first time I lubricated again, it was as if I had received water shortly before I died of thirst: total salvation! If my skin was so craving for cream, it couldn't be right to withdraw it, could it? I finally declared this therapeutic approach a failure once and for all.

However, doubt crept in, because the moment of relief after reapplying cream lasted only briefly. Already after a very short time the skin began to burn again and I did what I had always done in such situations—I smeared again and again.

But in Lahnstein? There I have endured three long weeks in the agonizing dryness of the skin desert. Then the first patch of healthy skin appeared on my neck. Since then, I haven't creamed my body at all. Only the areas where my skin was sometimes very dry were rubbed with a light lotion every few weeks. Until this also led to itching. I had been using a little hemp oil at longer intervals ever since.

Outside it had become dark. I lit a candle and looked into the flickering flame.

Suddenly I remembered the Bible verse, I got on my confirmation: "Enter by the narrow gate; for the gate is wide and the way is easy, that leads to destruction, and those who enter by it are many. For the gate is narrow and the road is hard that leads to life, and there are few who find it." (Mt. 7:13-14)

Our skin is different in every part of the body and therefore it has different needs everywhere.

The legs have a different skin quality than the face. Compared to the skin on the body, our facial skin is particularly thin and sensitive, the skin on the eyelids is the thinnest.

The skin on the back of the hand is also extremely flimsy because it has hardly any fatty tissue. In contrast, the skin on the palms of the hands and soles of the feet contains a lot of fat and connective tissue and is covered with a robust thick horn layer. This is also the reason why the skin is thickest there.

Because our skin is so different, it also has diverse needs and reacts differently everywhere. So a cream that is unpleasant on the face can feel good on the body. And a lotion that is pleasant on the arms burns in the face or causes redness and feelings of tension.

It's Getting Tight

I have walked many wide and comfortable ways in my life. One of my favourite Bible verse then reminded me always what it was really about. It already has shown me many uncomfortable and unpleasant truth about me and my lifestyle.

Wasn't the creaming an 'easy' way, too? And wasn't the renunciation of this aid the eye of the needle, the narrow gate that led to the healing skin and again to life?

What has been working on the neck and the whole body for a long time—why shouldn't it work on the face? Maybe the week of ointment and cream abstinence in summer was just way too short? For decades I have brought kilograms of mineral oil, plasticizers and preservatives through the pores of my facial skin into my body system. Probably it just took a lot longer to regenerate.

Should I try it again without any creams?

And then—no matter what would happen—hold on until I noticed that the skin really started to recover? As I had once experienced it in Lahnstein?

*I had two weeks of Christmas-vacation ahead of me.
I didn't have to meet anyone, nobody had to see me if
the skin freaked out again. Just my partner. And he'd
give me all the support and encouragement I needed
for this second great trek through the skin desert.*

Yes. I wanted to do it. My skin should again get the chance to become completely healthy without fatty creams. Even the small back door "olive paste" should not be there this time.

I got up from the sofa, blew out the candle and turned on the light. Then I fetched a bag from the kitchen and collected all the ointment tubes and cream pots scattered all over the rooms—in the hallway, in the bathroom and next to the bed—and put them in the bottom drawer of the nightstand.

That was on December 22, late afternoon. In the evening the skin tightened so much that I longed to take some cream out of the bag and lubricate it. But I resisted, went for a walk and stood up to the fact that my skin felt hotter and more tense by the hour. It rebelled already, but I wouldn't give in to its desires. Over the next two weeks my skin should return to its own strength. And besides the hope that this way would not lead to the rescue of my skin, I had nothing to lose.

The next morning was a terrible awakening. My face felt like it was cooking. It was glowing hot, pulsating and so swollen that I could hardly see out of my eyes.

Carefully I washed myself, made cooling compresses and brushed my in a way so that as little water as possible touched my sensitive skin. I avoided everything that might bother it.

Some parts of the face got wet anyway. I gently dabbed it dry with the towel, so that I would not rub the valuable sebum away, which had perhaps already slowly formed again.

The Fat Factory

December 24 came. My skin glowed and burned, it begged and begged for cream. Several times I was close to giving up, to walk to the chest of drawers to reach for the tube. I didn't do it. But I only managed to do so because I wasn't alone with my furious skin.

We went to the Christmas Eve Service, went for many walks and made ourselves as cosy and relaxing as possible over the holidays. As cosy as I could make it in my skin prison. I clung to the idea that things wouldn't go on like this forever. That this tough Christmas period was my new beginning. And that I would soon see how right it was what I was doing here.

Fortunately, this time I didn't have to endure cortisone withdrawal, I just had to endure the withdrawal of the fats. But that was quite enough.

And that my skin rebelled—of course! When it suddenly couldn't get its "drug" anymore, on which it had been able to rely on one hundred percent for decades. My skin was addicted to grease. A junkie. And I, his dealer, had canceled the delivery.

Once my skin realized that the external supply was no longer there, it would consider how to get what it needed so badly: fat and moisture. It would focus on its resources and get the old, rusty machines of its fat factory running again. In years of inactivity they were probably completely dusty and rusty. But they did exist and they still worked. They had proved this impressively years ago in Lahnstein.

Dehydration

During the next two weeks the temperature of the skin dropped a little and the "mask period" began. It felt as if a thick layer of hot earth was growing and drying on the face. I constantly had the desire to wash off this sticky coating, which felt so strange, hard and dirty.

The region around the mouth became numb like after an anaesthetic at the dentist. The lips dried out so much that they looked white and wrinkly and tore with every movement. For a few days I could hardly open my mouth, which made eating difficult. So I slurped pureed soups and smoothies from vegetables and fruits through the straw.

Does too much cream make the skin lazy?

Some experts say yes, others say no. But there are few studies on this question. Researchers at the University of Copenhagen believe that the skin's protective barrier suffers if you constantly cream over a long period of time. In addition the skin loses even more water out of the body, because the horny layer swells up with moisturizing cream and lets more water out.

However, this issue has not yet been finally resolved. The best thing to do is to be sensitive to how your skin feels and reacts.

"Wow!" my partner shouted after a week when I sat down at the breakfast table with a face that felt like a mask, "You have a completely different appearance!"

"Really?" I asked skeptically.

"Yes. So much more alive! And somehow healthier, too."

After eight days, the skin, which still stuck to the face like a dry, heavy clay mask, became paler in some spots and began to peel off. The feeling of inflammation, which had been constantly in the eyes for the last few months despite eye drops, improved and gradually disappeared. With the end of creaming I had also omitted the eye drops and put the bottle to the creams and ointments in the drawer. Until then, I had taken the drops daily.

> *Day 10: Still extreme tension around the mouth and this strange numbness. The lips are as dry as paper. But the redness between mouth and nose is no longer there. And under the jawbone, the skin is now smooth and soft. And no more itching at all!*

Should I take permanent showers again like in Lahnstein? But I suspected that the Munich water was not very good for the skin because of its hardness. So I decided against showering.

Since I had been interested in water quality for quite some time, I looked at the drinking water analyses of the cities where I had lived.

Why do babies in the south of England suffer more from atopic eczema than in the north?

The reason for this seems to be the lime content of the water. Because there are signs that the water hardness, the lime content in tap water, influences the skin barrier. The skin of patients with atopic eczema partly lacks this barrier function. Therefore, it often produces less sweat and sebum. In addition, many patients show a mutation in the filaggrin gene, which is responsible for the keratinization of skin cells.

Scientists at King's College in London examined 1,300 three-month-old babies for symptoms of atopic eczema. To evaluate the skin barrier function, the "transepidermal water loss" (TEWL) was measured in the skin, an indicator that indicates the water loss via the outermost skin layer. At the same time, the researchers wanted to know how often babies were bathed and determined the hardness of the bath water. The results showed that keeping babies at home with high water hardness increased the risk of developing atopic eczema by 87 percent. In addition, there was a clear north-south divide, as the water in southern England is harder than in the north. Children with a mutated filaggrin gene appear to be particularly at risk.

The researchers are now investigating whether the risk to develop atopic eczema is directly influence by the lime content of the water. Or whether factors such as the pH-value, which measures the acidity of a liquid and also depends on the lime content of the water, also play a role.

In the region of the Lower Rhine, where I grew up, the water was soft. In Cologne, where I lived while I was a student, it was hard. In Munich, too. In Frankfurt it was soft and in the City district of Hamburg where I lived for a long time, it was medium hard.

I always recognized the hardness of the tap water by how often I had to decalcify the kettle. In Munich I could do that every three days. I was very surprised when I found out that Lahnstein also had hard water. Perhaps the stimulus that hydrotherapy exerted on the skin was so strong that it made my affected skin really mobilize all its healing powers. And was thus able to rebuild a stable skin barrier—even under extreme conditions, such as hard water is on for atopic eczema.

Starting from the Beginning Again

When I drove back home after two weeks of Christmas holidays, my face was still very warm and reddened, but the blazing heat had been extinguished. Also the sensation of inflammation in the eyes was completely gone.

The skin was crumbly, scaly and brittle, in some spots it looked like parchment. Nevertheless I enjoyed the return journey in a train compartment with dust-dry heating air. To my own surprise this time I didn't care much when fellow travellers looked at me. How different I had travelled to Munich two weeks ago! Just for this relaxed feeling the stony way of the past 14 days had been worth it.

But not just for that. My skin had changed—I could not only feel it, I could also see it. Now I dared to look in the mirror every day and saw tiny, very tiny healing steps, which motivated me enormously to continue my way without creams.

At home the everyday life started again. A moving to a new flat was on the agenda, professional topics wanted to be organized, book projects to be completed. Only now did I realize how little energy I really had and how sensitive my condition still was. I had underestimated this during the retreat and rest in the Christmas period and in the euphoria of the return journey.

The heat in my face was gone, but the clay mask feeling was as gruelling as the hot skin. Besides, the mouth and lips still looked wild. And where they did not feel numb, they felt sore and hurt.

After a professional appointment on a dark and cold rainy day, I felt so weak and hungry that I bought myself a Turkish pizza. I am used to take my own food with me. But this time I didn't because I thought I'd be home sooner.

It was clear to me that the pizza was not the ideal meal concerning spices and other ingredients. Itching would be the logical result. Yet the thought of not eating pureed vegetables today made my mouth water. But there was no way to eat this pizza without using an ointment for the corners of the mouth.

I hurried to the nearest pharmacy and bought a small tube of Bepanthen. For the corners of my mouth so that I could open my mouth a little wider when I bite into this delicacy.

Excitedly I ripped the box open and the guilty conscience came up the same moment I opened the tube. But I creamed only once … that couldn't be so bad!

When the cream touched the corners of my mouth, this indescribable feeling of relief and salvation was immediately there again.

I enjoyed every bite of the pizza. And even if it were only these two mini spots on my face that relaxed—to me it seemed as if a new world opened up. Wow—this could be everyday life! You just do the things that are on your schedule and then eat spontaneously on the road. How great!

It didn't take half an hour until my skin was longing for the cream again.

And what did I do? I fished the Bepanthen from the coat pocket and smeared. To cut it short: I got back into the cream addiction faster than I could think. The Bepanthen only worked for a short time. So I tried all the ointments I still had at home and my skin looked exactly the same after a week as before Christmas. The only difference was that I felt much worse. Because I had destroyed in no time at all the recovery of the skin, for which I had endured so much in the last weeks—by the frivolous and comfortable reach for the cream tube.

Keep Moving!

The cream relapse was very bad indeed. But in the past three weeks I had experienced that the condition of the skin actually had improved. And that the way without creams and ointments, no matter how arduous and tedious it was, was the right one. I wanted to continue the journey even if I didn't know if and when I would arrive in the land of healthy skin. So on January 25 I collected all the creams again, put them in a box and took them to the attic.

And since that day my facial skin has not come into contact with any grease cream, ointment or lotion.

The exterior was one thing. My face looked completely unkempt with all the dandruff and dry skin. That's what it was like if you equate care with creams. But it was much worse to live with this permanent feeling of parched earth on the skin, to which a sour burning sensation had been added. It was extremely nerve-wracking. I just wanted to get rid of this mask, tear or wash it off to the last layer.

At the beginning of the skin drying process I avoided water on my face as much as possible. Except of course to wash my eyes and brush my teeth. Now the short instants in the morning when I dipped my face in two hands full of water were the only moments of the day that felt normal. But after the dry dabbing the relaxed feeling had gone again.

At that time I worked mostly at home and I didn't even ask myself if I'm allowed to give myself the peace and quietness that my body now needed for its enormous skin repair and regeneration work. It went without saying. Like I also took the time I needed to mentally let go of eczema. I wrote a letter to the atopic eczema thanking it for everything it had done for me. For decades the eczema had to serve as an excuse for many things that I did not like to do. And yet it enabled me to develop my strengths: to believe firmly in something, to improvise and also to enjoy life to the fullest. Above all I owe the eczema an immense spectrum of emotions. Whether to the dark valley of despair or to the highest summit of happiness—it had already led me everywhere.

I promised the atopic eczema that I would take care in the future of my needs even without its help. And if I didn't, I let it remind me. I also promised it not to condemn it for doing so but to understand the skin reaction as a signal to look after myself earlier.

Shedding the Skin

I felt like a snake shedding its skin. This was actually a good sign, because under the exfoliating skin the new one appears, in the best case a healthy one. But every time a layer of dandruff was removed, the new skin underneath was still red and hot.

It took a few weeks and several shedding procedures until finally paler skin became visible. It was very dry, but it was no longer inflamed. How wonderful!

"It will be all right," I said bravely to myself when I saw my red and white spotted face in the mirror, "just a little bit more patience. We're on the right track."

The lips dried out so extremely that they ruptured and bled at the slightest movement. At some point, it was too much for me. I applied a thin layer baby cream with zinc on my lower lip, which I usually couldn't tolerate. The hope that zinc could now be good was stronger than my concerns and my experience. And—oh wonder—my lips relaxed!

Immediately the temptation was there to lubricate the cream on the face. Perhaps then everything would heal very quickly?

This time I didn't do it. I had already come so far, the process of changing in my skin was obviously being at work and I did not want to disturb it again and set myself back for weeks again. My mirror ritual—smiling at myself every day—became as natural as brushing my teeth. And it was wonderful to watch how the feeling of affection and trust in myself gradually spread faster and faster and deeper within me.

"This gets under my skin", "he has a thick skin" or "she is very thin-skinned"—many expressions show how closely the psyche is connected with the body.

The science of psychoneuroimmunology investigates how our thoughts and behavior are related to our immune system and hormone production. Feelings can maintain health or even help restore it! For the conviction that a challenging life situation is meaningful and can be mastered creates a hopeful and full expectation. This in turn ensures that excessive immune defense and hormone production is reduced to the normal level. The resulting relaxation creates the physical conditions for well-being and health.

The best thing we can do for our health is to encourage ourselves as often as possible and be happy. Hormones of happiness are the purest medicine for the body and also prevent diseases. The best example of this are people who have just fallen in love—they get rarely sick.

Relaxation

In the middle of March I was invited to my girlfriend Susanne's birthday party. Her husband Thomas, who also suffers from atopic eczema and who hadn't seen me for a long time, looked astonished at me.

"Gee, you look great!" he cried enthusiastically. "What'd you do?" It was true. Compared to the beginning of the year, my skin was unrecognizable. The inflammation had completely disappeared from the face. It was no longer swollen, had no spots and my eyes were clear and no longer itchy. Apart from a few scaly spots, I looked perfectly healthy. What was even more important for me: I felt totally healthy! No burning, no "earth-drying-on-the-skin" feeling, no paralyzing heat.

The feeling of wearing a mask feeling had disappeared exactly one day before the celebration of Susanne's birthday. And—hooray—the numbness around the mouth too.

That morning I was sitting at the breakfast table, pouring myself coffee and suddenly I noticed it: the skin on my face was "silent", I didn't feel it! For the first time in weeks, in months, in years there was nothing that disturbed or impaired me. I was just there with my cup of coffee and a calm skin. What an experience, what a sensational, great feeling!

It was Susanne's birthday, but I also celebrated—my new skin! I enjoyed that I didn't care someone looked at me. For years I hadn't been as carefree and relaxed as I was that night. I completely enjoyed every second of this wonderful new feeling.

Although my skin was still dry, it did not stretch and kept recovering steadily from now on. At intervals of three weeks there were phases in which the philtrum—the small area between the upper lip and nose—became inflamed and scaled. I suspected cashew nuts or mustard. Because the better I felt, the more I ate the things I had avoided for a very long time. Now Cashew nuts and mustard were removed again from the menu for the moment. But the philtrum continued to inflame.

In the beginning such a mini eczema attack lasted two weeks, then ten days, at some point only three days. At the first of these small relapses I was very afraid that this again was the start of another long period of serious eczema. But I managed to keep my fingers off the creams and saw the skin recover by itself within two weeks. The intervals between these inflammations between mouth and nose became larger and larger. Until they didn't appear at all.

It was as if the skin and body went through several healing phases in which they transported decades of residues and harmful substances from creams to the surface. It helped me very much to imagine that any eczema mini relapse only served to give me another step to healing and health.

In winter I got brittle hands with painful fissures on my fingers. Since the skin on my hands had been wonderful in the last few months, I took the hand cream that I had tolerated best until then. The skin became smoother, but I had to cream in ever shorter intervals. At night, my fingers itched so much that I was awakened by my own inner voice that warned "don't rub". Nevertheless I had a sore skin in the morning.

I put one and one together. The result: total cream stop. So the hand cream migrated to the other creams in the attic and the drying process of the skin started all over again. But I knew it was only a matter of time: What had healed my face would also be good for my hands. I just had to be patient again.

Brittle, rough and cracked hands in winter are often also a problem for people who otherwise have no difficulty with their skin.

The dry winter air, temperature fluctuations, icy winds and an immune system weakened by infections put the skin in great strain at this time. This is mainly due to the fact that the body limits sebum production at an outside temperature below 8°C, which makes the natural protective barrier more permeable. Since cold air is also very dry, moisture is extracted from the skin additionally. This also happens with dry air through heaters in the office or at home.

For four weeks my fingers were very dry, rough and wrinkled and I didn't want to touch anything. But here, too, the reward for the endurance showed itself: the skin on the hands recovered, it became soft and elastic again. And the painful, bothering itching stopped completely.

Skin Miracle—Miracle Skin

Since I started living without creams and ointments four years ago, my skin has become more and more stable. I no longer have to get up hours earlier to cool my face, apply creams on it and decongest it. Neither do I have to prepare myself mentally to go among people. In the morning I wake up and feel good. Isn't that great? Isn't that a miracle?

I don't have to cancel appointments anymore because I don't want to be seen by others. On the contrary, I want people to see me! Today I like to go to invitations, I invite people and enjoy being together with friends and nice people.

I go to the hairdresser's, I can easily stand to be looked at. In the first summer after the cream withdrawal I swam in a seawater indoor swimming pool, of course without applying cream before or after. It burned slightly at first, but after a few lanes it was gone too. In the second summer the burning was hardly there. While I used to hectically apply my creams after swimming to lubricate my inflamed and burning skin, I now shower and dry myself in complete peace and quiet.

A hat with a wide brim, my big sunglasses and above all the right timing protect me at the seaside. When I'm planning extended hikes or longer bike tours, I'm not doing that exactly in the bright midday sun. And I do such actions anyway only after a few days of getting used to a new climate and the summer.

I jog, I sweat and the sweat doesn't itch unbearably anymore. In winter my skin is able to balance the temperature in heated rooms and can cope with the dry indoor air. I don't immediately look for the darkest corner in illuminated rooms, mirrors are no longer enemies. And what I never thought possible: I even like bright summer days now! What an incredible, great freedom to no longer experience my life and myself exclusively through the discomfort that my skin has caused me for so long.

A Ride of Hell

My way to my well-being skin was a tightrope walk. A venture I didn't know how it would end. A real ride of hell.

In the long term, no one but oneself can be expected to withhold the cream from the skin in cases of atopic eczema. And it might work only if you are prepared to show enormous patience, courage and hope. You need to have a lot of strength and perseverance during the hard and long phases when nothing seems to move, when you see regression rather than progress and continue to feel ill.

I was ready for it. Like a snake that grows all its life and feels when it is time for the next shedding because its skin, which cannot grow with it, has become too small. During the transformation process, the snake is very vulnerable. It withdraws to a safe place and then winds herself with great effort and patience out of her old skin. The snake gives the new one time to dry so that it can become stable and resistant. In this phase, the snake lives from its reserves. Until the reptile—now bigger and much stronger—can go back to its usual life.

Without my temporal and spatial refuge, into which I could withdraw during the first ten weeks of the ointment withdrawal, and without my "reserves"—the unconditional support of people who also believed in my way—I probably would not have made it. Although now I see and experience my healthy skin every day, it still sometimes seems like a miracle to me. But not like a miracle that has unexpectedly fallen into my lap. Rather like one that I have walked towards step by step on a rocky road.

I believe that the heavenly powers did not foresee an easy path for me, because I probably would have always been skeptical about how long my healthy skin would last and I would have caused myself a lot of stress with this doubt. So I had to get active myself. I'm glad I managed to do so by going through the narrow gate of the arduous way of total ointment and cream abstinence. The way that finally led me to the salvation of my skin.

And It Goes On

Through atopic eczema I have become the person I am and I also owe the eczema my rich, beautiful and so beloved life.

The countless experiences I have had with my injured and sensitive skin have become my great treasures and resources to which I have access at all times. This includes the many valuable encounters with people I might otherwise never have met. And also the confrontation with myself in a depth that would never have happened without my distress.

I discovered new dimension of myself again and finally surprised myself with the courage, the strength and the determination that my healing way demanded of me.

Of course, I don't know if that will ever change again. The tendency to atopic eczema is a challenge in my life, an "imposition", which gives me the chance to show courage and grow. That's what I want to do and what I will continue to do. Because if I want to feel comfortable in my skin, it is up to me to make sure that this is going to happen. To do this, I have to find what I need for my well-being every day anew. Often this is not easy, but worth the effort. My skin always feels best when I leave it completely alone and avoid everything that irritates it. It is a miracle of regeneration and strength, and I expect it will continue to be so in the future. But it's pointless to think about it now. Today I feel good in my skin because I don't use any cream. Should this change at some point, should I feel like offering a high-quality oil to my skin again or other care product made from the best ingredients, I will do so. And I will carefully check whether my skin likes it.

I have understood that one of my life tasks is to pay attention to the signals of both my skin and my body. And not only listen to myself when there's already 'alarm'. I should always ask myself as soon as possible: "What do I want? What do I not want? What's getting under my skin right now?"

In the many years with atopic eczema I have learned that a contented skin is always the result of how I deal with my body and soul. Just as an artist makes an artwork out of the material he wants to work with, is every day an invitation to evolve by its small and big challenges. And to shape my health at the same time. For which I have a lot of material and useful tools at my disposal.

Chapter 4

What I Can Do Today

Health is a gift that you have to give yourself.
Swedish proverb

Like my life my health is not in my hands. It's a gift, not to say a mercy. Nevertheless, I bear responsibility for it, because I can contribute a great deal to my physical and mental well-being.

I know now that I am the most important person in my life and that I depend on the quality of my self-care. The better I treat myself, the better I feel mentally and physically. Today I no longer perceive my skin as an unpredictable, insidious power that only aims to torture me and destroy my quality of life. My skin supports me, it wants me to be well. It belongs to me, that's why it is loved, caressed and admired. Again and again I am amazed by its enormous expressiveness, its incredible healing power and its enormous ability to change.

I have now confidence in my skin and trust it to take good care of itself. And that's what it does best when I pay attention to my needs and deal constructively with challenges. When I set healthy boundaries and change in my behaviour patterns which are no longer useful.

"It is the spirit that builds our body," wrote Friedrich Schiller in his famous work *Wallenstein*. Schiller, who was also a physician, had already recognized what neuroscientists are investigating step by step today: If our mind changes, the body changes with it. And vice versa, the same applies: If our body changes, the psyche also changes. I experience this all the time with my skin: If it is well, I am also well. If I am well, my skin will also be fine.

Body posture and movements also have a huge impact on our feelings and moods. New self-confidence develops out of the dejection by straightening the back and head. A brisk walk can change the world and everyone who does sports knows that exercise can make you feel better immediately.

Once you have started not to look at life as usual and behave differently than usual, you constantly make new experiences. It is fascinating how the perspective on things alone changes the world around us and, more importantly, within us.

Life is like a box of chocolates. You never know what you'll get.
Forrest Gump

Fortunately we cannot foresee life, it is full of beautiful surprises, but sometimes it also provides less beautiful ones. And just as the alternation of ebb and flow, day and night and the course of the seasons that determine nature, also our life follows a biological rhythm of tension and relaxation, healthy phases alternate with less healthy ones. Therefore there will always be stressful times that will bring us physically and spiritually to our limits. If we want to cope with this with a healthy skin, we need mental strength. It helps us to overcome disappointments, to overcome crises and to grow with them.

This mental ability is also called resilience—a term that steams from physics and describes the tolerance of a system against disturbances.

Our resilience is largely innate to us. One person has got more, the other had gotten less of it into the cradle. But just as we can train our bodies, we can also strengthen our resilience at any age. Setting goals, cultivating good relationships with people and repeatedly creating occasions for joy and success in life—all this strengthens and nourishes the life force. If we then take the needs of our body seriously and treat ourselves and others with respect, we create the ideal conditions for our mental immune system to be able to work optimally.

> *To say yes, to find creative solutions for what sticks and jolts, to constructively participate in my own life—that is what my life demands and expects of me every day. But not to spite me. Rather, to become aware of my possibilities. And to make the best of them.*

This chapter is about what I have found and learned in my recovery process. Like probably many people with chronic illnesses, I too have reached for every straw that offered a hope for healing. Fortunately, I now know what I need for my well-being. But I also get to know new sides of myself again and again. And if I find an interesting and convincing suggestion, I like to try it out.

Even today there are moments when I feel this unpleasant energy in my face again, this fine vibration and tingling that used to put me in an alarmed mood. Because these were mostly the harbingers for the next eczema attack. Sometimes my skin really gets more restless. But it's not the beginning of the end anymore. It calms down just as quickly as it got upset.

In such situations, the challenge is not to panic. First of all, I just realize that it's just the way it is and that my system only reacts to something. And then I have to make sure that body and soul get what they need to calm down and relax.

The following impulses, techniques and exercises could therefore all be under the great heading of "self-care". It shows once again that the way we treat ourselves touches every aspect of our being and decisively influences our quality of life.

1. Mental Hygiene: I Am What I Think (About Myself)

"Our life is the product of our thoughts", the ancient Roman Mark Aurel once put it in a nutshell. Health starts with thinking.

2. Stress Management: Balancing the Liveliness

Stress and health are connected, stress and illness also. Knowledge and techniques for coping with stress contribute significantly to the good functioning of our nervous, immune and hormonal systems. So the skin doesn't have to get excited.

3. Nutritional Concept: Eating What Is Good for You

There are many books about food and its effects on atopic eczema, as well as countless tips and information on the internet. I report here about my experiences with the kind of nutrition, which after years of experimentation has proved to be the most practical for me.

4. Skin Health: Care, Caress, Confidence

Since I no longer use creams, I have found other ways to lovingly care for my skin. It is also about the effects of water and soap, about sun, wind and fantasy.

Atopic eczema is very individual. Every person experiences it differently and everyone suffers from it in her or his own way. Those who are affected by atopic eczema must therefore find their personal tools to deal with themselves well. There are no miracle cures and there is no such thing as a miraculously working lifestyle. But there is a variety of solutions that you can try out and find the best possible way for yourself. Or the best possible ways.

1. Mental Hygiene
I Am What I Think (About Myself)

Meanwhile it has been proven that we create our personality and our reality with our thoughts, ideas and actions. With the help of brain scan, ultrasound and CT one can see exactly whether we are having fun or meditating, whether we are anxious or relaxed. Depending on the mood, different areas in our brain are active.

◢ Thoughts Guide Our Life
Feelings and thoughts can even be so powerful that they change genes. These in turn influence our body. Which means that if I keep thinking the same thoughts, acting in the same way, and reacting in the same way to my problems and circumstances, I will send the same signals to the same genes over and over again. They then keep my body and all my organs in their familiar state. My body in turn sends signals to my brain that let me act the way I have always acted. With the result that I will make the same experiences again and again.

I think that my skin will never get better. My body
picks up the signals of incurability and unsightliness
and tries to implement them as well as possible.
When this mechanism became clear to me, I thought
about what I had to change. My permanent need for
retreat, for example. On the same day I arranged to
meet my girlfriend Andrea, whom I had not seen for a
long time. When she accepted me as I was, I felt after
a long time how healing it was to be in contact with
people. So I invited friends or went to cafés. And
each time I felt a little better and safer.

If we change our thoughts, our brain naturally is puzzled.
"What, please, is this supposed to be?" it thinks and is
anything but enthusiastic. "We've never done this before!"

But if we do not allow ourselves to be deterred by its
resistance, it realizes that we mean business. Our brain then
sends signals for new behaviour to other genes, which can then
become active. If this happens many times, our physical
condition gradually changes. Very fascinating, isn't it?

However, what science can prove today with state-of-the-art
technology is not entirely new. Even the ancient Chinese knew
about the tremendous power of thoughts:

Pay attention to your thoughts, for they become your words.
Pay attention to your words, for they become your actions.
Pay attention to your actions, for they become your habits.
Pay attention to your habits, because they become your
character.
Pay attention to your character, for it becomes your destiny.

Putting new thoughts into action often costs a lot of attention and overcoming, especially at the beginning. The more often you do this, the less willpower you have to expend over time. Because every time we think differently, our brain expands the wires to new behavior and the more often we use them, the more powerful, faster and more stable they become. It's like crossing a jungle: At the beginning, there is no path and one laboriously makes a way through a narrow footpath meter by meter with a bush knife. If you walk it again and again, it becomes a trail, then a broad, comfortable way and finally a well-constructed road. Which you take automatically because it has become the shortest, most familiar and fastest connection to the other side.

If you want to change something in your behaviour or life, the following questions may help you:

🖉   What do I want to change?

🖉   What do I think about it?

🖉   What does the constructive idea look like?

🖉   What's my first behavior change there?

🖉   How can I integrate what's already working well my everyday life?

🖉   What support do I need? Where can I get it?

🖉   How do I know I'm back to the old way and act like I used to?

I am convinced that 10 percent of my life
consists of what happens to me and
90 percent of how I react to it.
Charles R. Swindoll

Tip

Decide what you want. Of what you want,
do more. Of what you no longer want, do
less.

■ *I Can Make up for It*

"Love yourself, then others will find you lovable," an old proverb says. What I have suffered through my skin over decades—I cannot undo it. But I can now choose to give myself the care, compassion and support that I once missed.

Today I understand that I was extremely challenged by skin and university during my first years of study and had no possibilities to make it easier for me. Once, I consciously set myself back in my student days and experienced a typical day in my imagination. How I let myself down because I was so ashamed of myself. And how lonely I felt because I didn't want to share my misery. I've forgiven myself. And I make up for this every day by believing in myself today and standing by me unconditionally. It is an amazing and touching experience to see how old wounds can actually be healed by making amends to oneself.

■ Taking Responsibility for Myself

By listening to myself I got to know my strengths and weaknesses, my wishes, needs, joys and sorrows better and better. In this way I can also react more quickly to fears or anxieties, so that they don't have to become overwhelming in the first place. The best way for me to do this is to retreat into silence and simply perceive what is going on inside me.

Listen to the whisper of your body,
before it starts screaming.
Ann Weiser Cornwell

Knowing my needs also means satisfying them appropriately without violating the boundaries of others. This means that I take responsibility for my life and how I deal with what happens to me. I always do this when I ask myself "What can I do to make me feel better in this situation?" Or "How can I use my abilities in a way that is useful for me and others?"

There are many occasions where I have the opportunity to change a situation in a way that makes me feel more comfortable. For example, I can avoid a conflict that "gets under my skin". But I can also address the problem in an open and respectful way and look for a solution. The issue of withdrawal also has a lot to do with responsibility. You can hide at home and shutting yourself off from life when you're not well. But you can also, if it is physically possible, go out and encounter life with its unbelievable possibilities and ideas.

Even a walk is enough to get home completely changed. When I walk with open eyes and an alert mind through the city, woods or parks, my brain is literally "aired" and the stink of old, used up thoughts, which so successfully cause bad feelings, will be removed.

■ My Best Mirror Girlfriend

The way I deal with my mirror picture says a lot about my relationship to myself. This is not about the vanity of the "mirror, mirror on the wall, who is the fairest one of all?"—it's about the inner attitude with which I look at myself: loving, friendly, willing? Or permanently critical and rejecting, as I had done for so long and with such great success that I could no longer bear my mirror image.

As I let the skin dry out, I took all my courage together, stood in front of the mirror, smiled and said, "Just the way I am now, I love myself." The first times it has cost me enormous overcoming, because I felt quite silly. But the more I did it, the easier it became. Today I smile at myself every morning in the mirror, wish me a beautiful, healthy, successful and cheerful day and don't want to miss this first daily beautiful contact with me anymore.

How self-love shows itself

💜 I stand by my strengths and weaknesses and I have a good feeling and opinion about myself.

💜 I promote myself and my capacities and make sure that my weaknesses do not harm me.

💜 I'll get support and help if I need it. And I support others if I want to. And if the balance between giving and taking feels right for me.

💜 I feel and know that my value does not depend upon my origin, my appearance and my performance.

💜 I have compassion for myself without sinking into self-pity.

💜 I am happy about praise and getting compliments. I also like to praise and compliment others. But only if I mean it honestly.

💜 I set my own limits by following rules that are good for me.

💜 I treat myself and others with respect and esteem. I expect the same from others towards me.

★ ★ ★

■ Rituals for More Self-love

There are many rituals that can be used to strengthen self-confidence and love for oneself. Here is a small selection:

Morning ritual

When you wake up in the morning, you tap your fingers gently on your breastbone and speak in your thoughts or loudly several times in a row: "I love, I believe, I trust, I am grateful and courageous."

The thymus gland is located behind the breastbone. It is regarded as the link between mind and body, which transports our thoughts into the body. It also controls the entire energy balance of the body. By gently stimulating it by tapping, it compensates disturbances and the life energy can flow again.

Patting yourself on the back

Another nice tapping ritual: Pat yourself several times on the right shoulder with your left hand and then on the left shoulder with your right hand and say: "I am good, I am precious." Then circle your right hand clockwise over your stomach while saying "I am happy and satisfied". At the end you embrace yourself with the words "Yes, I love me!"

Smile impulses

Paint a smiley on the bathroom mirror or stick a post-it note with a smiley there. This reminds you to smile every time you look in the mirror. To show you that you are so happy to see you again.

Tip!

Rituals work best if you practice them by yourself. Because if you're not quite sure whether they do you good and you feel a little silly at the beginning, you just have to stand it alone. When someone else smiles about the rituals, it's harder to go on. So only talk about them when you are convinced of their effect.

■ *It's turning out well*

Scientists have shown that people who look to the future with confidence, while keeping a relation on reality, feel better, are mentally and physically healthier, and even recover faster from disease. Optimism not only helps to overcome the current difficulties, but even influences the future. This happens because even the belief in the arrival of something good triggers positive feelings, which in turn have an effect on one's personal charisma and behaviour. This increases the probability that the expectation will actually materialize.

I have two proven slogans that help me to keep looking ahead again:

"Who knows what it's good for" and

"If it goes wrong, it gets better".

You can make an "It's turning out well"-can or small box. Write down your thoughts and worries and put them in there.

With this method you let go of the thought and gain physical distance to it. When you look at the notes again, after a while it's always amazing to see what you've been worried about. The worries have long been forgotten, because things had turned out well.

Collecting "gold leafs" also helps to focus on what is good. "Gold leafs" are the happy moments of the day that are so easily overlooked: The nice talk with the neighbour or the funny mail from the colleague. Later in the evening you write them in a "gold leaf book", which gradually becomes an always available source of good thoughts, optimism and gratitude.

Tip!

You can also put some peas in a small tin and take it with you wherever you go. For every nice and special moment you put a pea in your pocket. Before falling asleep, you look at these peas and remember every special and beautiful moment of the day that you otherwise would have forgotten.

■ Making Peace

Anyone who keeps thinking "how do I look" or "I'm not good enough" has stress. Feelings such as envy, bitterness, resentment and inferiority cost strength and they damage your health in the long run. Today we know that the movement and function of our immune cells in the body are essentially influenced by messenger substances and hormones that are produced in response to our thoughts. This is the way through which psychological processes such as stress, joy or anger reach our body's own defence system and can strengthen or weaken it.

If you now make peace with yourself or with the situation that triggers the negative feelings, you start the flow of energy again. Because the production of healthy hormones is stimulated and the body is thus offered the conditions to heal itself or to stay healthy.

Inner peace begins the moment we accept and acknowledge ourselves. And we decide that neither another person nor an event can control our feelings and moods.

Inner peace, of course, is also a question of trust in life. Depending on how strong we are emotionally, we have to work on it every day again and again. The more we strive for our inner peace, the more confident we will soon master situations that would have overwhelmed us earlier.

■ Recharging Energy

Joy is the health of the soul.
Aristotle

If I am in a bad mood or do not feel well and want to change this, then joy, gratitude and kindness in dealing with myself and others immediately brighten my mood again.

1. I can consciously turn to my body, or gently massage my skin like I'm applying cream. And thank it for everything that it is doing for me.

2. I can enjoy! A delicious hot drink, my favourite ice cream or a meal I wouldn't cook otherwise. Or I let my soul dangle again—by looking out of the window, taking a walk, or just being there and doing nothing.

4. I can find someone to hug me or someone I can hug. This contact is good and also gives the other person the feeling of being able to give something precious.

5. I think about what is good in my life and I'm grateful for it. Gratitude is a powerful source of power that immediately raises the energy level.

6. I can help someone who needs support. This gets me out of my self-centered attitude immediately.

Body postures can also change the mood. Just try them all out for a few minutes and then find your favourite pose.

If you go into this posture every now and then during the day, you will quickly notice that you have much more energy. Smiling at the same time increases the effect even more.

☺ Stand up, spread your arms and be as big as you are. It's like embracing the world. If you like, sigh loudly and deeply from the bottom of your heart.

☺ Place your hands on your hips and stand with legs spread. Breathe deeply into the abdomen.

☺ Sit back in the chair, relax with your arms behind your head and enjoy the feeling of sovereignty.

The Happiness Collage

A wonderful method of dealing with yourself and your own well-being is to create a collage with all the good things that the future should bring. This takes two to three hours and you need old magazines, brochures, photos, scissors and a glue.

Then simply select the headings and images that you like, cut them out and puzzle them back together on a large sheet of paper. You can also experiment with other materials, decorative pencils, water, oil or acrylic paints. This is great fun and in the end you have created a unique and highly individual artwork that gives impulses and new strength every time you look at it. And best of all: The place that your own worries had occupied is now filled with strengthening and inspiring images!

When I look at my collages after a longer period of time, I am always surprised to find out how many of the themes depicted have come into motion or have actually been realized. Like my healthy skin, which was always an important aspect in my collages. Because by dealing with a collage you create a playful access to what moves you inside. You translate your thoughts into images, so to speak, the subconscious understands them as orders and gently steers your own actions in their direction.

Nature has made sure, that it does not require a great effort to live happily. Everyone can make himself happy.

Lucius Annaeus Seneca

2. Stress Management
Balancing the Liveliness

Experts estimate that 75 to 90 percent of visits to general practitioners are due to complaints caused by stress. Not surprisingly, considering that almost every physical system and every part of the body can be affected and impaired by stress. The skin in particular. Some people become pale under stress, others get a red head or red spots. And the symptoms of atopic eczema can worsen.

■ *Stress and What It Has to Do with Atopic Eczema*

What exactly is stress? In general it can be said that stress is a physical reaction to mental processes that always occurs when we are strongly challenged in some way. If we think "this will work" because we have mastered similar situations well in the past, we will only feel little stress. But if we feel swamped and are afraid that we are not up to the challenge, our stress level rises sharply.

Researchers demonstrated in a study that atopic eczema patients under acute stress experience had a sharp increase in lymphocytes, a subgroup of white blood cells, and immune messengers (cytokines), which are essentially responsible for inflammation of the skin.

Life without stress doesn't exist. Our existence consists of permanent change, adaptation and development, dealing with unforeseen situations and encounters with people whose behaviour we cannot appreciate. Without stress we wouldn't even exist, because our ancestors wouldn't have survived the steppe. Their lives were constantly endangered by predators like the saber-toothed tiger with its pencil-long teeth. In case of an attack our ancestors had to decide between fight and escape. If they hadn't had such survival stress—they would have been easy prey and we wouldn't exist now.

Today, stress motivates us, among other things, to perform and to increase performance. Athletes could not perform at their best without the stress hormone adrenaline and some people need a tight schedule to get on with their work. But the dose makes the poison. Constant stress without recovery phases makes you ill. It's like an engine that has to run constantly at high speed: after a short time it is broken.

Even if today we no longer have to reckon with being attacked by a hungry predator on our doorstep—today's steppe consists of private and professional pressure to meet deadlines and perform perfectly, job anxiety, conflicts and overestimation of one's own capabilities. Our psyche and our body react to it with the same fight-or-flight-mechanism as in the early days of human evolution. By producing stress hormones, our system enables us to react accordingly.

If the stress situation passes quickly and we can recover sufficiently afterwards, the body absorbs the effects of the stress alarm. In the case of uninterrupted stress, however—which is caused by noise, sensory overload, frustration, anger, anxiety and also by a chronic disease such as atopic eczema—our body is on constant alert. Because we do not use up the stress energy through extreme activities such as fighting or fleeing, or through a sufficient recovery phase in the cave like our ancestors did, it remains in the body where it causes health damage in the long run. In atopic eczema, stress energy contributes to maintain the symptoms.

Stress is therefore primarily about redirecting stress energy, letting it flow away through sport, for example, and ensuring relaxation and recovery as often as possible. Positive feelings such as joy, calmness and trust also help enormously to reduce stress more quickly and to be able to deal better with future situations.

Atopic eczema often means chronic stress. Not only does one suffer because of the appearance—the unpredictable and uncontrollable course of this illness is also an enormous burden.

According to studies, inner tension, fear or hopelessness trigger new eczema attacks in about 30 percent of neurodermatitis patients. If the stressful situation continues and the psychological pressure becomes too great, more stress hormones are released. The already weakened immune system reacts extremely sensitively: Immune cells become more activated and the body's own defense system beats wildly. The consequence is, that the skin becomes inflamed and the itching tortures. However, many atopic eczema sufferers are also familiar with the phenomenon that the new eczema attack is just beginning to occur, when the stress phase is over.

Tip!

In case of acute stress, a simple but
very effective recipe helps: Breathe!
Inhale deeply and count to three, then
exhale deeply and count to six. While
doing so, drop your shoulders. You can
slow down the breathing rhythm even
further. Breathing in this way noticeably
releases the tension and relaxes the
muscles from the neck to the big toe.

★ ★ ★

Relax Physically and Mentally

The skin itches under time pressure, right after the exhausting
relationship crisis comes the eczema attack. For several decades, intensive research has been carried out into how our
thoughts and feelings affect our bodies. Among other things,
it was found that people who regularly experience feelings such
as love, joy and well-being have a better heart rhythm and a
lower risk of heart attacks. They become healthy more quickly
and their immune system even copes better with
inflammations.

*It is not the things themselves that worry
people, but the idea of things.*
Epictet

On the other hand, those who constantly feel insecure, restless and often afraid are under constant physical and mental stress. Tense muscles in turn have a detrimental effect on all bodily functions and also contribute psychologically to feelings of anxiety and insecurity.

The American physician Edmund Jacobson recognized this already in the 1930s and developed the "Progressive Muscle Relaxation", PMR, an effective relaxation method that is very easy to learn: Conscious tension and deep relaxation of the muscles ensure that the body activates its self-healing powers and can even dissolve fears.

What is absolutely practical about the PMR is that you can apply it almost anywhere and at any time and feel its beneficial effect immediately.

Tip!

There are many instructions for progressive muscle relaxation according to Jacobsen on the Internet. Some health insurance companies offer them as podcasts for download.

Even the famous Greek physician Hippocrates already knew 2,500 years ago about the power of the psyche and the body's own healing powers. He repeatedly administered his patients drugs without active ingredients—which his patients didn't know—and assured them that the strong medicine would be guaranteed to work. The ill people trusted him, believed in the success of medicine, relaxed and became healthy.

Hippocrates used what is today known as the "placebo effect", and which has now been well researched as a neurobiological process. In order to protect itself from harmful influences such as viruses and bacteria and to be able to heal optimally, our body needs above all an anxiety-free, relaxed and positive climate of confident attitude to life and trust.

To see joy, positive things in oneself, in others and in life is one of the essential and most powerful sources for our health.

According to psychologists, a bad event in the daily balance can be outweighed by five to fifteen (there are various opinions) positive experiences. Therefore, when we see the good things, collect the many moments of happiness, enjoy life and focus on our strengths instead of our weaknesses, happiness hormones will flow through our body. We are more relaxed and create the right conditions to stay or become healthy.

▪ Dealing Well with Our Energies

I always liked to do everything immediately and then one hundred percent, oh, one hundred and fifty percent. That can put a lot of pressure on you. Stress research has shown that it is not only the external triggers that can make us sick in the long run. Above all, it is how we treat ourselves.

Nobody can give 100 percent all the time. Often, 80 percent of our commitment is sufficient to achieve a goal. Here are some tips on how to use your energies better and—more importantly—healthier.

1. Reducing expectation

A first step to reduce expectations is to realize that you have unrealistically high expectations. And then you should gather the courage to lower expectations. The resulting space in between relieves and even contains room for creativity. Some decisive ideas could only be born because of this gap.

2. Keeping the big picture in mind

Professionally or privately—it's about the big picture that we should keep an eye on. Of course, the necessary care must be also taken with the details. But without getting bogged down in them.

3. Dealing with criticism

If you always want to make everything perfect, the fear of criticism often resonates. It costs strength and is at the expense of self-confidence. Criticism is perfectly normal in interpersonal processes, but we must learn to distinguish between justified and unjustified criticism. And we should not let the reactions of others dissuade us from treating ourselves well (see also page 163).

4. *Request for support*

Nobody can do everything alone. And nobody has to do everything alone. It is enormously relieving to get the competent support you need in time.

Tip!

> KISS means "keep it short and simple". In other words, don't complicate things unnecessarily. This saves a lot of energy. Things may also be simple!

★ ★ ★

Healthy Boundaries

Setting boundaries, saying "no"—many people have a problem with this. In atopic eczema, the inability to say no and not wanting to constantly satisfy the needs of others can also play a role. A friend who suffered also from atopic eczema once told me: "My skin became healthier when I could finally say *no* and realized that I could not do everything. And that I didn't have to do everything. And that I can have my own rhythm."

Saying "no" is often difficult because we are afraid of losing people's appreciation and affection. Sometimes feelings of guilt are added because you believe that as an employee, friend, good acquaintance or family member you cannot simply refuse a request. Even if it doesn't fit into your own planning at all.

But if we constantly put the needs of others and their demands on us before we take care of our own needs, we not only lower our self-esteem—we also lose our verve. Because always keeping pace with others and living against one's own rhythm costs strength. This energy is no longer available to ourselves to maintain or restore our health. The skin then sometimes says the 'no' that we did not dare to say.

There is a form of egoism that is so
nourishing for us that we have much
to give to others.
Marshall Rosenberg

To fulfill the wishes of others in order to be liked is childlike thinking. Today we are adults and have a right to our own interests, methods and dreams. We also urgently need them in order to stay healthy and to be able to develop. If we take our needs seriously, we get the good feeling to feel safe with ourselves and we regain our self-esteem. As well as the trust and respect of others. Because just when we allow ourselves to be ourselves, we contribute to sincere and balanced relationships and can manage to shape our lives according to our ideas. Not to mention the fact that an occasional friendly but clear "no" will keep us a helpful person anyway.

I discovered late how easy it is to just say no.
William Somerset Maugham

If we don't want something, we can practice the refusal in front of the mirror. Just say loud and friendly: "I'm so sorry, but I don't have time for that right now."

We don't have to justify our decision. If someone still doesn't let up, you can ask nicely which part of the "no" was not understood. Then the interlocutor knows that we know exactly what we want and what we don't want.

The mirror exercise might cost overcoming in the beginning. But the more often you pronounce your "no", the more understandable it becomes.

A "no" always means a "yes" to one's own life in the sense of "I do it for myself, not against you". This is how we express our appreciation of ourselves.

Setting healthy boundaries, to say "no", if you mean "no", is a real learning process and you need determination, perseverance and courage for it. But it's worth it. Because every time we don't bend or betray ourselves, our inner strength grows. And we gain more and more clarity about what we want and have more confidence in ourselves. And the others have it, too.

Tip!

```
The idea of a garden fence helps to keep
a distance. Everything that you do not
want to let get too close to you remains
outside the fence. You decide yourself
when to open the garden door.
```

■ Saying "Yes"

We sometimes also have to learn to say "yes". "Yes" to yourself, to your wishes and needs, to your feelings in general and to your gut feeling. Which sometimes sends uncomfortable messages that one would only too gladly ignore. But you should take them seriously if you want to feel good.

Saying "yes" to a job that may not always be fun, but that helps you to live the way you want, immediately removes blockages and makes life easier. Because the power that was once used for rejection is now available for other, more useful things and circumstances. It's all about the general "yes" to the things that do us good. In particular, this includes relationships and people. As much as you have to set yourself apart on the one hand, it is on the other hand very important to be together with other people and to be there for them. Of course always under the condition that we want to do that and that it feels right for us. And finally, a "yes" is shown by the fact that we also accept support when we need it.

■ Joy—the Silver Bullet for Coping with Stress

The best we can do against stress and for our health is to be happy as often as possible. Joy is pure relaxation and true medicine for the body. Scientists have shown that wounds heal worse under stress, but our immune system is strong and active when we are internally relaxed, comfortable and happy. And even if we just pretend to be happy, the immune system is stimulated. In an experiment, actors played emotional states such as sadness and joy. In sad scenes the number of defense cells decreased. But when the actors acted as if they were happy, the defence cells became more active. However, our immune system is smart enough to know that we can't always be in a good mood. Having a bad temper from time to time and not feeling good doesn't throw it off track.

Health is less a condition than an attitude. And it thrives with the joy of life.
Thomas Aquinas

Hearty laughing is like a health cure for the whole body. It loosens muscles, frees accumulated emotions, activates self-healing powers and releases happiness hormones. That'll make us feel better right away. Just two minutes of hearty laughing are supposed to be as healthy as twenty minutes of jogging, ten minutes of laughter should have the effect of thirty minutes of relaxation training. Research shows that laughing activates the abdominal and back muscles almost as much as intensive training. Of course we are not spared psychological challenges and difficult life events by humour. But laughter helps us to deal with them better and healthier.

Tip!

"What was I happy about today?" We should ask ourselves this question every now and then. It reminds us how important daily pleasure is for our well-being. For example, we can make ourselves a little present or spend a nice time with ourselves. And look out for humorous situations in everyday life. A playful approach to things and not always taking everything so seriously leads to spontaneous cheerfulness. And if there is really no opportunity to laugh or smile, you can watch funny films, read amusing books or hang funny cartoons over your desk. A daily laugh and smile program is balm for body and mind. How did Charlie Chaplin say it? "A day without a laughter is day wasted."

■ Dealing More Calmly with Criticism

Being criticized doesn't feel good. Especially when you're already "scratched" by your skin. Then you are hurt, offended, and maybe even ashamed. And it can take a long time to recover from it.

Especially when you start to care for yourself, when you set limits, say no and change your behaviour, some people feel insecure and react with criticism. And it is irritating indeed when someone suddenly, who otherwise always behaved rather conformist, has his own opinion.

Criticism of us or our behaviour can happen to us again and again. But we can learn to deal with it in such a way that it does not shake us to the core.

1) First of all, we should listen to the criticism calmly and not react immediately. If the criticism is unjustified, we reject it by summarizing what has been said and explaining our own point of view.

2) If the criticism is justified, it offers the chance to grow personally at this point. Asking "what exactly do you mean?" creates clarity and gives time to think.

Some critics are not able to say what it is about. You don't have to deal with this criticism any further. But if the critic replies in detail and if you can understand the points he complains about, you should ask what you can do better in the future. This often develops into a constructive conversation and you don't feel you have to defend yourself.

Tip!

It is also helpful to take the critic's perspective. You could say "I haven't seen it like this before." This shows your counterpart that you respect his opinion and that you are at eye level with him. What is criticized, however, is only one possible point of view—that of the critic. There are countless others. If you make yourself aware of this, you usually feel much better immediately.

■ Slow down

Everyday life is hectic and tightly timed: taking the kids away, working, and shopping. Getting the kids, playing sports or dating friends. In the long run, time pressure is harmful.

You may not be able to slow down every day, but you can always ask yourself whether you really need to stress like that. Then taking a deep breath and going on a little slower from now on is a big step in the direction of deceleration. Planning a day—for example a Sunday—on which you only follow your own schedule also takes off a lot of pressure. Little by little you will find your own personal well-being-speed, with which you can lead a much better, healthier and more intensive life.

"God, grant me the serenity to accept the things I cannot change, courage to change the things I can, and wisdom to know the difference."

The well-known prayer of the American theologian Reinhold Niebuhr helps many people to stay calm in turbulent situations. Here are some more ideas for more serenity.

▶ If everything gets too much—stop! Why is it so stressful right now? What's the most important thing at this moment? What must be done first? Becoming aware of the situation and concentrate on it gives back control.

▶ Get up and move! Climbing stairs, walking around the block, cycling. Movement brings us out of the head into the body. The stress energy is effectively redirected and the stress hormones in the body are reduced.

▶ "Count your blessings"! Count what you are blessed with and what good things have happened to you in life. To look at the good does one verifiably good. It has been also scientifically demonstrated that people who do not constantly compare themselves with others rest more within themselves and therefore are more satisfied and relaxed.

★ ★ ★

3. Nutritional Concept
Eating What Is Good for Me

Your food shall be your remedy.
Hippocrates

There is a veritable flood of information, recommendations and tips on atopic eczema and nutrition. On the one hand special diets for atopic eczema are advertised, on the other hand they are not recommended. This is confusing and extremely unsatisfactory, because it is not possible to follow general rules and diets. But whether you are concerned with skin healing or any other health issue, finding your own way of nutrition is always a big challenge. Last but not least, it is a question of personal life philosophy and the level of well-being you want to achieve. Because we are what we eat.

So if we want to feel good in our skin and our body, we cannot avoid paying attention to what we take in every day. And we have to find out which food is good for us.

■ What My Nourishment Has to Do with My Skin

For a while I ate only raw food, then for months only boiled food and finally both together. I avoided salt, hot spices anyway, coffee, tea, chocolate, cake and sweets. Eggs and everything made from milk. I used only hemp oil, ate several days exclusively rice with fruit. Then rice without fruit, then just potatoes. I don't even remember what else I've tried out.

Since I have been doing well, I have made the experience that my body can also cope with food that it does not tolerate so well. I also eat them from time to time so that I do not develop a defence against them.

Meanwhile it has been scientifically proven that permanent abstinence from certain foods and substances only increases intolerance.

So far, experts have advised parents to keep food allergens away from their children as long as possible. Today, a British study recommends just the opposite: if a child has a high risk of peanut allergy, for example, he or she should eat small amounts of food containing peanuts as early as possible.

I have heard of a man suffering from atopic eczema who got rid of severe atopic eczema and extreme citrus fruit intolerance by eating large quantities of lemons, mandarins and grapefruits for several days. I do not know if this is true. But there is at least some idea of how differently food can affect our physical condition.

In the meantime I know very well which foods I should avoid. If I really feel like it, I eat them now and then. I do that also because anything that forces me to consistently follow a rule promotes my inner stress and sooner or later tempts me to break that rule.

If I'm in an environment like a clinic, where are no alternatives to the food offered, and where the food choices make sense to me, it's easy for me to follow the nutritional suggestions. At home, however, the desire for certain food that is not on the agenda creeps in again. I have experienced this countless times and have since understood that I cannot pursue any particular form of nutrition. I know I could never find my recovery on a rigid diet, no matter how confident I had been of it in the beginning. I de need a form of nutrition that doesn't always make me feel guilty because I had again eaten something that wasn't on the "allowed" list.

After years of experimenting with nutritional concepts, healthy nutrition today means for me to eat what does not harm my body and my soul. As far as the selection of my food is concerned, I feel absolutely free today. Because I am no longer subject to any diet or dogma, but I avoid voluntarily whatever is not good for me. And I choose out of the same freedom what does me good.

On the following pages I have compiled the most common foods and substances that are repeatedly mentioned in the context with atopic eczema, and my personal experiences with them.

Alcohol

I don't like alcohol, so I don't drink alcohol. Apart from that, it does me no good physically and I prefer to experience the world with clear consciousness. But alcohol and skin don't really go well together either. Alcohol takes a lot of water from the skin and it has also a negative effect on the immune system. However, its function is particularly important for atopic eczema sufferers, as the degradation process of alcohol causes many toxic substances that put a strain on the body's own defence system. Chianti, champagne and Bordeaux also contain a lot of histamine, which promotes itching and the tendency to allergies and rashes in sensitive people.

Eggs

I have avoided eggs and everything that contains eggs for a long time. Because chicken eggs are one of the most common causes of allergy or food intolerance, along with cow's milk. Meanwhile I enjoy a breakfast egg every now and then and my skin likes it too.

Vinegar

I love sour, but vinegar doesn't work. Like everything that is processed with vinegar: pickled gherkins, olives, mixed pickles. Instead, I like to use pickled vegetables with lactic acid. But also not often, because my skin also likes to react sensitively here.

One time I followed the recommendation to drink diluted apple cider vinegar to relieve the symptoms of eczema by its effect on the metabolism. Apple cider vinegar helps many, but has made my skin more restless. Another thing is to apply diluted vinegar to the skin. It can have a soothing and disinfecting effect on itching and might help to prevent new inflammation.

Meat and fish

The question of meat and fish is a very personal question that everyone must decide for him/herself and according to his/her own criteria and values. According to naturopathy, meat—especially in larger quantities—is a burden for the organism and over acidifies the tissue. In connection with atopic eczema, there is a recommendation to avoid poultry, pork, fish and shellfish as they are often not well tolerated. Personally, I don't eat meat and very rarely fish.

Spices

Basically I avoid everything that is spicy. My skin almost always reacts irritated and fortunately I don't like spicy food either. All the more I enjoy the original taste of the food. It seems only logical to me that a quickly excited skin feels more comfortable with a low-irritant diet.

Grain

For a long time I was a fan of Max Otto Bruker's (the physician who founded the clinic in Lahnstein) fresh grain muesli and loved to eat bread. I now consume only a small amount of grain and believe that it is good for my skin and my body. Gluten, the gluten protein in cereals that, among other things ensures that the dough rises well during baking and does not crack. On the other hand gluten is repeatedly discussed in connection with skin worsening. Gluten enters the intestine through digestion, where its components can cause an increase in the permeability of the intestinal wall or even inflammation of the intestinal mucosa. As a result, important vitamins, minerals and other nutrients can no longer be absorbed properly. Celiac disease, sometimes also called celiac sprue, is a genetic food intolerance to gluten. Buckwheat, millet, rice, corn, amaranth and quinoa are gluten-free.

Food containing histamine

I didn't use to know why my skin itched from sauerkraut. Today I know it: Sauerkraut is a true histamine bomb. The substance is found in many foods and it is associated with itching, redness of the skin, runny nose, hives, migraines, nausea or diarrhoea. Everything that has been matured, fermented, smoked or frozen for a long time contains histamine. I avoid eating food with a high histamine content.

Coffee

From time to time I take a longer coffee break and enjoy it even more afterwards. Coffee still is a small miracle to science: More than 1,000 substances contribute to its beguiling aroma and the caffeine not only promotes concentration, it also stimulates the metabolism. But unfortunately this is unfavorable for atopic eczema because the increased blood flow to the skin also increases the itching.

The caffeine in coffee also feigns stress to the body because it signals the adrenal glands to produce more of the stress hormone adrenaline. Constant coffee consumption puts the body in a state of permanent alarm and this is definitely not healthy. In my coffee phases my skin is also slightly drier. As an alternative to coffee, I like to drink the lupine coffee, which is even gluten-free—an idea for those who want or need to consume gluten-free products.

Cow's milk and dairy products

I couple of years ago I quit eating yoghurt, kefir, quark and other dairy products. But from time to time I enjoy a piece of cheese and my favourite ice cream. It immediately catapults me to the peak of pleasure and it is pure happiness made of cream.

In the "Klinik Lahnhöhe" I experienced amazing changes in other patients by doing without animal protein as well as milk products. Traude, an elderly lady, had arthritic hands, she couldn't stretch out her thick fingers with cartilaginous joints anymore. She held them like claws. After six weeks of raw vegan food she was able to move her fingers again and the swelling had gone completely.

I know from many atopic sufferers that the abstinence of milk does them good. However, many do not notice any deterioration of the skin when they consume dairy products. And if they do, goat or sheep milk products are often better tolerated.

There is hardly any other foodstuff about which there are so many controversial opinions and studies as about milk. The fact is that milk, along with wheat, eggs and nuts, is the most common allergen and many children react to cow's milk with allergies or intolerable symptoms. The common argument that milk prevents osteoporosis—bone loss—because of its high calcium content has also been refuted. In the western industrial countries, where milk is consumed most, the osteoporosis rate is highest. In other countries, especially in Asia, where dairy products are rarely consumed, osteoporosis is practically unknown.

Cow's milk consists mainly of growth hormones in dissolved form. Nature has intended it for the rearing of calves. And not as a basic human foodstuff.

After the first year of life, we lack enzyme lactase, a special digestive factor in the stomach that makes milk usable by the organism. The consumption of dairy products therefore leads to abdominal pain, bloating, bloating, constipation or diarrhoea in some people. Those who have these problems but do not want to do without dairy products can take lactase as tablets, which makes the cow's milk digestible again.

However, a cow's milk allergy or intolerance, which often occurs in connection with atopic eczema, has nothing to do with lactose intolerance. In the case of cow's milk allergy, the body does not react to the lactose but to the proteins in the milk. They trigger the immune reaction, which manifests itself in allergic reactions, a deterioration of the skin or atopic eczema attacks.

Fruit and citrus fruits

Some atopic eczema sufferers have problems with apples and fruit, which contains a lot of acid. I, on the other hand, tolerate apples well, pears, cherries and raspberries too. Papaya—completely unproblematic for others—does not work for me. I know people with atopic eczema for whom citrus fruits are not an issue. Others must leave the room immediately when a mandarin is peeled. I have not eaten oranges, lemons, grapefruits or mandarins for decades and avoid anything that is made from or with them like jam or canned tomatoes, for example, to which citric acid is often added for preservation.

Fresh fruit is a wonderful food due to its vitamins and other valuable ingredients. However, the particularly sweet varieties also contain a lot of fruit sugar (fructose), which is just as harmful when eaten in excess as sugar.

Oil

High-quality oils such as hemp, linseed and olive oil belong to my daily diet. Hemp and linseed oil possess the anti-inflammatory gamma linolenic acid which is extremely important for the skin. It is also known from evening primrose, black cumin or borage seed oil, which is recommended for atopic eczema. Hemp oil contains the vital omega-3 and omega-6 fatty acids (gamma linolenic acid is an omega-6 acid) in an ideal ratio of 1:3. They regulate inflammatory processes, repair cells and strengthen the immune system. They are also responsible for the production of many important hormones and ensure the optimal functioning of the brain and nerves.

Sugar

For many people with atopic eczema, sweets often lead to itching shortly after consumption. But sugar isn't the sole culprit. The many ingredients and additives in sweet stuff can also irritate the skin. Countless studies have shown that a lot of sugar is absolutely unhealthy. Not only does it lead to tooth decay and obesity, it also robs the body of vital minerals and B vitamins, which are very important for the skin and it promotes the development of diabetes and arteriosclerosis. In addition, sugar provides the ideal nutritional basis for intestinal fungi, which can upset the balance of the intestinal flora that is so important to our well-being.

Germans eat 36 kilograms of sugar a year, Americans 55 kilograms. The front-runners in sugar consumption are the Cubans, who make it to a whooping 71 kilograms per year. In 1874, when sugar was still rare and precious, the sugar consumption was still around 6.2 kilograms. At that time sugar was still revered as "white gold".

I like to eat ice cream, cake and chocolates. All in all, however, I make sure that as little as possible of the "white poison", as sugar is called by scientists today, flows through my body.

Onions

I read in an article about nutrition in the Traditional Chinese Medicine (TCM) that onions have a heating effect and increase the dryness of the skin. And therefore they are not recommended for atopic eczema sufferers—despite all the good substances which they also contain. I then left out onions for some time and the itching on my fingers that kept reappearing disappeared. But now and then onions are no problem at all.

◼ Rules That Do Good

I find the following three simple rules very helpful both for my nutrition and my lifestyle:

80:20

To 80 percent I eat "healthy", to 20 percent I eat all that what I have an appetite for and what may be "unhealthy". Healthy means fresh food, lots of vegetables and fruit. And healthy is also the mental freedom to decide for food, which comes from the pure need for pleasure and without paying for it with a guilty conscience. But I also realize that my body has more work with food that my body is not in favor of and therefore I avoid it as often as possible. However, one of the most beautiful aspects of my recovery is that I no longer have to slavishly adhere to dietary rules.

Eating in peace

"When I eat, I eat," it says in Buddhist wisdom. So do I. No book, no newspaper, no television to distract me from the pleasure of the meal.

Nothing in between

A pause of several hours between meals is good for the body. It can then work the food ideally and one also experiences the living rhythm between satiety and becoming hungry again much more consciously.

4. Skin Health

Care, Caress, Confidence

Will I now always do without creams? I don't know. I started it because I wanted to calm my inflamed and raging skin. And I have succeeded with the ointment and cream abstinence. Today my skin signals daily that it doesn't need or want any fat ointment or cream. But maybe it will be different in a few years or even tomorrow, and my skin likes it when I use a cream again.

Turning to one's own skin is an important feel-good factor that affects our overall well-being. The easiest way is with fragrant baths and creams or lotions that are gently massaged into the skin. In the "Spezialklinik Neukirchen" I once had an almost solemn feeling of "anointing" when I applied a cream with incense for the first time. I imagined how it would heal me and made the application of cream a little healing ritual.

But since I don't use creams or other products, I had to find something else with which I could show myself affection for myself through my skin.

■ *Skin Hunger and Caresses*

Thunder and lightning. A little boy jumps out of bed, runs into his parents' bedroom and cuddles up to them. "God is taking good care of you," says the father, caressing his son in a soothing way. "Maybe," says the little boy, "but I prefer a real person now."

There's no better way to describe skin hunger than in this charming little story: It is the need of our skin and soul for care, caresses and protection. To fulfill it, you can stroke over the skin or you can exchange tenderness with your partner. Hugs or massages are also ideal ways of fulfilling the skin's desire for touch. All touches, if they are appropriate and welcome, do us good all around—the kiss of greeting on the cheek, the gentle touch of the hands or on the arm. They are precious gestures that signal support and assure us: "You are welcome and you are not alone."

Touches that we ourselves like to give and receive from others give us new strength because they recharge our energy and make it flow.

■ Sun Protection

My best sun protection is not to go into the glaring sun. If I can't avoid that—for example on holiday by the sea or in the mountains—I always wear something long-sleeved, long pants, a big hat and I even have an umbrella with me. At first I found this very silly, but the protection of my skin is worth this outfit.

Conventional sun creams also often contain many harmful chemicals, including carcinogenic substances such as retinyl palmitate, titanium or zinc oxides, which are absorbed through our skin and enter the body. Not to mention the fact that they are not recommended for the sake of the environment.

◾ Shower Daily?

Too much water—unless it is used for therapeutic purposes such as the permanent shower of good old Sebastian Kneipp—stresses and damages the skin. Our skin is covered with a layer of bacteria that it urgently needs to stay healthy. By daily showering and soaping this sensitive protective film, which is also called protective acid mantle, is destroyed and the sealant substance between the individual horn cells is attacked. This causes the skin to lose moisture and germs or harmful bacteria can penetrate into the body. After showering, it takes several hours for the skin to rebuild its protection.

We tend to scrub too often because we think the body is dirty. Today, however, scientists also see excessive hygiene as one of the causes of atopic eczema and recommend taking a shower once or twice a week at most. And on the other days washing with a washcloth and a mild, soap-free product. The skin is grateful for that. Especially in the winter months, when our skin is already extremely challenged by cold and dry air.

★ ★ ★

◾ Washing Hands, Protecting Hands

After I also stopped applying cream to my hands, I wanted to protect them in a different way. Whether I wash my hair, clean something or do the washing up—today I do everything only with gloves. My hands have recovered well. And in cold weather I always wear gloves if possible. This not only keeps your hands warm, but also protects them from drying out.

Under wool gloves I usually put on thin cosmetic cotton gloves so that the sensitive skin on the hands is not irritated by contact with the wool.

Regular hand washing is important to prevent infections and, of course, to have the feeling of cleanliness and freshness.

But the constant contact with water—especially with hot water and soap—removes the protective fats from the skin. It becomes brittle and cracked, which makes it more permeable to harmful external influences. It is better to wash your hands only with lukewarm water and a soap-free and skin-friendly wash bar without dyes or fragrances. It can be recognized by the fact that the label "pH 5.5" appears on the packaging. If the pH-value is higher or lower, the product would attack the protective acid mantle of the skin.

Scientists warn against the massive use of disinfectants in times of a pandemic like the one of Corona. This damages health and also the skin instead of protecting it. Regular and careful hand washing with a soap free cleansing bar is, according to expert opinion, completely sufficient even in this challenging times. As an alternative you can also wear gloves.

■ Hard and Soft Water

We consist of over 70 percent water and need two to three liters of water a day in order to stay healthy. The skin as our largest organ with its many functions—among other things, it protects the body from mechanical and chemical influences and pathogens, coordinates the water balance and regulates body temperature—is dependent on sufficient water supply.

In regions with harder water, atopic eczema occurs twice as frequently as in other areas. Researchers believe that the minerals calcium and magnesium, which hard water contains—the so-called "lime"—could irritate the skin. Even drinking mineral-rich water is said to contribute to the dryness of the skin. However, this has not yet been conclusively proven.

Another consideration is that you need more detergent and soap for hard water, which can also promote skin diseases.

Hair and skin feel different after contact with hard water than with soft water. This is because hard, calcareous water in combination with soap forms insoluble salts and this "lime soap" remains on the skin and hair. That doesn't happen with soft water. It gives a feeling of well-being on the skin, it becomes softer and the hair gets silkier and curlier.

Scientists have also found out that atopic eczema people who have access to soft water feel less itching. Also people with other skin diseases experience relief through lime-free water.

■ *Trusting My Skin*

"If you want to smell like a rose, you have to surround yourself with roses," an old proverb says. This is based on the experience that if we want to change, we have to imagine this change as vividly as possible and trust it firmly. Many scientific studies have proven the enormous power of imagination: It supports healing processes and contributes significantly to pursuing and achieving goals. Professional athletes, for example, put themselves mentally into the training situation and experience every single sequence of the movement they want to optimize. The lively, intensive imagination stimulates the muscles to micro-movements, which in turn create feelings. In this way, the subconscious, which is mainly influenced by images and emotions, receives essential information and creates the mental and physical prerequisites for the inner scenario to become reality.

We can also use the enormous power of our imagination for our skin. This works by retreating to the mental cinema for a quarter of an hour every day and watching the film "My Wonderful Life, My Beautiful and Healthy Skin!" We are playing the leading part and master all small and big adventures of everyday life courageously, humorously and successfully. The more intensely we experience ourselves with healthy skin and in perfect health, the more effective it is. For our subconscious mind does not know the difference between reality and vision. It does not doubt for a moment that we are what we feel in our imagination and what we trust in. And it will support us on the way there with its tremendous power.

End and Beginning

The end of my long journey to my healthy skin is also the beginning of the way to new life themes. Some I already know, others I will get to know anew on the way. The following words by Charlie Chaplin "As I began to love myself", which he is said to have written on his birthday on April 16, 1959, have become a valuable companion for me.

As I began to love myself I found that anguish and
emotional suffering are only warning signs that I was
living against my own truth.
Today, I know, this is AUTHENTICITY.

As I began to love myself I understood how much it
can offend somebody as I try to force my desires on
this person, even though I knew the time was not
right and the person was not ready for it,
and even though this person was me.
Today I call it RESPECT.

As I began to love myself I stopped craving for a
different life, and I could see that everything that
surrounded me was inviting me to grow.
Today I call it MATURITY.

As I began to love myself I understood that at any circumstance, I am in the right place at the right time, and everything happens at the exactly right moment. So I could be calm.
Today I call it SELF-CONFIDENCE.

As I began to love myself I quit steeling my own time, and I stopped designing huge projects for the future. Today, I only do what brings me joy and happiness, things I love to do and that make my heart cheer, and I do them in my own way and in my own rhythm. Today I call it SIMPLICITY.

As I began to love myself I freed myself of anything that is no good for my health—food, people, things, situations, and everything that drew me down and away from myself.
At first I called this attitude a healthy egoism.
Today I know it is LOVE OF ONESELF.

As I began to love myself I quit trying to always be right, and ever since I was wrong less of the time.
Today I discovered that is MODESTY.

As I began to love myself I refused to go on living in the past and worry about the future.
Now, I only live for the moment, where EVERYTHING is happening.

Today I just live in this moment where everything happens. Today I live each day, day by day, and I call it FULFILLMENT.

As I began to love myself I recognized that my mind can disturb me and it can make me sick.
But As I connected it to my heart, my mind became a valuable ally.
Today I call this connection WISDOM OF THE HEART.

We no longer need to fear arguments, confrontations or any kind of problems with ourselves or others.
Even stars collide, and out of their crashing new worlds are born.
Today I know THAT IS LIFE!

End and Beginning